Text Classics

PETER GOLDSWORTHY was born in South Australia in 1951. He grew up in various country towns, finishing school in Darwin.

Goldsworthy graduated in medicine from the University of Adelaide in 1974, then worked for many years in alcohol and drug rehabilitation. He began writing poetry, and has since the late 1970s divided his time between writing and general practice.

His story collection *Archipelagoes* was published in 1982 and, after two more volumes of stories, Goldsworthy's first novel appeared in 1989. *Maestro* was critically acclaimed and became a bestseller; in 2003 the Australian Society of Authors named it one of the top forty Australian books of all time. Goldsworthy followed the novel with *Honk if You Are Jesus* and the ambitious, controversial *Wish*.

He has won major literary awards in poetry, short story, opera and, most recently, theatre. His novel *Three Dog Night* won the FAW Christina Stead Award. Goldsworthy's novels have sold more than 400,000 copies in Australia, and along with his poetry have been translated into many languages. Five of his works have been adapted for the stage.

Peter Goldsworthy lives in Adelaide. Among his recent works are *His Stupid Boyhood*, a comic memoir, and the libretto for *The Ringtone Cycle*, a cabaret quintet.

JAMES BRADLEY is the author of three novels: *Wrack*, *The Deep Field* and *The Resurrectionist*, an international bestseller. He has also written a book of poetry, *Paper Nautilus*, and edited the anthologies *Blur* and *The Penguin Book of the Ocean*. His reviews and articles appear regularly in a range of Australian and international publications, and he was awarded the 2012 Pascall Prize for Criticism. James lives in Sydney.

ALSO BY PETER GOLDSWORTHY

Fiction
Archipelagoes
Zooing
Bleak Rooms
Maestro
Honk if You Are Jesus
Little Deaths
Keep it Simple, Stupid
Jesus Wants Me for a Sunbeam
Three Dog Night
The List of All Answers
Everything I Knew
Gravel

Non-fiction
Navel Gazing
His Stupid Boyhood

Wish
Peter Goldsworthy

Text Publishing Melbourne Australia

textclassics.com.au
textpublishing.com.au

The Text Publishing Company
Swann House
22 William Street
Melbourne Victoria 3000
Australia

First published by Angus & Robertson 1995
This edition published by The Text Publishing Company 2013

Cover design by WH Chong
Page design by Text
Typeset by Midland Typesetters

Printed in Australia by Griffin Press, an Accredited ISO AS/NZS 14001:2004 Environmental Management System printer

Primary print ISBN: 9781922147035
Ebook ISBN: 9781922148117
Author: Goldsworthy, Peter, 1951-, author.
Title: Wish / by Peter Goldsworthy; introduced by James Bradley.
Series: Text classics.
Dewey Number: A823.3

CONTENTS

Animal Form
by James Bradley

IT is difficult not to wonder how Peter Goldsworthy's publishers reacted when he delivered the manuscript that would appear in 1995 as the novel *Wish*. Already famous for his debut, *Maestro* (1989), Goldsworthy had established a reputation as one of the most clear-eyed observers of Australian middle-class life, yet here was a book that seemed—at least at first blush—more like science fiction than anything else.

That Goldsworthy was not entirely comfortable with narrow conceptions of his writing should have been clear from his second novel, *Honk If You Are Jesus* (1992), a bleakly acerbic riff on cloning technology that imagined the creation of a new Christ from traces of genetic material retrieved from holy relics. If *Honk* occasionally seemed like the work of a writer determined to resist the expectations of his readership, though, *Wish* was something else altogether: a fully realised exploration of love, language and the boundaries of personhood that just happened to centre upon the relationship between a human sign-language teacher and a biologically engineered gorilla.

At first blush it is a subject that is likely to prove challenging to many readers. Yet *Wish* goes further, not by escalating the science-fictional elements of its plot but by asking its readers to engage with the existence of systems of meaning and ways of being much closer to home, in the form of Sign language.

The reader's guide to this second—and in some ways more tantalising—world of meaning is the novel's narrator, John James. Better known by his Sign name, J.J., he is an anomaly: born to deaf parents, he learned to sign before he could speak, and even in his thirties is more at home in Sign and with the deaf than in speech and the company of the hearing.

Initially J.J. seems an unlikely candidate for the experiment he becomes involved in as the novel progresses. Recently returned to his native Adelaide, unemployed and still reeling from a bruising divorce, he is adrift, living with his parents on the seafront in Glenelg, his evenings spent watching television or—in a playful reference to the aquatic ape theories of Max Westenhöfer and Alister Hardy—floating, clad in wetsuit and flippers, in the silent water outside his parents' home. Then J.J. is hired by the zoologist and animal liberationist Clive Kinnear and his wife, the poet and veterinarian Stella Todd, to help teach Sign to Eliza—or, to use the sign name she soon adopts, Wish—a gorilla liberated from a laboratory in Melbourne by colleagues in the animal-rights underground.

Goldsworthy's fiction has explored the charged relationship between teacher and pupil several times, most notably in his 2008 novel, *Everything I Knew*, about a young boy's obsession with his teacher, and the short tale 'The Nun's Story', in which a boy's erotic feelings for his teacher collide with physical reality. These later excursions into this highly contested territory suggest a desire to tease out the complexities of such relationships, illustrating not just the ways in which both parties are often complicit in transgressing conventions, but the ways in which these transgressions can reverberate through both lives in unexpected and sometimes tragic ways.

These issues are present in *Wish* as well, but for the most part they are subordinated to a more complex set of questions about our increasingly unstable definitions of personhood and their ethical implications. Indeed, even as we are prompted to look past the more unsettling aspects of Wish and J.J.'s relationship we are being asked to grapple with deeper questions about Wish and her ethical status, questions that are made the more disturbing by the way her nature seems to elide so many of the categories we use to frame such discussions.

In this respect the novel has proven surprisingly prescient, its desire to explore the manner in which advances in genetic engineering and scientific understanding are forcing us to re-evaluate our assumptions about the boundaries between animal and human anticipating not just the burgeoning field of animal studies and the intensifying debates around the ethical status of great apes, but also books such as J. M. Coetzee's *Elizabeth Costello* and Sara Gruen's *Ape House*, and big-budget Hollywood movies such as *Splice* and *Rise of the Planet of the Apes*.

The genius of *Wish* lies not in its recognition that these dilemmas exist but in its deft marriage of them to the conflicts of character at the heart of the novel. Like much of Goldsworthy's work, *Wish* manages the not-inconsiderable trick of being both deeply felt and slyly aware of the contradictions and absurdities of the characters it portrays, allowing it to move effortlessly between comedy and compassion.

This lightness of touch also allows the novel to sidestep the temptation to moralise about many of the most unsettling questions surrounding the treatment of animals. Although J.J. is sufficiently appalled by Clive's descriptions of factory farms and intelligent pigs to give up bacon, these horrors are kept largely offstage, intellectual abstractions discussed and responded to but never experienced or described directly.

The book internalises and reproduces the rhetorical

strategy J.J. ascribes to Clive, his 'debating trick' of using a low voice and matter-of-fact descriptions as a means of 'having cake and eating it, his cool words only fuelling the reader's emotional heat'. At one level this is deliberate: if nothing else the average reader's tolerance for the visceral and confronting reality of the treatment of animals in factory farms and elsewhere is likely to be limited. But it also underlines the fact that *Wish* is as much about language as ethics.

Goldsworthy's poetry has shown he is fascinated by language, and its role in shaping thought and meaning. But in *Wish* this is allied to a larger investigation of the ways in which language shapes our identities. This is most obvious in the novel's treatment of Sign, and in particular its insistence that we engage with this often-neglected language, both through J.J.'s descriptions and through the many diagrams included in the text. At first glance these diagrams may seem little more than a gimmick. But they are intrinsic to the novel's design, demanding the reader step out of the realm of verbal language and engage with Sign as a physical, gestural system.

For those not fluent in Sign this encounter is likely to be revelatory and chastening. While it is difficult not to be amazed that a world of meaning so different from the one we inhabit lies close at hand, it is equally difficult not to be aware of how this amazement under-lines mainstream society's casual marginalising of the deaf and their culture—and how our ignorance of deaf culture points to a failure to comprehend the possibility of other, quite different ways of being that are all around us. For even as we strive to teach dolphins and birds to speak and apes to sign, our solipsism blinds us to the possibility that these creatures may exist in richly complex worlds of meaning quite unlike our own.

This recognition is the flipside of Wittgenstein's observation that once you teach a lion to speak it is no longer a lion. And it is also part of a larger ambivalence about language that pervades the book as a whole. Language, the novel suggests, is both liberating and confining, a creation capable not only of communicating but of isolating.

This is most obviously true in the case of J.J. and Wish, each caught between worlds by the ways in which their respective encounters with language have shaped them. But it is also evident in J.J.'s relationship with his parents, the way his ability to speak separates him from the two of them, and indeed the way in which their shared disability binds them together, 'two small, neat people in a small, neat house, most comfortable, finally, just with each other'. And—albeit in rather different form—in the novel's awareness of the tension between language and life, and the profane and the profound. Certainly it's no accident that Wish's first symbolic utterance is a scatological insult.

Nor is it an accident that *Wish* is both Goldsworthy's

most vernacular novel, and the novel in which his fascination with language and its possibilities is most intrusive. The fluid opening page swiftly conjures the instrumental poetry of Sign: 'The fist, thumbs up, is the Good Hand, shaper of good things. The Good Hand unfolding and tapping at the heart: Kindness. The Good Hand touching the brow: Knowledge...The observance of good is also in the exception. The Good Hand jerked over the shoulder: Fuck off.' Goldsworthy's prose is economical and powerful. Yet J.J.'s narration often evinces a curiously anxious, almost needy relationship with language: the noise of pipes is 'water-music'; J.J. in the ocean is 'a buoyant cork at the whim of the sea'; adjectives and similes abound, reminding us of the difficulty of pinning meaning down, and of the complexity contained in every description.

In the two decades since *Wish* Peter Goldsworthy has published three novels and several collections of short stories, as well as libretti and poetry, each of which has extended his considerable talents in often surprising directions. Yet in many ways *Wish* remains his greatest achievement, and the most eloquent distillation of his many interests. Brave, brilliant, as intellectually challenging as it is playful, it is testament to a restless and unpredictable imagination.

Wish

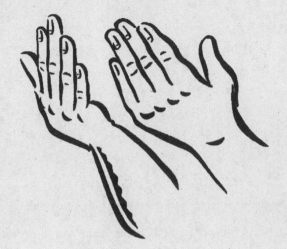

BOOK

ONE

I begin with a sign, not with words. The fist, thumbs up, is the Good Hand, shaper of good things. The Good Hand unfolding and tapping at the heart: Kindness. The Good Hand touching the brow: Knowledge. The fist's protuberant thumb tilted against the lips: Beer!

The observance of good is also in the exception. The Good Hand jerked over the shoulder: Fuck off.

First and foremost, the Good Hand is the shape of Greetings, of Hi, Hello, Good-to-see-you—the shape of welcome.

Welcome to my world, and to my language.

English is my second language. Sign was—is—my first. I still think in Sign, I dream in Sign. I sign in my sleep...

My ex-wife's favourite joke: she woke every morning black and blue all over. Bruised by Sign-language. It was a joke that soured towards the end; became, imperceptibly, a complaint, and, finally, grounds.

I'm not deaf, but I've always felt more at home in Sign. Both my parents are deaf. Deaf as posts. Deaf as adders, deaf as beetles. And proud as peacocks, Deaf Pride long before there was a word, or a sign, for it. I learnt to speak with my hands from birth; there was no other way of reaching my parents. The muttering of English—unnatural and unfeeling it seemed to me at first—arrived later, out of the mouths of others. The graft took slowly; even now I can say things with my hands that I could never squeeze into words.

But how to write of those things here? How to pin a pair of fluttering hands—the wings of a butterfly, a bird—to a flat page?

A year ago, almost to the day, I stood with my mother on the steps of the Deaf Institute on East Terrace. I had been away five years, lost, it now seems to me, in the foreign world of speech, in a marriage built on the shifting sand of spoken words. It was mid-summer, mid-morning—mid-life. Divorced and unemployed, I faced a new year empty of structure and responsibility, or the comforting routines of family life. Powerful feelings flooded through me as I gazed up at the big brick jail of the Institute, home-away-from-home for much of my childhood and a benevolent employer for the first years of my working life. I reached out a hand; my mother's hand was waiting, reading my body-language, as always, almost before it was uttered. Arm in arm we climbed the steps, a small white-haired woman, still agile in her sixties, and her more cumbersome middle-aged son.

I pushed through the door, overcome by trepidation and self-doubt. And here, as I scribble these words, I touch the heart of my problem: how, above all, to translate *feelings*, so easily and naturally expressed in the dance of Sign, so much a part of the actual vocabulary of Sign, into words?

It's tempting to sketch a single hand-shape in the top corner of each page, then flip them rapidly through, like the cartoon frames I once scribbled in the dog-ears of school-books and riffled into jerky animation.

But to tell my story in a flicker of page-corners would take forever. Even then, I'd be missing half the sense, and certainly all the passion, the ballet of eye and brow, mouth and tongue, the little shrugs and body-mimes, the complete performance.

Which leaves me stuck in the mud of words. I tend to speak English in much the same manner that I use Sign, but what is fluent in one is merely bad grammar in the other. My English lapses into the odd word orders and tenses of Sign; it stutters with qualifications, sub-clauses, modifications. *That's a person I don't know who it is. I like you—not. This book I will finish giving you.* In Sign any hand-shape is up for grabs, the smallest shift in direction or orientation of the hands can imbue flavour and nuance. My hands often move, involuntarily, as I speak, like the hands of an accompanist adding resonance to a singing voice. My written English is an improvement on my spoken—there is time to think, and fix—but even as my pen moves my free hand often twitches, qualifying the words as I set them down or expressing their sense more eloquently.

So perhaps the occasional cartoon sketch is better than nothing. This sign, for instance, which my mother shaped as I pushed open the glass doors of the Institute, and she released my hand and raised hers into the Signing Space between us.

The Wish Hand, fingers crossed: a single hand-shape which represents my state of mind that day far better than a thousand words.

'Welcome back,' Jeremy Hinkley said, in English.

He hadn't changed. He sat with his feet on a wide teak desk—a teak plateau—smiling, smug, full of himself. His hands, clasped behind his head, didn't move.

I signed an exaggerated thank you, a flowery two-handed salaam, but the sarcasm went over his head.

'How long has it been, J.J.?' he asked. 'Four years? Five?'

I held up the Spread Hand—five fingers, Sign-Esperanto—but still couldn't entice him to abandon his native tongue for mine.

'Time flies,' he said, a phrase that cries out for the greater beauty of Sign.

'Time is a bird,' I agreed: right forefinger tapping left wrist, both hands spreading and soaring like wings.

Morning sunlight poured through the big bay windows behind him, dazzling me. I felt spotlit, under scrutiny. I fumbled a pair of dark glasses from my coat pocket and slipped them on.

He smiled, indulgently: 'You might notice a few changes about the place, J.J.'

I raised my eyebrows, waiting. He leant back, wallowing in his armchair, savouring the sweetness of the moment: his former teacher sitting in his office, cap in hand. Soon he would offer me my old job; first I was required to sit through a speech.

'We've been developing a different…philosophy.'

His hands finally emerged from behind his head; he signed the last word, a half-familiar hand-shape, borrowed from Ameslan—American Sign Language. This also hadn't changed: Hinkley's weakness for foreign signs. His spoken English is the same, peppered with chic French phrases or highbrow mottoes from Latin.

But usually mispronounced, or misshaped. 'Miss-The-Point' Hinkley, his deaf friends, of which there aren't too many, like to call him behind his back.

'Different how?' I asked, in Sign. Auslan—Australian Sign.

Miss-The-Point stuck to spoken English: 'New directions, new…frontiers. A *lot* of changes.'

I gave a mock-terror sign: Claw Hand over the heart, white-eyes.

He kept his eyes fixed on mine, refusing to acknowledge the mime. This was his show; my role merely to be grateful. To salaam, perhaps even kowtow, from time to time.

'It may take time for you to, ah, re-orient, J.J. I've pencilled you in for Basic Auslan, Level 1. You can take the Wednesday night class.'

Another smug, high-beam smile. I had taught Miss-The-Point his first signs, and he wasn't about to let me forget it. Some debts are too great to repay, let alone forgive.

'I'd prefer to teach Advanced.'

I love to teach; I like to think it brings out the best in me. Given the disasters of my family life, perhaps my most satisfying relationships have been with students—with special students, gifted students. The best teacher–student bonds are a kind of love, I think, selfless and pure. And more equal than at first they seem—dependent on a likeness of mind, a journeying together.

'I'm teaching Advanced, J.J.'

I shrugged. 'So be it.'

He watched me, pressing the manicured fingertips of his slender hands delicately together. Hands are the voice you're born with if you're deaf: husky, whining, smooth, grating. Hands, and faces. I've watched hands so fluid that you can only describe their tone as musical, or melodious. I've watched bony, angular hands that give a clipped, exact kind of sign-speech. My own? A fat man's hands: podgy palms, fingers like nothing so much as little party sausages, bursting out of their skins. They speak a plummy kind of Sign, deaf friends tell me, but easy on the eye. Because hands, above all, must be things you see *through*, things that don't draw too much attention to themselves, don't get in the way of sense.

Hands of glass, I tell my students. The glass might be tinted a little, even stained, but it must always, finally, be transparent.

Miss-The-Point's hands were a huge distraction, especially to himself. The medium was the sole message. His voice was the same, all style, no substance: throaty and mellow, a newsreader's smooth voice. He had married into the Deaf world and come to Sign late; he used his hands mostly as an adjunct to speech.

'There are a few areas you might need to brush up on, J.J.'

I raised my eyebrows: Such-as, For-example?

'For example, we're encouraging Ameslan. I know it goes against your grain but we live in a global village. We can't separate our small community from developments in the rest of the world.'

A practised speech. Absence makes the eye grow sharper; we see more clearly what has changed. What I saw after five years was this: the timelag, the gap between intent and action, a gap of self-regard, self-absorption.

He said abruptly, irrelevantly: 'I was sorry to hear about you and Jill.'

'Always on cards,' I told him, sticking to Sign.

Signers keep their eyes at neck-level, taking in the face as well as the hands. He kept his eyes well above that, fixed on mine. An old battle, an old difference of priorities.

'It may not be my business,' he said. 'But I think you're well out of it. She must have been hell to live with.'

12

It *was* none of his business. Perhaps I agreed with him but I felt a lingering loyalty to Jill. She had been my wife for ten years, she was the mother of our daughter; he had been my employer for ten minutes. I wasn't about to discuss our troubles with Miss-The-Point Hinkley.

I wasn't about to discuss them with *anyone*, not even with myself. The split was still too raw.

'Both at fault,' I signed. 'Takes two to dance.'

I gave the dance-shape a little extra tango-twist, a once-off improvisation. It went over his head. The sign for 'miss-the-point' is a simple mime: the Flat Hand passing backwards over the head, skimming the top of the head, a sign so simple, so eloquent, that even the hearing world has learnt to use it.

'Till Wednesday then,' he said, and rose from his chair.

I followed him to the door, eager to escape, but he hadn't finished batting me between his paws.

'Feel free to take some of my classes, J.J.,' he said. 'I'd like to think I could be of help.'

Fuck you too, I thought. The Rude Hand quivered on the tips of my fingers, another Esperanto sign, universally understood. Somehow I managed to tighten my fists—*purse* my fists, keeping mum. To think the shape, to aim it mentally back at him as I walked from his office, was sufficient:

13

J-O-H-N J-A-M-E-S. A short name in English; a short story—a short novel—when the two words are signed, letter by plodding letter, in finger-spelling. Which is the problem with signed spelling, signed English; by the time you get to the last letter you've forgotten the first. Sign-spelling takes forever, but there's no single hand-shape—no hieroglyph—for John, or for James.

The deaf world calls me J.J. Sign shorthand: the J-shape, repeated. Or sometimes Double-J, Twice-J: the Two Hand, followed by a J.

Friends use the sign-name my parents gave me: a pet name, a family name. Frozen on the page it looks a little like this: first the Good Hand, touching the lips—Good-on-the-lips, meaning 'sweet':

Then the Point Hand, tapping the front tooth.

Sweet-Tooth. Self-explanatory, if out of date: my teeth are nowhere near as sweet as they once were. I gave up sugar years ago, trying, without success, to lose a little ballast. A sugar-free diet was Jill's idea, her reasoning, as always, unassailable. When the marriage ended I'd lost the taste. It still hasn't come back.

The name stuck: Sweet-Tooth. The Deaf like to give each other names like that, names that mean something, like Red Indian names, Japanese names, nicknames. Sitting Bull. Lotus Blossom. Miss-The-Point.

My mother invented endless pet names, nick-signs, for me. Butter-Ball. Little-Bear. Big-Ears.

This last was a gentle tease, shaped with mock sympathy and mock sorrow. I was one of the handicapped, I was given to understand, born with a pair of ears that let in noise.

'You hear, but you listen not,' she would sign, half joking. 'Your ears get in way.'

15

Congenital deformities, she liked to dub them. Ornamental flaps. Beneath the surface of those jokes lurked a great disappointment, even a minor family tragedy: I could hear.

Fear also lurked beneath those jokes. One day the world of the hearing, the wider world of speech, would surely take me from her, and never give me back.

Pressured by jokes and love, I tried hard to be deaf; tried my very best. The role was easy as a toddler, Sign comes effortlessly at that age: a pointed finger, a cocked eyebrow, a pursed mouth, the universal alphabet of gesture. It's part of our nature, more natural to us, Deaf Pride would argue, than speech. And much easier to learn. The hand is quicker than the tongue in the first few months of a child's life; the dumbest deaf babies learn to sign for 'milk' or 'mother' long before those with hearing can find the words to ask.

'Milk' is a simple milking mime, Spread Hand tightening into Fist Hand, tugging an imaginary udder:

Transparent, is the term used in dictionaries of Sign. My own preferred term: see-through signs. Even the non-deaf (poor handicapped cripples) can read the meaning in such simple hand-shapes, can see clear *through* them.

The Mother Hand is more opaque, a scout salute, roughly M-shaped if viewed with the eye of faith:

The Mother Hand, the Good Hand, the Spread Hand, the Flat Hand—these are the true letters of our alphabet; the building blocks of Sign. The plodding A-B-C of finger-spelling belongs only to the edges, the frontier with the foreign tongue of English, a last resort when all else fails.

4

I found my mother downstairs, sharing a table in a far corner of the common room with various cronies—an impromptu meeting of the Deaf Library committee. Always clairvoyant, she looked up at the precise moment I entered the room, and raised her eyebrows, an unmistakable question. I lifted my hands and answered from the doorway:

'Start W-E-D.'

Arms fully extended, high above her head, she shook her hands—Deaf-applause—then clasped them tightly together, a triumphant 'Congratulations!'

I filled a cup with water from the urn, stirred in a spoonful of coffee, and glanced about with growing confidence. The strange larynx noises and explosive laughter of the Deaf filled my ears, the bird-flutter of their hands filled my eyes. I knew everyone gathered in that large room, or everyone above the age of five. Heads began to turn towards me, smiles of recognition bloomed here and there, hands began to wave greetings.

'Welcome back, J.J.'

'Looking good!'

'Don't use all the sugar, Sweet-Tooth.'

I sipped my unsweetened coffee with one hand, and pressed the palm of the other over my heart: heartfelt thanks. Warmth welled from some deep internal spring, overwhelming me; I suddenly loved them all. I could even spare a small sentimental ration for Miss-The-Point, sitting alone in his upstairs office, practising his American signs.

I set down my coffee and returned those Good Hand salutes, thumbs-up, in two-handed stereo, both arms spread high and wide. It was, simply, wonderful to be back.

Less simple was understanding why I had left in the first place—but I had my excuses ready, a plausible version of the truth. Jill—my ex-wife—is a linguist, a student of Aboriginal languages. To learn the language of a Stone-Age people of the central desert of Australia, she was forced to travel to the Massachussets Institute of Technology, in America. Of course I followed—a loving, supportive husband. (This part would be easy to explain.) In Boston her honours degree became a masters, her masters grew into a doctorate—and love slowly contracted into duty. The struggle of those years—the imperatives of study, rearing a young child, scratching a living from a sequence of part-time jobs—still bound us together, but artificially. Each day brought new difficulties, or if not, we managed to invent them, as if sensing that we needed their glue. When Jill finally returned to Adelaide, a tenured academic, and I followed her back, less supportive than relieved, self-scrutiny could no longer be postponed. For the first time in our married lives we had time on our hands, time to find the differences between us, and leisure to argue over them.

The shape for marriage is a simple two-handed mime, the Okay Hand fitting a ring to the third finger of the Spread Hand.

Divorce is even more evocative: that imaginary ring ripped from the finger and tossed aside, hurled back across the shoulder, into the past.

20

5

I first learnt English—the noise of English—from television. I knew the look of English from books, but television
was my conversation partner for years. It arrived in the
living room when I was three, and from that day squatted
in the corner, permanently switched on, like background
music—muzak—for the eyes. This was long before the days
of TV captions, or teletext TV. My parents couldn't hear
the set but they liked to bask in its flickering presence, an
electronic fire in a corner of the room, warming them with
a constant glow. There was always plenty to see. Rare late-
night silent movies were a must: Chaplin, Keaton, Laurel
and Hardy. Sport was good to watch—any sport. They
liked dance movies, which were another kind of sport.
Fred Astaire and Ginger Rogers, ballet programmes on the
ABC, jive movies, rock'n'roll—their taste was catholic. The
music was beyond them, but not the rhythms. They turned

21

up the volume, pulled off their slippers and socks and pressed their bare feet against the vibrating floorboards like swollen ears.

My mother loved wildlife documentaries; my father preferred cartoons. *Road Runner* was his favourite. *Road Runner* was made for the Deaf, surely, probably made *by* the Deaf. He sat glued to the set each night, laughing his high-pitched laugh—the too-loud laugh he couldn't hear himself—and missing nothing but the quick gobble of the bird, that blurty empty beer-bottle noise.

They both watched *The Golden Years of Hollywood* every Wednesday night, and Movie of the Week every Sunday night. From the age of five I translated those movies, sitting on a cushion between my parents and the set, slightly to one side, cribbing English dialogue into the shapes of Sign whenever my father's toes pressed against the small of my back, prompted.

Foreign movies—movies with subtitles—weren't much use to them. They couldn't tell who was speaking the words that appeared on the screen. TV captions were a gift from heaven. My father bought the first decoder in the city, and possibly in the whole country.

'Expensive,' my mother signed, worried—an eloquent blend of the hand-shapes for 'money' and 'pain'.

Somehow they found the money and suffered the pain. A handyman, my father was always interested in devices for the Deaf. He works as a draughtsman—like many of the Deaf he has a special talent for design, a keen feel for the dimensions of space. He likes to tinker in his toolshed at night and on weekends. He once rigged up his own flashing-light door 'bells', and sold a few to deaf friends. He built his own baby-alarm when I was born: a small microphone screwed to my cot activated a vibrating device inside my mother's pillow. The Mark I alarm was a great success; soon he was selling Mark II to deaf communities all over the country.

The first signing videos, teletext decoders, and captioned programmes came as no surprise. He'd already thought of these concepts himself, he just didn't have the electronic nous, and possibly the working capital, to solder them together.

The shape for 'father': the letter F, repeated, an upper-case emphasis.

Of course something, perhaps everything, is missing from these cartoons I keep sketching among the words. Sign is lifeless the moment it hits the page: a language as dead as any hieroglyphs painted on the walls of a tomb. It's no longer even Sign; Sign moves and breathes, whispers, shouts, pirouettes, jives...

6

The shape for 'house' is a child's simple sketch, a finger-painting written in air:

My parents' house, exactly: a red-brick box on the Glenelg esplanade, as neat and square and orderly as a doll's house, and filled with little doll-ornaments.

The garden is equally well ordered, a smooth square of billiard-felt lawn, a single military rank of rose bushes behind the front fence. Atten-*shun*! Pre-sent *blooms*!

As always I could show this small, neat world much better with my hands. I could shape each room, each neat garden bloom, hold up objects in the bright light of Sign, turn them this way and that, polish them with gesture. I could almost shape the perfume of that garden.

Above all, I could show the world across the road, on the far side of the esplanade. The undulating Flat Hand of wave. The Spread Hand forward roll of collapsing surf. Sand: an invisible trickle between the fingers. I have always loved the sea; it seems my natural element, more natural to me than land, as if I am part-amphibian. Overweight and awkward on the shore, in the water, at least, I am beautiful. And unsinkable.

I swim each night, sheathed in a wetsuit, rubber flippers stuck to my feet, more seal than human. The sea soothes me at the end of the day; I like to think, to meditate, floating weightless in the dark.

My mother would use a different set of signs to describe the beach. She hates the crunch of sand underfoot in her house, the salt-blight in her garden. I have never known her to swim, or even paddle in the shallows. Her raised Flat Hand, a cruising dorsal fin, was a constant warning to me as a child.

She works part-time as a librarian, a perfect job for the Deaf. She runs the Deaf Library as a volunteer, after-hours; nine to five she works in the local council library. As a child I would walk there after school each day, and study or browse till closing time. She moved through those quiet aisles with the grace of a dancer—the Deaf can always dance—shelving books from trolleys, surrounded by mysterious notices on every wall: *Silence, Please.*

The hearing have a hush-sign for silence: a single finger pressed to pursed lips. The shape means nothing to the Deaf, it has no entry in dictionaries of Sign. What is silence?

Her library was my second home. I was a loner, a fatty, a bookworm; my best friends were the friends I met in books. Much of my childhood (the childhood I spent on land) was spent reading at those big wide tables, or borrowing books to read at home. Television taught me to hear, but the library taught me to read. It was a strange sort of reading—I wasn't to hear the sounds of many of the longer words I saw in books till much later. I never learnt to pronounce them properly; I still can't. I saw them rather than heard them as I read. They came through my eyes long before they came through my ears; I knew them by look, not sound.

Even when I spoke new words, I pronounced them wrongly. For years I said character as it's spelt. *Ch*ocolate, *ch*urch, *ch*aracter. I still hear it that way in my head: chattanooga character. I prefer to hear it that way: I think it has more character, a richer sound. Misled is the same. Others hear Miss Lead when they see the word on a page, I hear mistled. As in mistletoe.

Books mistled me. Classmates laughed out loud when it was my turn in reading-time at school, or when I spoke long words that no one could recognise.

My parents had no conception of this. How could they? And yet I blamed them—or began, slowly, to blame them.

My mother is a small, dainty woman; in part her dancer's grace is the compact grace of the small. My father is also small, but stockier—an athlete, a sprinter. A Roadrunner. He ran a close second in the Bay Sheffield in his teens, and a more distant third in the Stawell Gift. He would have won, my mother liked to claim, given a good start. He couldn't hear the starting gun, and lost precious time watching the other runners or waiting for the puff of smoke. A proud man, he spurned the shelter of such excuses himself. My mother has a drawer full of newspaper clippings from those glory days. He looks the same in every picture, a small, cocky bantam with a puffed out chest and ramrod back, staring the camera straight in the eye. 'The Deaf Dash', the sports headlines dubbed him. In his later footballing days, this shrank to 'Dasher'. Dasher James.

27

He took more pride in that. He didn't want any special favours, special adjectives.

Life had been easier for him than for most of the Deaf, his fast-twitch muscle-fibres had opened any number of half-closed doors. He had no patience for those who couldn't force their way through those doors. Always more willing than my mother to pass judgement, he believed firmly that those who were locked out in the cold belonged there, deserved to be there.

'Give all the money in the world to the poor, and... what?' he once signed to me.

I shrugged: what?

'After six months the rich have it all back again.'

My mother, overhearing—overseeing—threw up her hands in horror.

He had a repertoire of little sayings, or signings, like that: a cliché for every occasion. Sooth-signings. He was a champion on the football field, a quick little man who played a hundred-odd games for the local football club, and two for the state team. After work, he sometimes took me to the beach for kicks. He could hit me on the chest with a football from any distance. He could knock a crow off a Norfolk Island pine with a football.

I couldn't hit the side of the sea-wall. I always headed for the safety of the water as soon as his back was turned. Even then I was too slow and awkward on land. Too fat.

'Too cuddly,' my mother signed, reassuringly. She had her own two-handed mime for 'cuddle', a family sign, somewhere between 'hug' and 'bear', with a bit of 'love' merged in. Two fists, crossed tightly on the chest.

28

We had a family sign for 'fat' too, the mouth pursed tightly shut, the cheeks inflated: a mime of fatness. Or is it more a mime of the *cause* of fatness, a mouth stuffed full of food?

She never let my father criticise me. Hers was a much fiercer sense of injustice; many of the Deaf share that sense. Anyone who has suffered at the hands of the unimaginative shares that sense.

She would always back the underdog, any underdog. She always supported the bottom team on the football ladder. She took me most Saturdays to watch my father play when I was little, and he was nearing the end of his career. She barracked, signing frantically, for the team that was losing—'running second'—even if he was playing, as he usually was, for the team that was winning. He had no need for sympathy, he had never felt himself to be an underdog.

'Great vision,' a commentator once said on television, as we watched a footy show replay on Sunday morning, and my father stabbed some pass across his shoulder to hit a team mate on the chest. 'James doesn't need ears—he's got eyes in the back of his head.'

My father's toe jabbed my back; I interpreted, and they both laughed the explosive incontinent deaf-laugh that neither of them could ever hear; a loud tuneless alien laugh that made heads turn in public and embarrassed me no end.

I learnt the sign for 'embarrassed' early: the dominant Fist Hand disappearing behind the Flat Hand's screen— hiding its head in shame. Crawling into a hole.

Plus an even simpler, more expressive sign: the Flat Hand sliding up to cover the face. Sometimes with the shape for 'red' added: shame-face, red-face.

When I write the word 'embarrassed' on this page, when I remember those times, this is closest to what I feel.

This *is* what I feel. The sign is the thing it represents.

My parents' weird speech was another embarrassment, a speech they couldn't hear themselves, but pieced together from studying tongue and lip positions. It had a blurred, indistinct sound, a language of vowels, as if the edges of its consonants had been sanded smooth. It sounded like the speech of clowns, or spastics.

In my teens I found it difficult to be their son in public. My behaviour is hard to explain, harder still to excuse, but I seemed to change overnight. I still loved them, that went without saying—at home, in private. In public I was shamed by them. The two feelings—love and shame—fused together, and warped each other into strange new forms.

I insisted they keep their mouths shut in public, and only communicate with others through me.

I always walked several paces ahead or behind.

I bought a cheap guitar, taught myself a handful of basic chords, and sang my way through *The Bob Dylan Songbook*, a private world they couldn't share, or even enter.

I said things behind their backs, often shouted things behind their backs. To abuse my father after I'd been punished for some misdemeanor—to stand a few inches from the back of his head and shout *fuck you* and *hate you*, unnoticed—was a wonderful release. Perhaps it even helped me to pass more quickly through that shameful time.

I also lied to them. I played jokes at their expense. Once, once only, I even deliberately mistranslated the Movie of the Week, inventing the occasional line of dialogue at first, then faking whole scenes.

Both my parents could lip-read, partially, and both were highly sensitive to body language, but somehow my improvements—my lies—were overlooked at first. Shifting their attention between the screen and my hands meant that they were able to scrutinise neither perfectly, non sequiturs went unnoticed. They also saw exactly what they wanted to see; my mother was always more willing to believe in happy endings than sad.

The lies soon snowballed, uncontrollably, my leaky memory could not keep pace with the changes. As the end of the movie approached disappointment seeped slowly into my mother's face, spreading across her small neat features like a stain. I had overstepped the mark. She could tolerate being shunned in public, she could tolerate my private world of music, but this was a betrayal of trust. It took some time for her to accept what I'd done; finally, with tears in her eyes, she lifted her hands.

'Not funny,' she signed, 'cruel.'

Cruel: the Point Hand become a knife, slitting the throat.

That same knife was turning in my heart. I regretted instantly what I had done, and fumbled for excuses.

'Joke,' I signed, 'just joking.'

'Bullshit,' my father signed back: the Two Hand thrust from the mouth, double-speak, forked tongue.

He stood and slapped me hard across the face. For once my mother failed to defend me.

'You deaf—not,' she signed, sadly. 'You understand—not.'

The accusation was always there, barely beneath the surface: if I had been born deaf I might have been a better, more decent person.

When I remember those teenage years now, I'm embarrassed—shamed—only by myself. I squirm inside; my hands fly up to cover my face, involuntarily.

Sign puts it best:

7

Wednesday night, Basic Auslan, Room 101—my first class for years. I zipped my lips, theatrically, then tapped my watch twice. Not classical Sign, but the point was clearly made: no English to be spoken for the next two hours.

My apprehension was clearly mirrored in the faces of my students.

Twenty-odd beginners were scattered around the edges of the classroom, repelled from me and from each other by the powerful centrifugal force of shyness.

None were deaf. Basic Sign is aimed more at the friends and families of the Deaf, a course for the hearing. Social workers, trainee nurses and teachers help make up the numbers.

I plucked a book from the nearest desk, turned it this way and that with exaggerated interest, set it down, then demonstrated the sign. Two open palms, hinged together: two pages.

Heads nodded here and there, tentative hands began to mimic the shape. I walked among the scattered desks, pointing out other everyday objects, silently demonstrating their corresponding signs. Desk, window, pen—simple representations, all of them. See-through shapes.

'Are we late?'

A voice—a woman's husky contralto—jarred the silence; all eyes turned. Two late-comers were framed in the doorway: a thin, elderly man in corduroy trousers and coat, and the speaker, a plumper, younger woman in jeans and a khaki work shirt. A cigarette was jammed in her mouth; she removed it and spoke again, a small explosion of smoke.

'We *are* in the right place? Basic Auslan? Finally?'

A plump black dog pushed its head between her legs and gazed in, tongue lolling; a titter of surprise rippled across the class.

'This place is a maze,' she said.

I pressed a finger to my lips; realisation dawned, she turned to her older companion and smote her forehead with her fist: Stupid-me.

I liked her immediately, a natural signer. She had a comfortable thirty-something face, plenty of laugh-lines, a broad lopsided smile. The rest of her body looked equally comfortable, a collection of bulges unapologetically sheathed in those tightish denim jeans. A skewed bunch of hair topped her head, a kind of vertical spout, a punkish semblance of carelessness.

She looked from her cigarette to me, and raised her eyebrows quizzically. I shook my head firmly, she grimaced in mock pain, took one last exaggerated drag, then ground the butt beneath her heel.

More titters among my students; they were enjoying the performance.

She pointed to the dog, and lifted her eyebrows again, another unspoken question. I spread my hands and shrugged; I knew of no rules forbidding dogs from the classroom. She was wearing heavy work boots; the effect, as she tiptoed theatrically to a desk in the front row, was clown-like. Her plump black dog waddled painfully after her, its front and rear ends composed, it seemed, of disconnected halves.

Her human companion also followed. Despite his age and small stature, he too seemed to command attention. He sported a surprisingly youthful head of hair, but the face beneath was lined and leathery—it reminded me of a shrunken head. He walked with a slight forward stoop, choosing each step with care. His clothes had a vaguely academic look: brown coat, dark skivvy, brown cord-jeans. On his feet were a pair of white sneakers, an athlete's triple-striped running shoes, an incongruous touch.

Despite the clear age difference there was something in their body language as they sat together—practised intimacy, a kind of subliminal *pas-de-deux*—that suggested husband and wife.

The dog spread itself on the floor, resting its chin on her boot; I regained the attention of the class.

I tapped my chest, simplest of possessive pronouns:

My, I chalked in large letters on the blackboard.

Heads nodded; so far, so good.

Name, I added, then shaped the word with my free hand: an opaque sign made with the Hook Hand.

The class waited; I set down the chalk and finger-spelt, slowly, with both hands: 'J-O-H-N.'

I signed to the furthest student: 'Your name…what?'

She shrank further into her corner. I pointed to a wall-chart above her head—an illustrated finger-spelling alphabet—and coaxed a reluctant, misshapen J-O-A-N-N-A from her timid hands.

It took a good minute. I mimed exhaustion, boredom, melodramatically wiped my brow. More titters in the class. I signed an abbreviation—'J-O'—with a great show of relief. The students laughed, more loudly, the ice of shyness was slowly breaking. Inside another five minutes, all were practising standard introductions: greetings and names, finger-spelt.

'Hi.'

'Hi.'

'Pleased to meet you. My name J.J. Your name what?'

'My name S-T-E-L-L-A.'

The latecomer in the front row smiled, pleased with herself. She was easily the most fluent of the students. She sprawled comfortably in her chair, legs apart, her body language relaxed, open, interested—a sharp contrast to the rest of the class, still terrified of making fools of themselves.

Her companion, or husband, was also quick to grasp the shapes, if not quite as quick as his wife: 'My name C-L-I-V-E.'

There was something measured and overcontrolled in his finger-spelling. His legs were crossed, rather prissily, his posture was more upright, more feminine, than his wife's. He struck me as the type who might pull out a pipe mid-sentence, tamp in tobacco, apply a match, and puff, meditatively, before finishing.

'Good-to-meet-you C-L-I-V-E.'

His leathery face seemed familiar but I couldn't quite place it. I scanned the class-roll on my desk, surreptitiously. His surname also had a familiar tang: *Kinnear, Clive.* Immediately below it: *Todd, Stella.*

'B-I-N-K-Y,' Stella finger-spelt, and pointed to her dog, flattened like a seal against the floor, staring up with mournful spaniel-eyes.

37

I signed hello to Binky; she thumped her tail sluggishly against the floor; more titters.

I steered the class further into the usual beginners' repertoire. Signs for 'yes' and 'no'. 'Please' and 'thank you'. The beard-shape for 'man', the long-hair shape for 'woman'. I opened the window, mimed the shivering-fists of 'cold'; closed the window, wiped my sweaty-brow: 'hot'.

More laughter, and a smattering of applause.

I shook my head with mock horror at those clapping hands, cupped my ear, shook my head again. Puzzled faces all around; I demonstrated deaf-applause: the hands raised high above the head, shaking, shimmying.

The class followed suit, smiling, nodding.

I was on familiar terrain, increasingly at ease. I shaped the numbers one to ten, ten to twenty, twenty to a hundred. I shaped the sign for one thousand, an elegant economy I've always loved: a single finger 'one', followed by the twist sign for 'comma'. Two thousand: two, comma.

The class was gradually relaxing, unfolding. Sign has that effect; it brings people out of themselves. It brings *me* out of myself; switching from English to Sign I become less awkward, more extroverted.

I become myself.

If time is a bird, the bird is surely a swift; as of old the lesson flew by, students began glancing discreetly at their watches.

'Any last questions?' I chalked on the board.

Stella raised her hand; I nodded.

'Can we ask them in English?'

Her words, the first spoken words for two hours,

sounded overloud, almost hurtful to the ear. Or perhaps it was her voice, a smoker's voice, abrasive, sandpapery.

I answered her in Sign: 'In lessons—only Sign. Speaking—banned.' The sign for 'ban': emphatic, unmistakable.

I added, in English: 'But since the lesson is officially over...'

She exhaled, exaggerated relief. 'One last question then,' she said. 'What is the sign for asparagus?'

At first I thought I had misheard: 'The sign for what?'

'Asparagus.'

Another titter rippled across the class; Stella ignored it, waiting. I pursed my lips, furrowed my brow. I knew of no single sign. I was tempted to improvise—long-green-veg, green-pencil-veg. In the end I finger-spelt: A-S-P-A-R-A-G-U-S.

'Long way,' I added, apologetically. 'Slow way.'

As the room emptied she approached me with another request: could she bring a video camera to the next lesson?

'With your permission, of course. Taking notes is fine to a point but so much of the...*dynamic* is lost.'

Close up, she seemed slightly older than I had first thought. Mid-forties, possibly. Her face had the looseness of a well-worn garment: a lived-in face, crinkle-eyes, floppy cheeks, a generous smile.

'Our adopted daughter is learning to sign. It would be useful to have the videos at home.'

'Your daughter is deaf?'

'She's mute. She's not deaf—just dumb.'

I was puzzled: 'Your daughter can hear but she can't *speak*?'

Her body language seemed suddenly shaded with reticence; she turned to her elderly husband for help.

'Eliza was born without vocal cords,' he said.

There was something a little too calm about the way he looked me in the eye as he spoke. The body is its own polygraph: a visual display—a leakage—of signs and shapes that tell the truth despite what emerges from the mouth. The body always betrays the voice.

His forced calm gave me pause; made me think things through. A child born without vocal cords? I'd heard of no such disability, ever. I waited, curious; no elaboration was forthcoming. I felt I didn't know them well enough to push.

I asked: 'How old is she?'

Stella resumed control of the conversation: 'Eight.'

'I take it she has the basics of Sign already?'

'She's been taught a little. At the, ah, Home. Not much, but needless to say she's streets ahead of us.'

'Then perhaps *she* should be taking this class.'

40

More evasive language was written on Stella's body.

'Eliza's very shy,' her husband murmured, more controlled and deliberate in his movements, and in his speech. 'We hoped that she would agree to come but perhaps she's not quite ready.'

I knew that I had heard that quiet, precise voice somewhere before. I knew that I had seen the face, but where?

'Feel free to tape the lessons,' I said, 'but no copies can be made. Sign classes are a source of revenue for the Institute.'

He waved his hand, a little dismissively: 'It goes without saying that we would never record your material—your intellectual property—for anything other than personal use.'

Stella said, jokily: 'We promise not to sell the tapes to Hollywood, J.J.'

She slid her arm in Clive's, and steered him towards the door. As I followed them out I realised for the first time that he was wearing a hair-piece: a ginger toupée, well-camouflaged at the front, but clearly, artificially separate from the leathery skin of the back of his neck. This touch of vanity, or insecurity, finally confirmed, surely, my hunch that he *was* married to a woman young enough to be his daughter.

8

Like many of the fat, I love to drive; wheels offer a freedom and mobility that legs can never match. Wheels are a kind of compensation. And also a kind of sanctuary: a warm cocoon, often filled with music. Like the sea, they provide a good place to think. Things often come to me, driving.

I tried to place the half-familiar face of Clive Kinnear as I drove away from that first lesson. Friend of a friend? I had no friends apart from the Deaf. My former friends had turned out to be Jill's; friends after the divorce she seemed to have been granted custody of all our friends, if only by the friends themselves, choosing up sides. Had I seen him on television? A celebrity face? Stella's loose smile also itched somewhere inside me, but the more I strained after those memories, the deeper they hid, knocked a little further out of reach with each clumsy mental grab.

I set the problem aside. The night was warm, I was weary, I drove with the windows wound down. The humid air rubbed my face like balm, the ocean awaited me, cold and refreshing, I could think of nothing but immersion. A red light halted my progress at the top end of Jetty Road, at the bottom end the moonlit ocean glinted like beaten metal; I revved the motor impatiently.

FREE-RANGE CHICKEN

The words, painted on the plate glass of a corner butcher shop, somehow caught my eye and the connection was made instantly: Clive Francis Kinnear.

The lights changed, a car tooted behind me, I turned the car into the kerb, and sat there, stationary, thinking. More keys were turning, more doors opening, a chain of associations. I remembered a television news item from some months past: the picketing of a chicken-battery somewhere in the Hills. Vague images came back to me of flour bombs, torn fences, activists chained to the axles of freezer-trucks.

'Animal liberation,' I had translated to my father, watching with me at the time, prodding my back with his foot.

First, the two-horned Animal Hand:

Then the see-through sign of bound hands, unshackled:

He had laughed an angry hyena laugh. 'Animals themselves,' he signed. 'Hairy, shaved-not, washed-not.'

Content with his lot, comfortable with the life he had made for himself, without help, or charity, he had no time for fringe opinions. Or for people, or animals, who might need help.

My mother gave him a disapproving look. He corrected himself, jokily: 'You right, Mother. Unfair to animals. Animals keep clean.'

He laughed again, this time even she joined in, a pair of hyenas, guffawing out of tune.

I've set down my parents' signing as a kind of pidgin English, but of course it was more than that. Far, far more. I could never do it justice in English—the nuances, the shadings, the movement—so perhaps it's best to settle for this: a transcription of the physical hand-shapes, rather than a full translation of their freight of sense. That would be a re-creation, a new kind of poetry.

We had watched the news a little longer. The screen was filled with skinny vegetarian types in torn jeans and Indian smocks and Rasta dreadlocks, shouting and chanting. My father waved a handful of his usual opinions. It was the same rent-a-crowd he had watched storm an American satellite base the day before, he claimed. The same crowd that had chained itself to trees in a Tasmanian rainforest the week before that.

I ignored him as best I could, more interested in the news than in his editorial. Clive Francis Kinnear had been the odd face out on that screen: an older, calmer talking head in brown academic habit, clean-shaven among the beards. I had been impressed by the way he refused to raise his voice—he *lowered* it, if anything, to gain attention, to make people lean forward and strain to hear his words.

I remembered this, also: he had been at pains to distance himself from some of the actions committed by his followers, although he was careful to add that he fully 'understood' their anger.

My father had made the sign for 'saint', sarcastically, tracing a halo with his forefinger above his head.

The halo-sign came back to me as I sat in my car outside the Jetty Road butchery. It seemed a perfect fit: St Francis of the Animals.

I pulled out into the traffic again and drove home. My parents were still up, sitting each side of the kitchen table; my mother pretending to read a book, my father poking a screwdriver into the innards of the toaster. They maintained the pretence for several minutes as I fossicked for supper in the fridge, but I knew they had been waiting for me. My mother's patience gave way.

'Good first lesson?'

'Great!' I signed back. 'Feel great!'—two Good Hands welling up from the stomach, exploding out from the heart.

A slight exaggeration for her benefit, but not much. I was weary, but also happier than I had been for many months. Sign, as ever, had lifted me, and brought out the best in me.

She smiled, immensely relieved.

'Work tomorrow?'

'Work whole day. Morning—Deaf Clinic. Medical translations. School—afternoon.'

'Busy, busy,' she signed, a simple carpentry mime, a sawing and chopping of the hands.

My father, head down, half-watching from under his brow, nodded with gruff approval. Over the years I had chipped away steadily at whatever love he had once had for me, sometimes intentionally, mostly not. Growing too fat to play sport was merely the first of many disappointments. I had married the wrong woman, then compounded things by leaving her. Neither of these last two life errors he could forgive, especially the second.

His interest in the outcome of my first lesson was mostly self-interest—now that I had a secure job, I might find my own place to live. He turned his attention back to toaster repairs; I ate my supper in Sign silence, aware of a growing awkwardness in the room, despite my mother's reassuring smile. I remembered that I still had a question to ask.

'Sign A-S-P-A-R-A-G-U-S how?'

She looked surprised: 'You hungry still?'

I shook my head: 'You teach me sign.'

46

She glanced to my father; he shrugged and set down his screwdriver and wriggled his fingers, the sign for finger-spelling.

She shook her head firmly; finger-spelling English was always her last resort. She pondered for a moment, then made the sign for French or France: the tweak of a stylised moustache.

'French sign?' I asked.

'Perhaps. Look library—tomorrow.'

Awkwardness filled the room again, stilling our hands, turning our arms to lead. I felt out of place, a cuckoo in a small cramped nest.

'Swim,' I signed—using my preferred shape, the fish-tailing of the Flat Hand:

My mother furrowed her brow and raised her own Flat Hand, the cruising dorsal fin that I had long learnt to ignore. I pulled on my wetsuit in my bedroom—a rolling action, akin to the application of a condom—then had to face them both again as I waddled out a few minutes later, carrying flippers and goggles.

My father set down his tools and made the sign for seal, two flippers flapping together, derisively.

'Arf, arf,' I barked, loudly, but only of course to myself, and left them sitting together: two small neat people in a small neat house, most comfortable, finally, just with each other.

9

I arrived early at the Institute the following Wednesday. St Francis was already seated in the front row; he waved a Flat Hand as I entered, and added the letters of my name: 'J.J.' He was wearing the same brown habit of corduroy, the same white running shoes and ginger toupée. His hands were the hands of an old man, gnarled and blotched. Their shapes looked slow and stilted, but precise, and carefully rehearsed, the Sign equivalent of a synthetic computer voice.

Stella stood at the back of the empty classroom, fixing a video camera to a tripod. Her black dog Binky was lying at her feet, adoring. She was wearing the same jeans and work shirt, but her hair was loose on her shoulders; the effect was to broaden her wide face even more.

She smiled warmly, and waved the broad Thumbs-up salute: 'Hi!'

Their different characters was clearly written even in those beginner-greetings: Clive's hands coolly methodical, textbook-exact; Stella's less precise but more generous, more open, more flamboyant.

'Asparagus,' I said aloud, and showed her the French sign: a witty penis-variant.

She laughed huskily, her hands copied mine.

Other class members trickled in. Some signed hello; one or two greeted me in English, then remembered, and covered their mouths—Oops!

I demonstrated the official Oops-sign: the fist banging the forehead, a more formal version of Stella's improvisation at the first lesson. Smiles all round; a more relaxed class.

Am, I chalked on the board. *Is. Are. Were.*

I obliterated the words with a duster, a single broad wipe. No verb 'to be' in Sign, I wanted it understood.

Clive watched intently; Stella nodded from behind her video tripod; the rest of the class looked more or less blank.

I chalked two further phrases on the board: the English *I am a teacher,* and its Sign equivalent: *Me...teacher.*

I added a second, more emphatic version: *Me teacher... true.*

Awkward looking, written out in English, but spoken with the hands anything but. I signed the phrase, fluently— then more slowly; I gestured for each member of the class, in turn, to rise and sign, inserting the shape for 'student' in place of 'teacher'.

The deft hands of Stella and the precise hands of Clive stood out from the rest. They were both quick learners, surprisingly quick for adults. The brain is a language-sponge, some claim—it learns language with ease. That's what it *does,* it's hard-wired for words, for grammar. Under a microscope it probably even looks like language, has the same anatomical shape. The problem is, the wiring gets faulty with age. Or the sponge is too soggy, saturated with junk memories and ancient history, unable to soak up anything new and fresh.

Clive and Stella might not have had the fluency of children but their hands were as intelligent as the hands of any beginner-adults I'd seen.

I found myself talking mostly to them, a class within a class; a teacher, two teacher's pets. They followed me effortlessly through a maze of basic grammar, word orders, pronouns.

At lesson's end they approached me again. The rest of the class quickly evaporated, but they were both still brimming with questions. Already they attempted to say, or ask, as much as possible with their hands.

Using my own hands I invited them to the common room for a drink; repeating the invitation, slowly, several times, but eventually getting through.

Clive looked at his watch meaningfully but Stella ignored him: 'Can I smoke?'

I nodded; she shouldered her video camera bag, lit a cigarette and followed me downstairs, inhaling deeply. Binky followed, lurching from step to step.

Several tables were occupied; people were chatting in rapid Sign, a blur of hands punctuated by an occasional hyena-laugh, or too-loud spoken phrase, its consonants

51

bevelled smooth. Miss-The-Point was sitting at a far table, alone; he glanced up and waved, hopefully.

We stood at the counter; I offered my guests the usual choice. The jiggling-bag mime of tea:

The fist-grinding mime of coffee:

A slight misnomer, since the coffee was instant, but Stella beamed with the pleasure of another new discovery, and furiously ground her fists. Clive rotated his more sedately. The sign was still new to me, also—a borrowing from American Sign that had gained currency in my absence. I had stuck stubbornly to the old Auslan 'C' for coffee for some months, but resistance was futile. No one remembered, or understood.

I hoped that Miss-The-Point wasn't watching.

I demonstrated the milk-mime; Stella laughed—a small

explosion of smoke—and shook her head; Clive followed my example, more slowly. Sugar—the Good Hand at the lips—more shaking of heads. I spooned out the coffee, tapped three cups of water from the urn. My guests were distracted, watching the various small groups huddled around gesturing hands as if around the flames of a silent, flickering fire.

'It's a beautiful language,' Stella murmured in English.

'It can be ugly,' I told her. 'It can be anything it pleases.'

She touched her camera bag. 'Would people mind if I videotaped them—for Eliza?'

'You could ask.'

'How can I ask?'

'You could ask me to ask.'

She laughed. 'Maybe not tonight. They look...pre-occupied. I wouldn't want to intrude.'

I lifted the coffees onto a tray and added a plate of ham sandwiches from the cabinet shelf.

'Would you like something to eat?' I said, then added: 'We have vegetarian meals.'

Clive stared at me, surprised.

'You know our work?'

'I've seen you on television, St Francis,' I said, cheekily tracing the halo-sign above my head.

A small risk, but I was feeling more comfortable in their company. They both laughed—the first real laugh I had heard emerge from Clive's prim mouth.

'Don't believe everything you see on television,' Stella said.

'Perish the thought.'

She selected a cheese sandwich; they both followed me to an empty table, as far from Miss-The-Point as possible. I passed out the coffees; we sat, and sipped.

'Clive's books are his real work,' Stella said.

'I must read them.'

'All good bookshops have them,' he said.

Stella added, timing-perfect: 'And a few of the bad.'

It seemed a practised joke; the performance of a double-act, a tag-team. Stella took a bite from her sandwich then passed the rest under the table to Binky; Clive's attention wandered again, distracted by the signing at a nearby table. His lips moved, barely perceptibly, as he caught snatches of a phrase, and made the translation into English.

I said: 'Ah…About your daughter…'

'Eliza,' he reminded me.

'Eliza. When will she begin classes?'

'We're working on it.'

'She's…eight?'

They both nodded, I pressed on: 'The first years of language acquisition are crucial. She should immerse herself in Sign as soon as possible.'

An invisible current passed between them; Stella finally spoke for both: 'She is *very* shy, J.J. Maybe a classroom is not the right environment. We hoped—we realise it's a lot to ask…' She paused and took a deep breath before continuing. 'We hoped that you might consider taking her as a private student. Tutoring her.'

'For a trial period,' Clive added.

I was flattered, but there were strict rules about such arrangements, proper channels.

'Jeremy Hinkley, the Director, takes the Advanced class. He's sitting over there. I could introduce you.'

They looked towards Miss-The-Point; he smiled and waved; they turned back to me.

Clive said: '*You* wrote the textbook.'

'Years ago. It's out of date.'

These days I try to keep it quiet: *Sign for Beginners*, a primer of basic hand-shapes I wrote—or mostly sketched—in my twenties. To call it a textbook was to invest it with false authority, it was little more than a stapled pamphlet, albeit a best-seller in the Deaf world, briefly.

I said: 'Johnston's dictionary is far more up-to-date.'

He insisted: 'We want a teacher, not a dictionary. We've been told that you are the best qualified.'

Stella smiled, and signed: 'You good teacher...true.'

More flattery, but I was susceptible. Separated from my wife and daughter, alienated from my parents, I was more in need of love than flattery—but beggars can't be choosers. The company of friends, the small verbal love-bites of their flattery, these at least provided a surrogate love, a temporary sustenance. Especially when their flattery agreed with my own self-flattery. For surely I *was* a good teacher—my best student had clearly learnt that day's lesson in Sign grammar.

'Congratulations,' I signed to Stella—my left hand shaking my right hand, more a self-congratulation.

She caught the irony and laughed.

'It's short notice,' she said, in English. 'But why don't you join us for a meal on Saturday night? We could work on you over dinner.'

Clive turned to her sharply, the invitation had clearly not been canvassed between them.

'I'd like that,' I said, before she could withdraw it.

'And your—partner, of course,' she added, more a question than an invitation.

I found it easier to answer in Sign, grasping my ring finger.

'You're married?' Stella interrupted, pleased with herself.

I shook my head violently, and finished what I had been about to sign, plucking that imaginary wedding ring from my finger, and tossing it aside.

'Oh,' she said, not knowing whether to laugh or sympathise. 'I'm sorry.'

I shook my head: 'Don't be.'

Clive looked at his watch again; this time Stella acknowledged the hint. 'We should be off. Saturday night, J.J.?'

'I'll look forward to it. And meeting Eliza.'

Another barely perceptible exchange of glances passed between them; Stella spoke again: 'That might not be possible, J.J. She goes to bed early.'

'Shall I come in the afternoon?'

Clive rescued his wife: 'I don't think that's appropriate at this stage. She has a strict daily routine.'

Stella added, brightly: 'Come at seven. We live in the Hills, it's a bit hard to find. You have a car?'

I nodded.

'I'll fax directions to the Institute tomorrow morning,' she said.

10

I didn't sleep well on Friday night. The night was hot; a mix of anxiety and anticipation added several more degrees to my mental weather. I don't make friends among the hearing easily. I blame my size, the social barrier of fat. I find social occasions—occasions that don't have some kind of inbuilt, pre-stressed structure—near impossible. A classroom is fine, teacher–student roles are clearly defined and demarcated. But drop me into a party and I'm lost. People look past you, look through you, when you're fat. A strange thing: somehow *you* embarrass *them*.

Excuses, excuses? So Jill liked to claim. She often held up examples, fat role models, that I would do well to emulate.

'Gerry Swain is fat—he's always the life of the party.'

'Overcompensation,' I diagnosed.

'You use your size as an excuse, John. The simple truth is you don't like *people*.'

'I like people. I just don't like some of your friends.'

Of course there was a kernel of truth in what she said. Fat is a convenient substance to hide inside, a convenient wall to hide behind.

I slept fitfully; around five I extracted myself from my tangled bedsheets and pulled on my wetsuit. I sneaked out through the back door, crossed the esplanade and waddled down the beach steps. The sea was smooth as glass, bone-cold, refreshing. Floating far out of my depth, suspended between the blackness of the night sky and the black deep of the Gulf, I decided to prepare properly for my meal with Clive and Stella. I decided to *study* for it.

Around six the eastern sky was beginning to lighten, the racket of the early birds carried to me across the still water. I emerged from the sea as the first kitchen lights began to flick on up and down the esplanade, our own among them. My mother was fussing in the kitchen, preparing breakfast.

'Up early,' she signed as I entered.

'Busy day.'

'Wash feet,' she added, sternly. 'Outside.'

After breakfast I followed her to the library, fending off her surprise with the answer 'research', a kind of scratching in the dirt, repeatedly—literally 'search-again'.

Another American loan-sign.

A single copy of C. Francis Kinnear's *The Rights of Animal* was listed in the catalogue, I claimed it from the Biology section. My mother stamped the book without

58

comment; my reading had always ranged widely, even weirdly.

I spent Saturday hiding in my small first-floor office at the Institute, studying. The severe look of the book—plain cover, hymnal black—matched its contents. A photograph of Clive stared out from the inside flyleaf, but it was a flattering photograph of a much younger Clive. The meditative eyes were the same, and the prim down-turned mouth, but he was wearing a full head of his own hair.

A pipe poked from the breast pocket of his jacket.

Beneath the photograph a biographical note offered further clues:

> *Clive Francis Kinnear spent twenty years escaping from the educational care of the Jesuits, finally abandoning his theological studies on the brink of Holy Orders to take a degree in zoology at the University of Sydney. He continued his studies as a Rhodes Scholar at Balliol College, Oxford. He currently holds a Personal Chair in Zoology at the University of Adelaide. Together with his wife, the veterinarian and celebrated poet Stella Todd, he is regarded as one of the founders of the Animal Rights movement.*

'Escaped' from the Jesuits? On the 'brink' of Holy Orders? Those light touches sounded more like Stella than her serious husband. It seemed a safe bet that she had written this brief biography, including, surely, that immodest self-description of 'celebrated'.

For Stella was printed on the dedication page.

The book proper was clearly all Clive's own work, a written version of his cool, compelling voice. His measured speaking tones could be clearly heard from the opening paragraph of the preface:

In writing this book it would be all too easy to appeal to the emotions of readers; to describe the cruelties perpetrated by humans against animals in highly charged language. But emotional responses fade, they are rapidly replaced by new and different emotions. My intent here is to convince the reader with logic. I have attempted to describe, in precise and uncoloured language, the treatment of animals in various human industries: the meat industry, the medical research industry, the animal products industry, the pet industry, the fishing industry. I have also attempted to arrive at some sort of logical ethical basis which might underpin our future relations with animals. In each of my arguments I leave the reader to draw his or her own conclusions from the material provided— although I believe those conclusions to be inescapable.

The preface was followed by a 300-page catalogue of horrors and cruelties—crimes—against animals. Vivisections, tortures, neglects, imprisonments, deprivations. Genocides. The low temperature of the language, the matter-of-fact descriptions only added to the horror. In retrospect it seems a brilliant trick, a debating trick: Clive having his cake and eating it, his cool words only fuelling the reader's emotional heat.

This reader, certainly. I swore off meat that day for life. And the use of leather products. Also drugs tested on animals. Gelatine. Lard. Whale perfumes. Bone, ivory. Dairy products. Wool.

I even renounced silk—silkworms, St Francis claimed in chapter 7, were boiled alive in their cocoons.

I arrived home that afternoon filled with zeal—exultant with zeal, high on zeal. No one was home, I had the house to myself. I began in my own room, among my own things. I emptied out my chest of drawers, and summarily judged and separated the items. My woollen socks and pullovers, and my single silk tie, I stashed in a garbage bag.

I ripped open the lining of my parka, searching for duck-down. My pillow, likewise—it proved to be made of foam rubber. Vegetable, not animal. Or even mineral: polythene, or polyester. Having decontaminated my bedroom, I moved out into the rest of the house. Clive's horror stories still filled my mind; I emptied out the larder cupboard, the tins of sardines and salmon and tuna, the canned pea-and-ham and chicken-noodle soups, the jars of my father's favourite anchovy paste. His reactions were the least of my concerns: if anything, there was an added thrill in anticipating the later arguments and recriminations. For once I would have right on my side; I would be lecturing him from a higher pulpit. I cleansed all milk and butter and cheese and yoghurt from the fridge, and finally, lastly, I purged the freezer of frozen chicken. I could barely bring myself to look at the unspeakable substance, free-range or not.

I lugged the full garbage bins to the front gate, ready for collection. I defrosted the fridge, and scalded the chopping

61

boards on which so much animal flesh had been hacked into tiny pieces.

I had purified the entire house. I had washed out its mouth with soap. But *I* still felt soiled. I stripped, stepped into the shower and scrubbed clean my entire surface area, then dressed myself in one hundred per cent cotton clothing, and scribbled a note of righteous explanation, or excuse, which I left on the kitchen table, paper-clipped to my library copy of *The Rights of Animal*.

11

The long drive into the Hills tranquillised me. The steady rush of air and the soothing hum of rubber on bitumen always has a calming effect. I drive a bubble-car, a tiny Fiat, one of the few possessions I salvaged from the wreckage of my marriage. Jill, tiny herself, a compact, no-nonsense shape, preferred small cars. (I seem surrounded by small, compact people.) Big cars, she persuaded me, were wasteful.

Jill collects small objects of every kind. Our life together was spent amid a clutter of tiny ornaments, miniature pot-plants, bonsai trees. Our bed was too narrow; I was often forced out onto a mattress in the spare room. The clothes she bought for my birthdays or for Christmas were always several sizes too small. Our meals were frugal. Perhaps it was a sensible economy: eat less, wear less. After Rosie's birth we had three mouths to feed, and half a job between us. I was teaching part-time at the Institute, she was tutoring at the University, there was never any money in the house.

Were those small clothes also an expression of hope, or encouragement, that I might shrink to fit them? I shrank to fit the Fiat: a one-person car, a loner's car, little more than an item of tight-fitting clothing itself. When I drive it—when I wear it—I feel I've slipped into something snug, and supportive, a wetsuit of beaten metal.

Indignation faded as I drove; the usual objections to vegetarianism began to form in my mind. There was an obvious appeal to natural law: animals eat animals, why shouldn't we? As for animal experiments: is or isn't a single human life worth more than the lives of any number of animals? Answers to these questions were buried in Clive Kinnear's book—convincing answers, answers spelt out step-by-step, with iron-clad Jesuit-trained logic—but I couldn't seem to remember them. I remembered only the accusation in the last lines of his preface: *A tour of the abattoirs might put a visitor off his or her dinner, but he or she will usually manage a hearty breakfast of sausages and bacon the next morning.*

I followed the fax-map up the long incline of Greenhill Road, struggled over the main ridge of hills, then coasted down into the Summertown valley beyond. Late summer, daylight saving—8 pm belonged more to late afternoon than evening. The eastern slopes of the valley, tessellated with vineyards and cherry groves, were still drenched in golden afternoon light, the western face was mostly in shadow. Stella had suggested I allow forty minutes driving time; it was nearer sixty before my Fiat turned into the last dirt track.

64

Thick bush lined one side of the road, a fence and stubbled field the other. I turned a small bend and was confronted by a wooden gate in the fence. A miscellany of animals grazed beyond: several sway-backed horses, a small flock of goats and sluggish grey kangaroos, two ancient donkeys, and a single hobbling red deer that was missing an entire hind leg. None moved freely; none, certainly, could have possessed any commercial value as stock. The sense of a veterinary retirement home—of animals put out to pasture—reassured me that I had reached my destination, that Stella was close at hand.

Beyond the gate, the dirt track crossed the field, skirted a small muddy-looking dam, then climbed a nearby hill, vanishing into a large stand of native pines and bush. The vegetation, rising abruptly from the shaved stubbled scalp of the hill, had a shorn-off mohawk appearance; the suggestion of a house could be glimpsed here and there through the trees.

PLEASE CLOSE was inscribed on a metal plate wired to the gate—but first there was the problem of opening it. The latch was operated electrically; an intercom was embedded in the wooden gatepost. I pressed the buzzer; a scrambled version of Stella's contralto shortly issued through the speaker:

'Push the gate, J.J.—it's open.'

At the sound of her voice the head of every animal grazing in the paddock lifted, ears pricked, and turned towards me— then, as if disappointed, bent back to the stubble.

The dirt track beyond the gate looked treacherous; I left my car outside and walked rapidly across the field, ignored by the animals. Another fence marked the boundary of field and trees; I opened a second gate and entered the mohawk stand. A car tyre was suspended by a thick hemp rope from a high branch; a child's perma-pine tree-house crouched in the fork above: dangerously high, I would have thought.

The house revealed itself, brick by brick, through the thinning trees: a two-storey bungalow, its upper level clearly a later addition. A jeep was parked to one side, a rust-bucket, mud-spattered, open-topped. Stella was sitting on the edge of a long verandah, a cigarette glowing in her mouth. She was clad in grimy overalls and muddy farm boots, this was a working farm, apparently. Two fat, rheumy-eyed dogs lay on the paving each side of her, as I approached their tails wagged minimally.

'Welcome to Fort Knox, J.J.'

I was panting a little, overexerted by the short climb: 'You like privacy?'

'We have the animals to think of.'

The dogs lay low, watching me, flattened even further against the verandah floor by their own obesity. She rubbed the ears of one; the other growled and nipped her thigh, jealously.

'And of course our work has bred enemies. We have to change our phone number *daily:* nuisance calls, even the odd death threat.'

A third dog waddled from the house, as if drawn by the sound of her voice.

'You've met Binky before,' Stella said.

'A former patient?' I guessed.

'Her family decided that Binky was past it—they asked me to put her down.'

'And you couldn't?'

She bent and pressed her nose lovingly against the dog's: 'Could you?'

The other two dogs staggered to their feet, and nudged at her, demanding equal attention.

'Chester,' she introduced them. 'And George.'

'More refugees?'

She puffed at her cigarette, averting her head to exhale, as if concerned by the possible effect of passive smoking on the health of her pets.

'George was a stray, some local kids found him and brought him here. Chester needed a little operation. I saved his life and his fucking family reneged on the bill.'

She paused, looking up at me.

'I kept him in lieu of payment,' she finally said, a small smile playing on her lips.

Just in case I might have some false notion that she was a soft touch, a sentimentalist. Or perhaps her words had a slightly different emphasis: she was a soft touch for dogs but no pushover for humans.

She unlaced her work boots, pulled them off, and ushered me inside. A living-cum-dining room opened off the wide hall; at the far end a small kitchen sheltered behind a wide bench, as if in the crook of an elbow. The impression was of cluttered squalor; I picked my way carefully among a miscellany of dog bowls, stacks of newspaper, empty wine bottles, and half a dozen shoes, none of which apparently made a pair. Three walls of the room were lined with bookshelves, tight-packed, floor to ceiling; books and journals were also stacked on every horizontal surface – coffee table, speaker cabinets, chairs.

Several children's books were among them, plus various brightly coloured balls and soft toys, but there was no sign of the foster-child, Eliza.

Clive, wearing an apron—A WOMAN'S PLACE IS IN THE HOUSE: AND IN THE SENATE—was chopping something white and slippery on the kitchen bench. The jokiness of the slogan seemed incongruous; it was not the kind of thing he would say. He waved his knife in welcome.

'Smells delicious,' I signed: two see-through hand-shapes.

'*Tastes* delicious,' Stella signed back, fluently. She had clearly been doing more homework. 'Take a pew,' she added, in English. 'Make yourself comfortable.'

The dogs had occupied the entire length of sofa; I sank into the nearest leather armchair, a little surprised to find such an unspeakable substance in that house.

Stella read my mind, or my face: 'Relax, J.J.—vinyl.'

Clive carefully carried out a tray of drinks: a flute of foaming champagne for me, another for Stella; a glass of soda water and bitters for him.

'Cheers.'

'Cheers.'

Stella, still sipping, took his place in the kitchen nook— one member of the tag-team relieving the other—and began fussing at the steaming, fragrant pots. Clive shook a white cloth across the table and set three places. His movements were unhurried and deliberate, due less to the handicaps of age, I now suspected, than to temperament.

I said: 'Eliza isn't joining us?'

'She's asleep.'

'I'm disappointed. I was looking forward to meeting her.'

'Do you have any children, J.J.?' he asked.

I held up a single forefinger; he shaped, questioningly, the beard of boy, the long-hair of girl.

'Girl,' I answered.

'Her name—what?'

I held an imaginary flower to my nose, and sniffed.

'Fleur?' he guessed, aloud.

I shook my head; waiting. In part I can't help being a teacher; in part, Sign seemed my one chance to be an interesting, or at least different, dinner guest.

'Primrose?'

'Close,' I signed: two forefingers closing a gap.

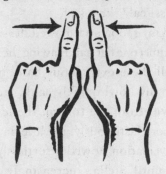

'Violet?'

The exchange was beginning to feel too much like a game of charades; Stella rescued us, planting a tureen of steaming soup in the centre of the table.

I shaped a question: 'Asparagus?'

She laughed again at the green-penis shape, and finger-spelt: 'B-O-R-S-C-H'.

They waited, watching me; the word was a challenge I couldn't meet. I raised both hands, open palms: 'I surrender'.

Clive ladled out the soup, then passed around a basket of hot bread rolls. Stella took four—one for herself, and one each for her dogs. Flopped at her feet, chins flat against the floor, their fat jowls had spread about them like puddles. Their tails thumped gratefully against the carpet as she tossed down each scrap.

We made small talk for a time between mouthfuls. I demonstrated a few more signs: spoon, bowl. Stella guessed a shape for 'soup': the ladle of Spoon Hand lifted towards a sipping mouth.

'Close,' I signed again, then added, in speech: 'but the real thing is a little more stylised.'

'A little *less* real,' she joked.

I set down my spoon and showed the sign for 'bread': a bread-slicing mime; one flat hand sawing the loaf of the other.

Despite all these extraneous hand movements, the borsch-level in my bowl quickly sank. Stella replenished it, and her own, from the tureen; the level sank again. Clive sipped more fastidiously; the level in his bowl barely changed. Conversation flowed effortlessly—English and pidgin Sign—until Stella, increasingly fidgety, shook another cigarette from the pack at her elbow.

'Can I have one too?'

She smiled at my request. 'I'm not corrupting you am I, J.J.?'

'I hope so.'

I tucked the offered cigarette between my lips, and bent my face to her lighter. She watched me inhale, amused.

'For Christ's sake *suck* the thing, J.J.'

Clive cleared away the soup bowls; Stella distributed the leftover crusts to her friends beneath the table. Their mournful eyes seemed to have migrated to the tops of their heads, like the eyes of flounder, watching, waiting.

'You like dogs, J.J.?'

'I guess. I mean, I never had a dog.'

'People are either dog people or cat people, don't you think?'

Clive was watching from the kitchen; I had the sudden distinct feeling that the question was some sort of test, or personality assessment. Which was I—dog or cat?

'Clive is a cat person,' she said, and blew a languid smoke-ring in his direction.

'I *admire* cats,' he said. He slopped a glistening mass of spaghetti into a colander to drain. 'I admire their sense of purpose. Their detachment.'

Stella chuckled, throatily. It was another routine, I saw. He was talking about himself; half mockery, half an affirmation of the thing it mocked.

'Dogs are a good character test for people,' she said. 'Dogs see the inner person. People reveal their true selves in their attitude to dogs.'

'Here, boy,' I said to Binky, and bent and rubbed his ears affectionately. 'Good boy.'

Stella laughed, then added, 'She's a girl.'

She poked another crust beneath the table. I asked: 'The dogs are vegetarian?'

71

'Of course.'

'But that's unnatural. Dogs are carnivores.'

She shook her head. 'Omnivores, like us. Eat anything.'

'Have *you* always been vegetarian?'

'The endpoint of a long journey,' Clive said from the kitchen.

He carefully carried in a huge dish heaped with the steaming spaghetti, then a second dish filled with a thick red sauce.

'With Clive vegetarianism is an intellectual duty,' Stella said. 'With me it's pure pleasure.'

He ladled out the sauce: chunks of onion and tomato and red and green peppers. It seemed the most delicious food I'd ever eaten. The dogs, staring up from their supine positions, drooled, open-mouthed.

'He converted you?' I asked.

She shook her head: 'It kind of crept up on me.'

She ground fresh pepper over her bowl, pondering. 'I always ordered vegetarian meals when I flew. Or sometimes Halal food. Kosher food. It didn't matter. The point was to order something personalised, something made with care. Anything except the standard plastic airline shit. I guess I found it was the same with cooking vegetarian at home. You have to work a little harder at it. There's more *love* in it.'

'So the pleasure came first—then the theory?'

'What theory?'

She laughed, and glanced teasingly at Clive. He seemed to enjoy her irreverence; perhaps he sensed that he needed it.

'This is delicious,' I told him.

'Stella's recipe,' he murmured.

She sucked several loose strands of spaghetti into her mouth with noisy relish: 'When I first met Clive his idea of a vegetarian meal was birdseed and mineral water. It was a *penance* for him.'

He managed another small, tickled smile.

'Clive's not big on pleasure,' she said.

'I like it in theory, my dear,' he said, his first joke for the night.

He turned towards me, scrutinising me. I sensed that I was still undergoing an audition, that he was measuring my responses.

'We detested each other when we first met,' Stella was saying. 'Chalk and cheese.'

'She thought me an old fuddy-duddy,' he murmured.

She leant over and rubbed the back of his neck, fondly: 'You *are* an old fuddy-duddy!'

'And I thought her a troublemaker—an opinion not entirely undeserved.'

She took mock umbrage at this: '*Who* is the trouble-maker?' She turned again to me: 'Let me tell you about His Holiness here...You know he banned animals from his Zoology Department?'

I shook my head, amused.

'Did the excreta hit the fan! I mean, you can ban animals from a Physics Department. You can ban animals from a French Department...But Zoology? The University shifted him sideways. A so-called Personal Chair.'

Clive said, mildly: 'It means you have no power.'

He rose and methodically cleared the table, stacking the two empty pasta bowls, with the third—his own,

73

largely untouched—on top. He uncorked another bottle of red wine, and brought out a plate of assembled cheeses: blue-moulds, smoked-browns, a single large wedge of camembert.

'You eat dairy products?'

'Hand milked,' he said.

Stella cut a sloppy slice of camembert, shovelled it onto a cracker, took a bite, pursing her big mouth appreciatively.

'Nice cheese,' she said. 'Very cunty.'

I didn't know where to look. Clive remained unfazed as she reached below the table and distributed a handful of crackers. He worshipped her: she could do no wrong. My earlier hunch that he liked a little unpredictability, a little extra colour, in his life seemed confirmed. Conversation moved on; more of their life together, their shared beliefs. They argued, continuously, playfully—not so much over those beliefs, as over how to arrive at those beliefs: which route to take to an agreed destination. Clive argued from the point of view of 'the cosmos': a place in which all sentient creatures had certain rights. The avoidance of pain was his key premise; on this foundation all else was constructed. There was no appeal to a higher authority than human reason, certainly no vestige of his religious training was in evidence. His body might be ageing but his mind was razor-sharp, as youthful as the wig that warmed it. Stella wasn't much interested in theoretical foundations for notions of right and wrong; she *knew*. We *all* know, she argued. The evil *know* in their hearts they are evil, given time to think.

'I take that as given. I'm interested in how, not why. Effects, not causes.'

74

She was still smoking steadily, her conversation, increasingly, could be seen as well as heard: each syllable emerging from her mouth, surrounded by a puff of smoke, like a talk-balloon.

'Stella is the ultimate pragmatist,' her husband said, not without pride.

'To know and not to act,' she said to him, 'is not yet to know.' She turned to me, and added, with disarming self-mockery: 'Confucius say.'

I listened, mesmerised. It was the most fascinating discussion I'd heard, or seen, in years; it raged back and forth, both sides appealing to me from time to time for agreement, or for adjudication. I felt in need of a referee's whistle, although I would have been far too indecisive to use it. I agreed with whoever was speaking at the time. Then was won over by the opposite argument a few seconds later. I had longed for years to take part in discussions such as these. I listened avidly, excitedly—too excitedly, perhaps. I was also drinking far too much; around midnight my wineglass slipped from my fingers and smashed on the tabletop. The dark wine spread through the white cloth as if through blotting paper.

'I'm sorry, how stupid. I'll get a sponge.'

'Leave it,' Stella said, airily.

'No, I'll mop it up. Sprinkle some salt.'

'It's nothing,' she said.

She reached out and deliberately knocked over her own glass. A second, larger redness bloomed in the linen cloth.

Clive was less interested in the spilled wine than in my reaction to his wife's act of weird generosity.

Embarrassed, I fossicked in my pocket for my car keys. 'Perhaps it's time I left.'

Clive, who had drunk nothing but soda and bitters all night, insisted that I shouldn't drive home. 'Take a cab, J.J.'

'From here?'

'It's less expensive than a funeral.'

Stella restored her intact wineglass to the vertical, and refilled it.

'*I'll* drive you home,' she announced.

'I couldn't allow that, my dear,' Clive said, as mildly as ever. 'You've drunk more than J.J.' He held out his open hand, palm up: 'Keys please, J.J.'

I handed them over; this old brown mouse of a man had a presence, an authority, that could not be denied. He rose, and walked to the phone on the kitchen bench. Stella leant across the table and whispered, with drunken sarcasm: 'Thou shalt always act responsibly. Thou shalt always lead a rational life.'

Clive murmured into the phone then replaced the receiver. 'Twenty minutes,' he told me.

'What *is* the sign for drunk?' Stella asked.

I demonstrated: two wobbly fingers, stepping unsteadily across a Flat Hand.

'I *love* it,' she said, laughing. 'Shit, I love this language.'

Clive stood at the bookshelves, head tilted, searching for a title. Stella pressed on, drunkenly enthusiastic. 'What I love most about it—it's so *true*. So natural. You couldn't tell lies in Sign.'

'Of course you can tell lies,' I said. 'Some would say that's what makes it a language.'

Clive tugged, with difficulty, a book from the tightly squeezed pack.

'You might like to borrow this, J.J. Much of the ground we've covered tonight is amplified here.'

He slid the book across the table: *The Rights of Animal,* a familiar black hymn book. I slid it back.

'I have a library copy.'

Stella, incredulous, said: 'When did you borrow it—this morning?'

My face betrayed me; she laughed loudly, a gotcha-laugh: 'You *did!*'

Clive managed a smile: 'I'm flattered.'

He hammered the black book back into the tight-packed shelf with the flat of his hand, briefly scanned a lower shelf, and eased out another, thinner book.

'I doubt very much that you have got a copy of this.'

'Everyone's got a copy of that,' Stella said.

'Take it,' he urged. 'Stella's animal poems are very... insightful.'

'It's not compulsory, J.J.' she said.

I took the book, a stapled booklet of her poems. *Selected Friends.*

'I set this book on the Zoology I syllabus,' Clive said.

'A book of poems?'

'One of the last executive acts I was permitted. And probably the last straw. But a book like this, for all its faults...'

'*What* faults?'

He smiled, semi-apologetically, at his wife's interjection: '... for all their faults these poems show science how far it has to go. One of the main reasons I fell out with my colleagues, J.J.—I came to see that the study of animal perception, of animal consciousness, was being completely ignored. We could dissect our millionth Sprague-Dawley rat and still have no idea what that rat *thought* about it all.'

I waved the book: 'This will tell me?'

I was joking; he wasn't. 'It's the nearest you'll get in English.'

'What he means,' Stella said, her huskiness increasingly slurred, 'is that the book was written by a rat!'

The intercom buzzer drowned her loud laughter; Clive rose and spoke into a wall-panel microphone. 'Coming.'

I heaved myself to my feet; Clive ushered me towards the front door. Stella followed; her three dogs, too torpid to move, remained beneath the table like beached seals. Clive lifted a torch that was hanging from a nail on the verandah post; we followed a wavering path of light through the trees to the first gate.

A taxi waited, engine grumbling, across the open field beyond the second gate; various pairs of eyes—red, yellow—glowed back as Clive played the beam of his torch across the darkness. The night was moonless, black as pitch; there seemed little point in a Sign farewell.

78

'A wonderful night,' I said aloud. 'Thank you. Both of you.'

The cabbie, a giant of a man, leant across and opened the passenger door. I eased myself carefully in.

'Where to, squire?'

'Glenelg.'

'You win the lottery?'

I opened Stella's small slim book, and read, hunched forward, by the light of the dash, as the cabbie navigated the dirt road. Her selected friends all seemed to be animals; each poem was about a different animal, as if written *by* an animal—an attempt to get inside that animal, to see the world through animal eyes.

I read through the first poem, *Dog*. I didn't understand a word, but the wacky syntax intrigued me. It seemed very . . . Stella. The wine had dissolved my normal reserve; I read the poem through again, this time aloud, trying to make sense of it. And slowly, like solving a puzzle, or cracking a code, it came to me. I *got* it—some of it.

Outside calls me every Sun:
new Sniffs out there, tangled Sniffs
I've never sniffed before.
Sun makes all Sniffs loud
until Sun hides and then there's Wet.
I hate all Wet: small hits of Wet
that fall from High, long ropes
of Wet that come from dry ropes
in the Green. Shake off Wet
and run inside, I sniff the Sniff

of Two Legs opening White Door:
the Cold Kennel where Meat lives.

I looked up; the cabbie was glancing at me nervously. His head brushed the roof, his huge belly was wedged hard against the steering wheel. I warmed to him: one of the Brothers, another fatty who liked to drive, combining work and pleasure.

'What do you think?' I said.

'What is it—a kid's story?'

'A poem.'

'Never had much time for poetry.'

'A friend of mine wrote it.'

'You can tell him I like the line about the cold, white kennel.'

'Her.'

'Tell her. Yeah, I like that. The kennel where meat lives. I'm a bit partial to the cold white kennel myself.' He glanced my way, appreciatively: 'You look like you might be of the same tendency.'

Fat Pride. We're not embarrassed among ourselves.

'Mind if I smoke?' he said.

I shook my head, willing to forgive him anything. With one hand he shook a cigarette from a packet on the dash, with the other he pulled the dash lighter from its plug-hole; meanwhile he steered the cab easily through a corner with a slight sideways movement of his belly pressed against the wheel.

'Power-steering,' he said.

He was showing off, one Brother to another; a kind of belly-dancing.

'Like one?'

I shook my head again; I was more than happy to sit back and admire the skill of his belly for the rest of the trip.

My mother was waiting up, sitting at the kitchen table, fidgeting. A fresh pot of tea brewed in a knitted cosy; tea-leaves emptied from the previous pot still faintly steamed in the sink.

The garbage bags I had packed with animal products earlier in the evening stood on the table, ripped open, emptied. The tinned animal flesh had apparently been restored to the larder; the items of woollen and silken clothing were stacked neatly on the bench.

'Why?' she signed, puzzled. 'We thought...burglar.'

The carnivorous burglar. I kissed the apex of her head from behind, rested my elbows lightly on her shoulders, and signed in front of her face, a few inches from her nose.

'You read note?' I signed, using the compass points of her body instead of mine as part of the signing, a kind of ventriloquism.

'Yes. But understand not.'

'Animal Freedom,' I explained.

She turned to face me: 'You alright?'

'Wonderful,' I signed, hamming up the pronunciation, but only a little. It *was* how I felt.

She paused, searching for something to say, or wanting to keep me there a little longer for interrogation, or rebuke: 'You where tonight?'

'Dinner with friends.'

A hint of pleasure softened the worry-lines—relieved-mother pleasure: 'Which friends?'

'Famous friends,' I signed: literally 'know-everywhere friends'.

The Rights of Animal still sat unopened on the table, black as a bible; I reached across and flipped it over. Clive's younger face peered up from the back cover, meditative, calm.

My mother pointed; I nodded. Her worry-lines tightened again; her hands began to fidget, became still, twitched again, then stilled themselves again. Something was on the tips of her fingers—what was it? A warning?

'Worry-not,' I signed, planted another kiss on the summit of her head, then scooped up the book and headed for bed.

I read for a time, but without concentration—unable to scan more than a few sentences without the faces and voices of my new friends interrupting, inserting themselves into my train of thought. Wine had addled my brain, certainly, but excitement also provided its share of distraction. The evening's conversations replayed themselves again and again, as if on some continuous spool. Exciting conversations, to me—conversations about things that mattered, important ideas. My friends in the past, apart from a few gifted students, had been Jill's friends; work colleagues mostly, their talk had been shoptalk, or academic gossip that meant little to me, an outsider.

I reached for Stella's book of poems; her smaller, bite-size pieces of writing, not requiring extended concentration, seemed better suited to my limited concentration span. I read several through again, aloud, enjoying the feel of seeing the world through different eyes: slitted cat-eyes, wide owl-eyes, eyes with transparent lizard-lids.

A small game to pass the time: I covered the title of each poem with my hand as soon as I turned the page, and tried to guess the animal from the contents—tried to *feel* myself that animal.

You with Feet keep clear from me;
I hear You coming thumping.
The earth's my ear, my tight-stretched
Drum, I hear you, Big Feet, Club Feet, beating
Through the grass: two big bass drums,
ten small side-drums. Up, the view is
wrong; Down, the air is cool,
the view is wide enough. Enough:
Stay clear, you, You; I have two
Sharps; I like the taste of heel and toe.

Finally I slept, drifting drunkenly in and out of wakefulness through the night. I was time-travelling, jerkily. I opened my eyes; the digits glowing on my alarm-clock had jumped forward an hour. My lids closed, and opened again: another hour.

I could hear the sound of the waves outside my window: a soft, steady concussion; the sea massaging the shore. A cool, refreshing sound; a beckoning sound—but for once I was too weary, or merely too drunk, to respond.

1 2

I opened my eyes; bright light was squeezing about the edges of the drawn blind. The digits on my alarm-clock had jumped forward in time to 12.00.

A phone was ringing somewhere. The door to my bedroom opened; the noise increased, painfully. My mother's silhouette appeared; the red light of the phone-cum-fax flashing in the hall beyond her.

'Phone,' she signed, a simple representation using the Ambivalent Hand: half Good Hand, half Bad.

I struggled from bed to find Stella's husky contralto at the other end of the line.

'How are you this morning, J.J.?'

'Fine,' I lied.

'I thought you might be a little worse for wear.'

'A little, but thank you. Both of you. I had a good time.'

'So did we. But we feel guilty: I plied you with alcohol, Clive bullied you into abandoning your car. We thought—I might drive down and pick you up later. You could stay for dinner—then drive yourself home.'

'I wouldn't want to put you out.'

'No trouble at all. I'll be down in the city anyway. A small detour. See you at eight?'

The phone rang again as soon as I had hung off; second thoughts, perhaps, or a change of time.

'Stella?' I said.

'Are you aware of the time, John?'

Jill's tone was mild, but the formality of my given name, seldom used, jarred. Years of marriage had accustomed me to a range of tender nicknames, or nicknames which had once been tender, and later, at worst, were a comfortable habit. J.J. itself, of course—used also by the rest of the world for as long as I can remember. Sweet-Tooth. And once, a long time ago, sweetheart.

'Your daughter's been sitting on the front doorstep since breakfast, John.'

The name sounded like she was handling me with tweezers.

'I'm sorry, Jill. I must have slept in.'

'I had plans.'

'I'll be right over.'

'I can't really see the point.'

'I thought you said you had plans.'

'I've had to cancel those.'

'I'm sorry.'

Sign has countless shapes for 'sorry', far more shapes than there are words of apology in English. Perhaps the Deaf apologise more often than the hearing. The Flat Hand placed over the heart is simplest, a James family sign, but there was no way of transmitting its meaning, its force, through a phone line. Disembodied, stripped of the support of gesture, my voice had no chance.

Not that Jill sounded angry. Her tone, as always, remained calm; if pressed she would claim that she was merely stating facts.

'Is being sorry enough, do you think? Isn't saying you're sorry a little too easy? It doesn't seem to stop it happening again.'

This kind of sweetly reasoned rebuke had always produced an immense rage in me towards the end of our marriage; more distanced now, I managed to bite my tongue.

'I can only try. I'll be there as soon as I can.'

I hung up, then remembered the obvious: I had no means of transport.

'Shit!' I shouted, loudly.

My mother continued clearing breakfast things, unperturbed. I waved my hands to get her attention; she turned.

'Me borrow car?'

'Your car where?'

'Broken down,' I signed, a blend of the head-on smash of 'accident' and the collapse of 'wear out'.

She eyed me suspiciously; it might not be impossible to lie in Sign, but it can be difficult.

'Please?'

'Ask,' she signed, and nodded in the direction of my father's workshop.

I could see no point in that. He would tell me to walk, tell me that I needed the exercise.

I signed: 'He needs car—not. Urgent. Rosie waiting... Please.'

The appeal to grandmotherly instinct met with more success. She held out the keys to me, dangled them reluctantly for a moment, mid-air, as if having second thoughts, then dropped them into my cupped palm.

13

'You're late, John.'

Rosie was sitting on the front fence. I'm not allowed inside the house; she always waits outside.

I leant across and opened the door. 'Sorry, sweetheart. I slept in.'

She nodded—sleeping-in seemed a perfectly plausible excuse, probably the only permissible excuse—and slid off the fence. She was wearing a tank-top and baggy jeans, her thick hair was stuffed beneath a baseball cap. As she climbed into the car I saw that her lips were painted purple, horror-movie purple.

'Does your mother know you're wearing lipstick?'

'She borrows it from *me*, Pop.'

Amused condescension is my daughter's preferred mode of relating to me, and to her mother. Even that 'Pop' has an ironic, distancing effect that I can't quite put my finger on. She never apportioned blame for the divorce; condescension was surely a safer outlet, a way of avoiding blame and the need to choose sides. We have both been deemed, even-handedly, too silly, too eccentric to blame.

'What's on the agenda today, Pop?'

'The zoo?'

'Gee, that sounds like fun.'

Eleven, going on nineteen—theatrical, precocious, and very demanding. She twiddled with the radio tuner; rap music suddenly filled the small car. We've both spoilt her terribly—the usual overcompensations, the usual displacements of divorce-guilt. Even though we understand the process, it doesn't seem to keep it from happening. Knowledge, even self-knowledge, doesn't help us change.

'What did I just *say*, Dad?'

'Um…Something about your violin teacher?'

She likes to test me, keep me on the alert with little comprehension tests, impromptu oral exams, from time to time.

'You weren't listening, Pop.'

'I was looking for a parking space.'

I parked; we climbed out and passed through the zoo turnstiles. I bought two double ice-creams from the zoo kiosk; we visited the big cats. Rosie humoured me by demonstrating the hand-shape for tiger: a pair of paws. We moved on to the next cage, she shaped a lion's mane. The leopards: a blend of paws and spots. Then she found an ocelot in a nearby cage, and turned towards me, smirking, arms on hips: a what's-*this*-then? challenge.

'Little-spotted-paws,' I signed, smoothly.

Another round of ice-creams, the giraffes, the polar bears. The feeding of the seals. A ride along the river on paddle-boats, a late afternoon visit to Hungry Jack's for burgers. We sat opposite each other in a small bright booth. She ate steadily through large fries and two cheese-burgers; I sipped a coffee.

'Can I be frank, Dad?'

'Of course.'

'You won't be hurt?'

Our day together always softens her attitude towards me. 'Dad' slowly replaces 'Pop', affection displaces condescension, by evening she occasionally even takes it upon herself to offer snippets of advice, little prescriptions for my self-improvement. Dietary recommendations are frequent, grooming suggestions, guidance on my choice of clothes. Once, memorably, there had even been a small homily on Personal Freshness. I prefer to take these words of wisdom as signs of love but remembering my own adolescence, they might equally be signs of embarrassment.

'As long as it's not about my weight.'

She smiled and shook her head, sucked briefly and noisily at her Coke, then turned to me, suddenly serious: 'I think I'm getting a little old for the zoo.'

'You're only eleven.'

'Nearly twelve. I'm very mature for my age.'

As if to prove the point, she took a motherly interest in my lack of appetite: 'You're not hungry, Dad?'

'I'm meeting some friends for dinner.'

'Do I know them?'

'I don't think so,' I said, and glanced at my watch. 'Better bring the rest of your meal with you, sweetheart.'

A younger girl, with simpler needs, peeped out, briefly from beneath the purple lipstick: 'Dad! I wanted a *thick* shake!'

'You can have two next week.'

'You *are* in a hurry. Is she someone special?'

Is television to blame for such precocity: the mannerisms, the adult-speak, the innuendo? How much does she understand and how much of it is merely the parroting of style? I drove her home—to her mother's home, my former home, a neat bluestone cottage in a leafy Norwood side street.

'Wait here, Dad. Mum wants a conference about the holidays.'

Jill and I always talk sitting in the car, in the street. I haven't been permitted back in the house since the day I left. I can't recall the cause of our final argument that day—a cause that was quickly swamped by effects. I remember waving my hands about. I remember Jill, as always, reasoning quietly. That sweet reasonableness was the final straw. I packed a suitcase after she had left for work and loaded my Fiat with a few precious possessions. I tried to write a farewell note, tried to get my anger down in words; words failed me. Still seething, I fed the garden hose through the window of our bedroom, set the lawn sprinkler in the middle of the bed, turned the tap on full, and drove away.

I surprised myself far more than Jill. She certainly forgave me more quickly than I forgave myself. Perhaps she read such actions as merely a more expressive form of Sign, not so much body language as thing language—bed, sprinkler and water droplets become temporary body parts or at the least, exclamation marks. The injunction, she explained pleasantly, was as much for my protection as for hers—to protect me against myself. To prevent it happening again.

I said to Rosie: 'Tell Mum I'll call her. I haven't time to talk today. See you next Sunday, sweetheart.'

'Don't be *late* next week, Pop,' she said, and thumped the door shut and ran up the drive without looking back.

The afternoon's concentrated fathering had exhausted me, but it was a delicious exhaustion, eased also by the promise of a reviving dip in the ocean before my evening out. I had been out of water, my natural element, too long; as I turned into the esplanade I could think of nothing else.

Stella's battered jeep was parked in my parents' drive. So much for swimming. I found her holding court in the lounge with my parents, an empty sherry glass dangling from her hand. Binky was lying on the carpet, a puddle of spreading black dog flesh, her chin resting on Stella's right foot.

'Sorry, J.J. *Mea culpa*. I'm early. But I've been practising my signing.'

She turned to my mother. 'Good teacher,' she signed, and pointed back at me.

My mother nodded, a little fixedly, and bent and stroked the dog. A frustrated dog person, she clearly found it easier to relate to Binky than to her owner. My father is neither a cat person nor a dog person—nor, for that matter, much of a person person. His disapproval was clearly written on his face, although Stella hadn't noticed, shaping her crude beginner-signs as though she were doing her reluctant hosts a grand personal favour.

The sherry glass was still dangling from her fingers, getting in the way. My father refilled it from a decanter, if only to silence her hands, then signed rapidly to me, deliberately too fast for our guest to follow:

'Already mother cook dinner—you tell not you eat with friends tonight.'

Among my answering apologies I covered my heart with my open palm, a meaning that even Stella comprehended.

'Am I in the way?' she asked, in English.

'No problem,' I said. 'I just forgot to report all my movements to Headquarters.'

14

Stella drove her jeep staccato fashion; jerky, impatient gear changes, frequent braking, fast cornering. Binky, standing on the seat between us, front paws on the dash, lifting her head into the rush of air above the windscreen, somehow maintained her footing. I didn't find it so easy, tossed side to side, swaying back and forth.

'I read your poems last night,' I said, trying to distract Stella. 'I couldn't put them down. They were wonderful.'

'Thank you.'

'The animal voices were totally convincing.'

'Of course Clive doesn't fully approve,' she said.

I waited; she elaborated: 'I commit the sin of anthropomorphism. His Holiness feels it's wrong to give animals human thoughts. Like dressing them up in human clothes—it's undignified.'

'But they're not human thoughts, they're animal thoughts. The way an animal would see the world exactly.'

'Maybe not *exactly*, J.J. They *are* written in a human language.'

'But those words are only symbols. Translations. The perceptions are animal perceptions. I think they're wonderful.'

'Light me a coffin nail, will you?' she said, weary of my repetitive praise.

I pulled a cigarette from the pack on the dash, lighting it with some difficulty as she swerved between lanes, impatient with the sluggish flow of traffic. I removed the cigarette from between my lips and jammed it gently between hers.

'Well lit,' she said, inhaling gratefully. 'I don't think I've ever tasted a cigarette that was better lit.'

This small fix of nicotine seemed to calm her; the car slowed, just a little.

She said: 'I like to think the best of my poems are close—or as close as we can *get* in words—to how an animal might think, or at least perceive the world.'

She stopped abruptly at a red light, and sat tapping her fingers against the wheel.

'What's the sign for red?' she said.

I shaped my lips into an O, and traced their outline with the Point Hand.

'Lipstick,' she said, pleased. 'I like it!'

She ground the remnants of her cigarette into the ashtray and turned to me with a wicked glint in her eye.

'What's brown, then?' she asked, and shifting her weight onto one buttock, reached her own Point Hand beneath the lifted cheek, circling the approximate region of her anus.

She hooted with laughter, highly amused; once again I didn't know where to look. I had blamed the excesses of the previous night on alcohol, but today? After two sherries? I began to dread what she might have said—signed—to my parents.

'I do believe you're blushing, J.J. Or are you trying to show me another version of the colour red?'

The light changed; she accelerated across the intersection, still chuckling.

'You can only blame yourself, J.J.—you've been very remiss in your duties as a teacher. You haven't taught us *any* of the colours. Not even black and white.'

An opportunity to restore equilibrium; I shaped the sign for white, an opaque shape, a variation played on the Okay Hand; she peered sideways at my hand, puzzled.

'I don't see it.'

'Look at the road,' I said.

'But I don't see any connection with the colour white.'

'You don't *have* to see it. It's an opaque shape. It doesn't mimic the colour white—it *is* the colour white.'

'I prefer shapes with a bit of poetry, like red. I like to see their origins. Light me another coffin nail, will you?'

I was beginning to enjoy lighting her cigarettes, there was an intimacy in the gesture, a kind of proxy kiss. I felt a thrill, a turbulence in my veins, as I jammed that second glowing cigarette between her lips.

'You give good cigarette, J.J.' she said, teasingly, aware, surely, of the effect on me.

'I try to please.'

The easy glibness of the phrase—something a movie character might say—surprised me. It was uncharacteristic, I had no idea where it had come from.

Stella returned to her theme: 'Surely your white shape represented something, *some* time. It must have had some natural connection to its colour.'

'Why should it? Spoken words have no natural connection with the thing they represent,' I said.

'Moo,' she lowed.

'Except for the occasional onomatopoeia.'

Unconvinced, she steered with one hand, shaping the Okay Hand with her other, turning it this way and that, glancing at it from time to time, puzzled.

'Maybe the number zero,' she mumbled through smoke. 'Zero colour.'

'Possibly. I did read somewhere that it had to do with pallor—the pale face of illness. As in, are you okay, or are you ill?'

She laughed: 'That's a long shot. Show me some other colours.'

'You'll like blue. The sign is more see-through—blue veins on the back of the hand...'

1 5

Her other two dogs were waiting, sharp-eared, at the second gate. I climbed out and pushed it open, Stella drove through into the trees. The dogs pressed about the jeep as it stopped, their rear ends wagging. Stella's short walk from shed to house was slow, retarded by mutual displays of affection. We found Clive kneeling in the lounge, twiddling knobs on a small portable television set that squatted on a video recorder in a corner of the room.

Eliza was still nowhere in sight.

Stella bent and kissed him on the toupée, a perfunctory greeting which struck me as being at odds with the affection she had shown her dogs.

'Did you tape the interview?'

'Got most of it.'

'Eliza in bed?'

He nodded, still preoccupied. 'I'll go up and say good-night,' she said.

'Shall I come?' I asked.

'I'll check first if she's awake.'

She lifted a key hanging from a hook in the kitchen and headed for the stairs. I watched, startled. Did they lock their mute foster-child in her room at night? It didn't seem polite to ask—yet.

Clive fiddled with the tracking control of the video recorder; I sat on the sofa and watched the screen swim in and out of focus. The soundtrack at least was coherent, a discussion of the fertility of great apes in captivity.

Stella descended the stairs. 'She's asleep. Sorry, J.J.'

I wasn't surprised, but the absences and evasions on the subject of Eliza were beginning to irritate. I could smell something in those gaps: something freshly bricked behind a wall of excuses. She tapped two glasses of red wine from a cask and handed one to me.

'Chateau Cardboard,' she said, 'but it works for me.' She turned to Clive. 'Let's replay the interview before we eat.'

The screen stopped flickering; the flat, reddish-brown face of an orang-utan appeared, staring past the camera with an expression of infinite boredom. A voice-over, its animation sitting oddly with the indifference of the ape, excitedly announced that Fatima was a previously infertile ape, artificially inseminated by a gynaecologist. A series of more talkative heads replaced Fatima's: the surgeon himself, a zoo keeper, a veterinarian.

'I'm next,' Clive murmured.

His familiar face abruptly filled the screen. 'In my opinion such procedures should only be performed with the ape's informed consent.'

99

The interviewer—a standard-featured beauty, mid-twenties, perfectly groomed—was bemused. 'I'm sorry, Professor?'

'Gotcha,' Stella chuckled behind me.

'I don't think she saw it coming,' Clive murmured. 'So bound up with self-congratulations about saving an endangered species.'

'Fatima may not *want* to be a mother,' his earlier, interviewed, self was saying, simultaneously, on the screen.

The interviewer was lost, floundering. 'But what about the survival of the species, surely that is an issue?'

'It would be regrettable if the species became extinct. But the rights of a particular individual of that species are far more important—far more tangible. I believe that we should be able to define those rights much more precisely under law. The client ape should be fully acquainted with the pros and cons and allowed to make an informed judgement.'

The interviewer laughed, but uncertainly. It sounded like a joke, but she wasn't sure; Clive's prim, deadpan face was giving nothing away.

'An orang-utan giving informed consent?' she asked. 'Surely you're not serious, Professor?'

'Extremely serious. It's a very serious issue.'

'But how can a monkey give consent?'

'Not a monkey,' Clive told her, patiently. 'An ape.'

'How can an *ape* give informed consent?'

'Various methods of communication have shown promise in recent years. I would have thought this was well known. Several keyboard languages have been developed for use by apes. You have perhaps heard of Yerkish: a language invented at the Yerkes Primate centre in the United States...'

The interviewer's face, full-screen, was relieved, amused, patronising. Apes being taught to speak? *This* she could handle: St Francis Clive Kinnear, crackpot patron saint of animal rights, making a fool of himself on cue.

'That's it,' Clive said. 'They cut the rest.'

Stella rose and switched off the television, then lovingly rubbed the back of his neck.

'You shouldn't antagonise them,' she said. 'You have to learn to milk them. *Use* them.'

'I only told the truth,' he said. 'The argument is unassailable.'

He rose and stepped behind the kitchen bench, lifted a pot lid, stared inside.

'The idea is a little surprising,' I said. 'It *sounds* a little off the planet.'

He replaced the lid: 'There's nothing new in what I said, J.J. There's quite a body of published work now on ape languages. Bekoff in Colorado has been suggesting some sort of public guardianship arrangement—State-appointed guardians—for the great apes for years.'

If I had seen the argument in black and white I might have agreed, if it had been a petition I would probably have signed, but something in his spoken tone got my back up: that cool assumption of agreement.

'Apes *have* been taught to sign,' he said.

I knew a little of this, a hot issue in the Deaf world several years before. To many it seemed an insult that

101

their—our—beautiful language should be taught to apes. It re-opened an old wound: the once-common notion that Sign wasn't a real language, more a primitive pidgin, an amusing pantomime, a game of charades.

I drained my glass and said: 'I understood that it was more a kind of imitation. Monkey-see, monkey-do.'

'Not monkeys. Apes.'

His correction, once again, was patient, matter-of-fact; there was no trace of recrimination. Clive seldom laughed; I sensed that the expression of anger was even more infrequent.

He stepped out from behind the bench; Stella took his place, the kitchen tag-team.

'It was *far* more than imitation, J.J.,' he said. 'The chimps had vocabularies of several hundred words. And used them creatively.'

'There's some dispute about that,' Stella put in, taking the words from my mouth.

'Not in my mind. It's conclusive. Washoe, the first of the chimps, was offered a radish to taste. She invented her own composite sign-word: "cry-hurt-food". She called a watermelon a "drink-fruit".'

'A poem!' Stella called across the bench.

'A metaphor, at any rate, my dear.'

I said: 'I heard that there was only one native signer on the Washoe project. And she was not very impressed by many of the so-called signs that the chimps learnt.'

'There were exaggerations,' Clive said. 'Of course. The number of signs. The sentences.'

I dredged up another criticism from some mental recess. 'If you put a chimp in a room with a typewriter, sooner or

102

later, among all the other permutations and combinations of letters, it will bang out Hamlet—by sheer probability. Maybe the so-called signing of the apes was nothing more than that.'

Clive nodded, clearly bored by the old argument, but as patient as ever. 'I grant that much of the work wouldn't stand up to statistical analysis, the claims are exaggerated. I grant that the trainers had an incentive to discover signs. But I've examined the evidence closely over the last few years. There is a core, a kernel, that seems beyond dispute. It seems clear that the great apes share many of the characteristics we would regard as human. An awareness of self. An awareness of the future—even a sense of time, and of death.'

'*That's* what you should have said in the interview,' Stella told him, carrying out a large bowl of food.

'I *did* say it in the interview. It was cut.'

Stella set the bowl, stir-fried greens, in the centre of the table; I smiled at the sight of it and lifted my hands into neutral Signing Space.

'Asparagus?'

Stella answered in speech. 'Eliza's favourite food. We eat a lot of it.' She offered the wine bottle, I covered the glass with my hand after she had half-filled it. The discussion might bore Clive but it intrigued me, I wanted to keep a clear head. I also sensed the stirrings of a new urge inside me: to needle him, to ruffle those smooth feathers.

'Do apes have an awareness of the dangers of artificial insemination?'

'Perhaps, if properly explained.'

103

'It might depend on who was doing the explaining.'

He shrugged. 'Perhaps on *how* it was explained.'

'But surely *you* wouldn't want to teach a chimp Sign-language?'

He watched me, puzzled, waiting. I pressed on.

'I would have thought you'd regard it as wrong. A form of exploitation, like dressing apes in circus clothes. Turning them into performing monkeys...'

He sipped his soda and bitters, thoughtfully. 'Perhaps,' he said. 'But that's a separate issue.'

My turn to be puzzled. Stella interpreted: 'The work has already been done by others, J.J., whatever its morality. Apes *have* been taught the rudiments of language. The work might be immoral but Clive feels it would be illogical not to make use of the results.'

A sudden, weird notion came to me—call it inspiration—of why I was there, and why they had befriended me. *Auditioned* me.

I said, abruptly: 'Your foster-child is a chimpanzee.'

Clive looked at me, clearly surprised; for once I had caught him off-guard. I had caught myself off-guard—even as I uttered it the idea seemed irrational. But his body language—and that of Stella, behind him—told me, shouted at me, that my inspired guess was right.

'Eliza is a chimp!' I said.

It was more a conclusion than a question but they answered it.

'A gorilla, in fact,' Clive admitted, after a time.

'A *gorilla?*'

Stella added, quickly: 'A very special gorilla.'

We sat for a long moment, silent, becalmed in the aftermath of revelation. I had astonished myself as much as Clive and Stella—perhaps more so. The cogs of my brain, momentarily frozen, finally ground on again, slowly. 'You want me to teach it Sign-language.'

'Her,' Clive corrected, calm and unruffled again. 'Not it.'

Stella was excited. 'We *need* you, J.J. Eliza is developing so quickly we can't keep up. She needs a proper Sign teacher.'

Another elongated moment of quiet. I sipped my wine on autopilot, thoughts churning. Two emotions were struggling inside my brain: amusement, yes—these people were clearly out of their minds—but also a growing disappointment. I had assumed I was being courted as a friend; it now seemed that their dinner invitations were nothing more than job interviews.

'It's a very important project,' Clive said. 'Eliza's education is crucial to the movement.'

He was speaking even more slowly and carefully than usual, as if to a child. 'We see her as a spokesperson for her whole species. Her whole *genus*.'

Stella risked a typical joke: 'A kind of spokes-animal.'

I didn't laugh; I felt used. I found it difficult to say so, however. I could tell them only obliquely.

'Then aren't you *using* her? Aren't you making her the subject for another kind of animal experiment? Exactly what you are opposed to.'

Clive heard me out impassively. 'Perhaps. But perhaps *she* will agree that the ends justify the means.'

Stella's argument was more direct. 'You're right of course, J.J. But we can't turn back the clock—can't make her *forget* what she knows. We certainly can't put her in the wild. She's grown up with humans—of sorts.'

'Where?'

She glanced at her husband; he shook his head, almost imperceptibly; she continued: 'I don't think we can say more at this stage. Let's just say her early life was... deprived. We want to offer her a real human home. And teach her, among other things, about the plight of her fellow animals.'

'You must be out of your minds! Crazy!'

My hands, as often during moments of high emotion, moved involuntarily as I spoke: a flurry of gestures underlining the words. Or were the words mere noise, underlining the gestures? 'Out-of-your-minds': the fingertips at the forehead opening out, *exploding* out; the shape of reason gone, vanished, flown away. 'Crazy': the Point Hand circling off-temple, stirring furiously, an ancient Esperanto-insult from the schoolyard.

Stella reached across the small table, took my hands in hers, and stroked them gently, as if trying to calm a pair of panicking birds.

'I'm sorry we couldn't be completely frank with you, J.J. We needed to get to know you first. And...for you to get to know us.' She smiled: 'We like you. Both of us. We think you're perfect for Eliza.'

I sat, stony-faced, resistant.

'Please, J.J. It *has* to be you. You're a very special person. Just meet her, that's all I ask. Decide for yourself.'

106

The flattery did its work, slowly; the suggestion of friendship buttered the hard bread beneath; curiosity reasserted itself. '*If* I agree, and I'm not saying I will, when can I meet her?'

'As soon as possible.'

'Tonight?'

A look of satisfaction passed between them; they knew they had me.

Clive said: 'We don't like to wake her—she sleeps sunset to sunrise. Why don't you stay the night? You can meet her first thing in the morning.'

I was tempted, momentarily. 'My parents would worry.'

'Phone them,' Stella said, then caught my glance and banged her fist against her forehead. 'Sorry. What a stupid thing to say...*Fax* them.'

'They might not see the fax till morning.'

'I'll phone you another cab,' Clive said.

'No,' I insisted. 'I'm fine.'

'You've been drinking again, J.J.'

'Half a glass?'

'The amount isn't always important.'

I raised my voice, needled. 'It's my decision, Clive, not yours. I'm perfectly capable of driving.'

I refilled my empty glass. Clive turned to Stella for support; she merely laughed. 'Yay, J.J.—way to go!'

He shrugged, rose and fossicked in his desk instead, and pressed a pile of loose A4 pages into my hands.

'Some bedtime reading. The manuscript of my new book. It's still in rough draft form but if you have any doubts about the project it might help convince you.'

I stared, incredulous, at the title page: *Primate Suffrage*.

'You want to give apes the *vote?*'

'The title is a simplification. The publishers wanted something marketable, something catchy.'

'*Who* wanted something catchy?' Stella said.

He smiled his minimal smile. 'Stella came up with the title.'

'Poetic licence,' she told me.

'Of course it overstates the case,' Clive said, then added, after a pause: 'Although I think some of the great apes may well be given voting rights in due course. There would have to be some kind of screening test. General knowledge. Comprehension.'

'Maybe they could stand for Parliament,' I suggested.

Stella's turn to laugh out loud: 'They might do a better job.'

Clive said: 'They might see through the bullshit. There *is* often a kind of wisdom in simplicity.'

His calm brain was working it through, placing one implacable fact in front of the other, refusing to leap to conclusions. He reminded me of a competitive walker, one foot always touching the ground before the other was lifted.

'Of course, to vote they would have to become Australian citizens. Which means—if they were treated as normal immigrants—passing a basic comprehension test. Which would solve the problem.'

This time I was reasonably certain that he was joking, sending himself up. His sense of humour, when it attempted to show itself, was what might be called 'droll'—meaning non-detectable, almost non-existent. Sign, usually so eloquent, has no equivalent. A certain limp-wristedness in the shaping of 'funny' might come close.

'What about apes born here?' I said, still determined to rile him. 'In the zoo, say? Wouldn't they automatically be Australian citizens, by birth?'

A wide smile creased Stella's face; she saw clearly that I was making fun of her husband. He was staring absently beyond us, unfocused, thinking it through, following each path to its logical conclusion, then returning to follow the next.

She winked at me behind his back. I extracted a cigarette from her pack, lit it, and reached across the table and jammed it gently between her lips. She smiled.

'Thank you, J.J.'

'A pleasure.' An especial pleasure, weirdly, in full view of her husband, as if placing that cigarette between her lips was some kind of illicit act.

'Just read the manuscript, J.J.,' he was saying, unperturbed. 'I like to think it's very persuasive. Even if you don't think a cow, or an earthworm, say, should have rights—read about the great apes.'

Stella tacked in from a different compass point. 'Read what *they* think about death, about pain—about themselves.'

'One other thing,' Clive said. 'Until we've discussed it further, I would ask that nothing we've said here goes beyond these walls.'

'It's a secret?'

Stella zipped her lips. 'Please, J.J.—it's very important you tell no one. At least for the time being.'

We rose together; as Stella preceded us through the front door and out into the night Clive took my arm, retarding me slightly. His voice was low, an aside meant only for me.

'I don't like to encourage Stella in her smoking, J.J. I hope you will support me in this—it's such an irrational habit.'

I read Clive's manuscript that night, cover to cover. I began in bed, later I rose and decamped to the kitchen, partly because the loose leaves were too awkward to read in bed, mostly because I was soon too agitated to stay there.

The book was another collection of horror stories, told with extreme coolness; a book that first made me squirm, then made me want to shout out in indignation. Once again there was nothing emotive, no easy appeal to righteousness in the style. It was exactly the kind of book I had come to expect from C. Francis Kinnear, a logical accumulation of cold facts. Ape-facts. Yet the final effect was one of fierce angry heat.

The stories were largely interchangeable, variations on a single theme. The medical experiments were worst of all. Conscious chimps smashed repeatedly in the base of the skull by mechanical devices, to study the effects of concussion and fractured skulls. Rhesus monkeys shot in the head from point-blank range to investigate gunshot wounds. The spines of baboons broken, mechanically, to allow study of paraplegia...

Many of the stories came from spies, Animal Rights activists working as deep throats within various research institutions: military, academic, industrial. Others came from experimenters who just couldn't stomach their work anymore.

These same stories were repeated throughout the book, with various more or less inventive tortures, different species of primates, larger quantities. *Huge* quantities: somewhere between 200,000 and 400,000 primates a year had been shipped from tropical homes to temperate-zone laboratories in the 1950s, I read, declining a little to 50,000 a year at present. Millions of primates, an Auschwitz of primates.

Do I sound like a teacher, repeating these figures? Chalking them on the page? I am a teacher.

The last few chapters of *Primate Suffrage* were less disturbing but no less riveting. Here were documented the stories of all those great apes—chimps, gorillas, orang-utans—with whom attempts had been made to communicate in language. Koko, signer of Ameslan. Donald and Gua, talking to each other through a keyboard language. The tragedy of Washoe, raised as human, abandoned among zoo-chimps, desperately signing to any passing human, begging to be set free, demanding to know what she was doing among these 'black bugs'.

There were photographs in the book; portraits of young apes, quick-eyed, intelligent—beautiful. And here was the only trace of sentimentality. The photographs were not quite as dispassionate as the narrative. The camera never lies? The portraits had been culled, surely, for cuteness—to find some human essence in the apes, a kinship with which the reader might identify.

The photographs, if not the narrative, had committed that cardinal sin of anthropomorphism.

Not that I saw it as a sin. The effect of those photographs, coupled with the cold horror of the narrative, was powerful, and undeniable, the only possible conclusion was that apes should be given the vote.

Or at least placed under the protection of some sort of public guardianship.

I slept in fits and starts, winding myself in my sheets, a walrus tangled in a deep-line net. At first light I pulled on my rubber sheath, slipped out of the house and down the beach steps. The sea, as still and heavy as oil, calmed me; I floated weightlessly for some time, close to shore, unwilling to make any move that might dent or disrupt the limpid surface. Buoyed by fat and rubber, I floated upright, hands at my side, head well above water. I might have slept there, vertical, comfortably suspended—but to the east, beyond the roof tops, the sky was filling with light; the ridge of hills, backlit, knife-edged, was silhouetted against the coming day. Each time my head, bobbing gently, rotated in that direction I felt a small kick of excitement.

I emerged from the water as the sun peeped above Mt Lofty, climbed back up to the house, sluiced my wetsuit beneath the garden hose, and hung it out to dry. My mother was preparing breakfast; the whole house was steeped in

113

the stink of sizzling bacon. Pig bacon was being fried, not chimp bacon, but I pushed my plate aside.

'Hungry-not?'

I rubbed my belly, and gave her the Bad Hand sign:

A mirror-image of the Good Hand: little-finger extended instead of thumb. I was sick, I was telling her—but I meant sickened, not merely ill. Sick, sickened: the different meanings share the same shape in Sign, and the same sound in English. The bacon smell nauseated me. I'd always thought that tastes and smells had some sort of absolute intrinsic worth. Other senses—colours, shapes, sounds— were more subjective, but a particular taste was actually, morally, either good or bad. Shit stinks evilly. Flowers smell…decent.

The smell of frying bacon had always seemed an abso-lute mouth-watering good, but somehow reading the words of C. Francis Kinnear had altered my perception of the flavour.

'Stay bed today,' my mother advised.

I shook my head. I was apprehensive about what faced me in the Hills, but I was also excited. And I knew that my apprehension could only be cured by contact with its object, to postpone the moment would merely magnify it. As I drove towards the rising sun, I was overcome again by body turbulence: shallow, tight respirations, fidgety hands. The sign for anxiety is exactly those tense, fidgety hands. The drug of the ocean had long worn off. My heart pounded as loudly as the four small struggling cylinders of the Fiat as I crossed the last ridge beneath Mt Lofty, and coasted into the Summertown valley beyond—although I still half-expected to find that Eliza would not be at home, or would still be in bed asleep, or otherwise engaged and unavailable.

BOOK

'It is a great baboon, but so much like a man in most things, that though they say there is a species of them, yet I cannot believe but that it is a monster got of a man and a she-baboon. I do believe that it already understands much English, and I am of the mind that it might be taught to speak or make signs.'

SAMUEL PEPYS, 1661

TWO

1

She entered the living room hesitantly, keeping close to the wall, walking upright, on two legs, but awkwardly, a side-swaying waddle. I smelt her instantly—a feral scent but not unpleasant, sweetish and musty, familiar in a way I could not immediately identify. Her long arms brushed the carpet from time to time, but merely to maintain balance. She did not appear to use those arms as forelegs, levering herself as if between a pair of crutches, chimp-fashion.

She glanced up at me, then quickly away, then back again—desperately curious, I sensed, but not wanting to intrude, or threaten.

She was larger than I had expected, almost five feet in height, stocky, barrel-chested, powerfully muscled. And thickly furred, covered with a sleek black pelt, thickest and blackest on the shoulders and upper arms.

Sign has a two-handed mime for richness, or extravagance: the thumbs and fingers stroking the lapels of an imaginary mink coat, feeling the quality.

A perfect description for Eliza's coat, there is no English equivalent.

'Try not to stare,' Clive murmured in my ear. 'Staring is not considered polite among gorillas.'

His expression remained as earnest as ever, his thin mouth devoid of humour, but how could I not stare? The sight was astonishing, disorientating. Eliza's head was still half-averted; her nose broad and squashed looking, almost one-dimensionally flat, more an opening directly into the front of the head than a nose. I was reminded of the nose-hole in a human skull.

The ears were small and delicate, fine elf ears, bearing no resemblance to the Dumbo-flaps of chimpanzees, or cartoon-apes. They would not have been out of place on a young girl.

Her black eyes were the most human feature of all. Once I found the eyes, I could look nowhere else for some minutes. They returned my gaze on and off, shyly, lingering a little longer each time.

Clive and Stella waited, expectant but unhurried, not wanting to prompt—wanting their charge to speak, or sign, spontaneously.

Her eyes darted from one to the other, then back to me. She was still standing side-on, reluctant to face me completely; her gaze, steady now, seemed thoughtful and curious. There was still no sign of intelligence in her hands, no trace yet of any movement which could be interpreted as Sign.

I remembered the comments of the Washoe-sceptics: Washoe scratching her nose interpreted as a sign for 'scratch', Washoe poking a random finger in her mouth interpreted as the sign for 'drink'.

Clive still waited, impassively, but Stella, more restless, could restrain herself no longer.

'Good morning,' she signed towards Eliza.

No response. Stella repeated the sign, a little more urgently. Her own signing was crude, rough around the edges, and too expansive; she was shouting, without realising it.

'Perhaps she's shy with strangers,' I suggested, embarrassed.

'You're her first stranger.'

'Then she's probably terrified.'

Stella turned back to Eliza, her signing far too slow and far too loud, as if speaking to a parrot which refused to recite.

Those dark, glitter-black eyes looked from Stella to me, then slowly, reluctantly, the hands moved for the first time: 'Good morning.'

121

I had been expecting her to sign, *waiting* for it—but the effect was still electrifying, beyond the full reach of expectation. It was as if a dog, a cat, a horse had suddenly spoken aloud.

Or was she merely a parrot after all? I tried desperately to contain that first surge of wonder, to keep an open mind. Surely those hand movements were merely a form of mimicry. Words without meaning.

I managed to find my own hands, and give back another version of 'Hi!': the Mother Hand saluting from the temple.

She copied the gesture, slowly—aped it, I still couldn't help thinking—repeating the simple salute several times. Her hands were partly shielded by her body, the gestures minimal, a sign-whisper. Her palms were black and hairless; the fingers were short stumps, more thumbs than fingers; the thumb itself was more like a little finger, a slender appendage, set at an awkward angle to the hand. Her signing had the sense of someone speaking with a thick accent, or a speech impediment: a swollen tongue, or hare-lip.

Stella pointed at me, then slowly finger-spelt the letters of my name, in full: J-O-H-N J-A-M-E-S.

No response. Stella repeated the sequence, with reasonable accuracy. The gorilla's eyes found mine again, then slid quickly away. Stella's hands continued to move, pleading for an answer; her foster-daughter retreated further into her corner, and finally, abruptly, turned her back.

'You're hectoring her,' Clive admonished his wife, mildly.

'I want J.J. to *see*.'

'My dear, this is exactly what we decided not to do. She's obviously not comfortable.'

'She's fine.'

'She's *not* fine.'

A strange thought came to me, watching that broad black back: that Eliza might feel embarrassed by her nakedness, sitting among the three of us, fully clothed.

'Does she like to wear clothes?'

'She does,' Clive said. 'But we think it demeaning. The effect is merely comical.'

Did he ever use the word comical without that qualifier: merely?

'We let her dress up as an occasional treat,' Stella added, quickly.

Of course Eliza was dressed, in a sense: clad in that thick glossy pelt. Her breasts were naked, and large-nippled, but seemed, in human terms, more masculine than feminine. Her genitals were totally hidden in hair. Surely she had no awareness of nakedness, of its social meaning. Had she sensed the embarrassment of humans in similar circumstances and appropriated the emotion without the proper cause? Or merely aped the signs, the body language, without either emotion or cause?

'I suggest we expose her to your presence more gradually, J.J.,' Clive said.

He paused, waiting; it took me some time to grasp the implication.

'You want me to leave?'

'I hope it doesn't seem too rude, having just arrived. Eliza has the run of the house during the day. It's very much her private space. It might be best if you come back tomorrow. My suggestion would be that we increase your contact time a little each day.'

One last argument from Stella: 'But he doesn't believe us, Clive. We need him to *believe*.'

'I've an open mind,' I said. 'I'm happy to come back tomorrow.'

In truth, my mind had closed, my opinions hardened. I would return partly out of curiosity and partly for the sake of friendship, but the sense of wonder, the sense of something new and astonishing that had filled me when she first entered the room had faded. The hard facts were surely these: those thick animal hands, those *paws,* might ape the odd hand-shape, but were incapable of putting sense to the shapes, let alone linking shapes into fluent Sign.

Eliza turned her head slightly, watching from the corner of her eye.

'You sign goodbye,' Stella urged, with her hands.

Eliza ignored her, wedged in the corner, unmoving. I felt the stirrings of sympathy; her destiny was beyond her control, whether she could speak of this or not. She looked distinctly human, especially in the delicacy of her facial features: a cross-species, cross-primate childishness. She was almost adult sized, but her face was surely not the face of an adult gorilla. Her forehead was less protruding, her head disproportionately larger and more rounded—a child's big head.

Stella repeated the request, more sternly in English: 'Say goodbye, Eliza.'

'Perhaps that's enough for today,' Clive murmured.

As we turned away, the ape finally raised her palm.

'There!' Stella said. 'Did you see that?'

I smiled reassuringly, but she seemed merely to be brushing away a fly.

Clive carefully locked the front door after us, Stella pulled on her muddy work boots, the two of them walked me through the trees to the first gate. If Clive was disappointed, he wasn't saying; Stella's disappointment was all too clear in her forced, jollying tone of voice and in the nervous puffing of her cigarette.

We passed through the gate and out into open paddock. Various grazing animals lifted their heads and began moving in our direction.

'She's just a little shy, J.J. When she gets to know you you'll be *amazed*.'

My curiosity had turned from the question of whether Eliza could sign, to more mundane matters. 'How did you get your hands on her?'

'We rescued her.'

'Stole her,' Clive corrected.

'She's *stolen?*'

He felt the need to be even more precise: 'Abducted might be a better choice of word.'

We halted at the second, outer gate. I waited, hoping for more clues; their eyes met, deciding. The three-legged deer arrived, hobbling with surprising speed, and nuzzled at Stella's hands; she fished a treat from a crevice in her overalls.

'Eliza was a laboratory animal, J.J.,' she said.

Clive filled in the details. 'We had reports of a company in Melbourne working with primates. *Rhesus macaques* mostly. The usual horror stories.'

'Which company?'

'It's probably best if you don't know the name. Let's just say that one of the primatologists became disenchanted.'

'An attack of the guilts,' Stella said.

More animals arrived; Stella, distracted, knelt among the nuzzling, bunting noses, distributing sugar cubes and caresses and words of love. She knew each invalid by name; as she whispered into ears and rubbed noses she seemed, momentarily, one of them herself, a warmhearted mother-mammal, wide-mouthed and big-breasted, distributing love like milk.

Clive, thinner, more cold-blooded, ignored the gathering menagerie.

'The primatologist in question was a former student of mine.'

'You trained him well.'

He shrugged. 'We kept in touch over the years. He didn't like what was happening.'

'What *was* happening?'

'Foetal surgery. I'm not sure I *did* train him well, J.J. The principles of the research didn't seem to bother him—more the methods. Lack of adequate anaesthesia. And the fact that the research was moving up from *rhesus macaques* to great apes, getting too close to home.'

Stella glanced up, half-hidden in the press of big twitchy ears and furry heads. 'One night he took Eliza home—and didn't take her back.'

'He stole a two-hundred pound gorilla?'

She laughed. 'She was a bit smaller then.'

'What about the police?'

'The, ah, abduction hasn't been reported to the police.'

She turned back to her friends, allowing me time to process this news. Once again it was Clive who filled in the gaps. 'The company are still lying low. The last thing they want is publicity. It's become very difficult to experiment with primates in the current climate.'

'For which we like to think we can take some of the credit,' Stella said.

Clive waved his hand dismissively, the allocation of credit was of no importance to him. 'The company had an import licence for macaques, but not in a million years would they be granted permission to house a gorilla. The Federal Police would be *very* interested in their activities.'

'So you could dob *them* in to the police? Or whoever.'

'National Parks and Wildlife. There is a watchdog body, the Vertebrate Pest Control Committee. The police act on their advice. If we turn the company in, we turn ourselves in. Eliza will be taken from us and put in a zoo. There's a gorilla colony in Melbourne—and that's the last place we want her.'

'Why? Surely she would be happier among her own.'

'*We* are her own,' he said, patiently.

Stella stood up abruptly, less patient, more indignant. The animals shied away from her, startled.

'J.J.—you've met her. You've talked with her! And you want to put her in a zoo? A *jail?*'

Chastened, I passed through the gate; they followed. The autumn sun was high and hot, an Indian summer sun, beating down, an actual physical pressure on the face and head; I felt in need of the ocean.

'This company,' I asked, a last parting question. 'What kind of foetal surgery were they doing?'

Another barely perceptible exchange of glances; Clive elected to answer: 'As I said, J.J., it might be best if you didn't know the full story, at least for the time being. The legal position is unclear.'

Stella said: 'If she *is* stolen, we would be in possession of stolen goods. You would be an accessory.'

'I prefer to think of her as an illegal immigrant,' Clive said, 'rather than goods.'

'A political refugee?' Stella suggested, less seriously.

We reached the car; I fumbled in my pockets for the keys. Clive grasped my forearm, gently: 'Once again we would ask that you keep our confidence. Not a word of this to anyone—please. Can we rely on you?'

I nodded, but felt the need to add: 'I don't know that I can give any long-term guarantees.'

2

Had Eliza raised her hand to wave goodbye? Perhaps, but what did a single hand-shape prove? Glancing back through these pages, at the cartoon shapes I've sketched here and there among the words, I sense I've still failed to make one thing clear. To repeat: Sign is no mere pantomime of see-through shapes. My sketches are the figures of a crude alphabet, nothing more; they cannot pretend to be a language.

Granted, these single signs are more natural than the letters of an alphabet; most have a clear mime-meaning, a particular resonance and beauty. But the sum of language is always greater than the parts. The parts become irrelevant. The last thing on a native signer's mind is the beauty, or even the meaning, of each separate sign.

In fluent hands the language becomes smoothed out, more stylised; the printed block letters of the child's alphabet become the flowing script of adult cursive.

These thoughts preoccupied me as I drove away—thoughts stained by a sense of disappointment. Distracted, I found myself heading the wrong way on Greenhill Road, driving further into the Hills. I didn't turn back. The sun shone; the compact glasshouse of the car trapped and magnified its warmth; I soon felt pleasantly baked. The rhythms of the car engine massaged me gently to and fro, my mood slowly lifted. I chugged on through wooded valleys and over sunburnt ridges until the country began to flatten again; the car struggled to the top of a last small rise and I found myself looking down over an immense plain. The Murray River glittered in the distance, a meandering silver ribbon as far as the eye could see; I wished that I had brought my wetsuit, and considered, momentarily, swimming without it.

Instead I pulled to the side of the road, tilted back my seat and slept for a time, overcome by drowsiness. I dreamed that I was walking on the beach at home, wading in the shallows. A commotion disturbed the water: two whales roared out of the surf like locomotives and beached themselves each side of me. They spouted steam. Their hides were as thick as rhino-hide, scarred and barnacle-encrusted. Their low-set eyes, positioned near the corners of their huge mouths, were blinking, swivelling frantically about, looking at each other, looking at me. Their lips twitched, moving rapidly as if mouthing words—but no sound emerged.

No whale-moo; no sonar-squeak.

As I stared at those twitching lips, inspiration struck; the secret of whale communication. Of course! Whales *lip*-read! It seemed so obvious, why hadn't I seen it before? Their eyes were positioned near the corners of their mouths to allow them to watch their own lips as well as the next whale's—to hear themselves, in a sense, speak.

It seemed a major breakthrough, I knew that it would make me world famous. 'Known-everywhere.' The problem was: I couldn't understand what the whales were saying. It must have been important, a message they had beached themselves to tell me, had given their lives so that they could tell me.

I've never learnt to lip-read. Born with a pair of working ears, it's a skill I've never needed. I stared at those violently twitching lips without the slightest inkling of their meaning.

3

Eliza was wedged in the same corner when Stella ushered me into the living room the next morning, a black Buddha, immobile and impassive. Had she been squatting on her haunches all night? At least she had turned her back to the wall and was now facing the door. I had the impression that she was waiting, for me.

'J-O-H-N J-A-M-E-S,' she finger-spelt, slowly, and turned to Stella, seeking approval.

Stella smiled, smugly—but to me, nothing was proved. Perhaps they had spent the night in parrot-work.

I pointed to Eliza, and raised my eyebrows: 'You...?'

She sat, motionless. I glanced back to Stella, my turn for smugness. And then, in the corner of my eye, without warning, came the first small miracle; I turned in time to catch the last letters in a sequence: Z-A-K-I-N-N-E-A-R. The various letters were misshapen, but her hand movements

were rapid, the most rapid finger-spelling I'd seen—
a fast-forward blur, the hands of a pianist playing some
difficult, closing passage.

Astonishment, extinguished the day before, flared
inside me again. If the movement of her hands was merely
a form of aping, then it was a very superior aping. Lost
for words, lost for signs, I retreated into the banality of
speech.

'Longwinded name for a gorilla.'

Stella answered: 'Clive believes the usual clown names—
Koko, Bobo, that kind of thing—are too undignified.'

'Circus names,' he confirmed.

'Sign again,' Stella signed in the direction of Eliza.

She watched us, suspiciously. Was there also a hint
of resentment in those sharp, black eyes? Her name might
not be a circus name but she was still expected to perform
tricks.

Stella finger-spelt again—E-L-I-Z-A-K-I-N-N-E-A-R
— and Eliza copied again, in full, the same rapid blur of
finger-spelling, although it still took far longer, of course,
than the words, spoken.

I signed an 'E'. And added a 'you'—the Point Hand,
aimed.

She watched, puzzled.

'Short name,' I explained, in Sign, not expecting
her to follow the argument, but not knowing what else
to do.

'Short' was even beyond Clive and Stella. I tried a more
universal shape, the Hook Hand pincers of 'little':

'Waste time—not,' I added.

She copied my movements fluently, without the speech-impediment of her earlier hand-shapes. A realisation: the slurring of her sign-speech had nothing to do with odd hand anatomy, or the limitations of ape intelligence. She had merely copied, faithfully, whatever she had been taught. Her teacher or teachers had not been native signers.

There was still no evidence of anything beyond aping, however—no evidence of comprehension.

I said aloud: 'If she can sign, and I'm not saying yet that I believe she can, then she should have a sign-name.'

Blank stares this time from Clive and Stella: please-explain.

I tried: 'A single sign—or two. A pet name.'

'She's not a pet,' Clive insisted, always the literalist.

I conceded the semantic point. 'Bad choice of words. I meant, she should have a family name. A nickname. For ease of signing. Something simple.'

They waited for suggestions.

'For example, Mink,' I said, and shaped the fur-coat sign.

Stella was horrified. 'You want to call her after the skin of a dead *animal!*'

134

I said quickly: 'No hurry. Another name will come to us. Something that's right for her, something that fits.'

In the corner E. was motionless again, watching, waiting. Her broad black hands rested in her lap; no amount of pleading from Stella could coax further movements from them. We had taxed her enough for the day, Clive suggested.

I waved from the door, this time the answering gesture of her hand was unmistakably 'goodbye', if merely the goodbye of a parrot.

Once again she turned to Stella for approval; I wondered, not for the first time, what pressure she was under to perform.

Stella's goodbyes were far more meaningful: disappointment attempting to hide beneath its opposite, false enthusiasm. She talked me all the way to the gate, pushing her way through the cluster of following animals. I waded after her through the herd; as we reached the gate she stopped and turned and beat her fist against her forehead, a now-familiar part of her repertoire.

'In all the excitement I forgot the video,' she said to Clive.

'Shall I get it, my dear?'

'I'll get it.'

We waited for her return, leaning against the outer gate. The animals kept their distance; they seemed to have no affinity for Clive, their chief defender and spokesman in the human world. I found the sudden silence awkward, but Clive seemed relaxed, unfazed. He wasn't the kind who wasted words; he spoke only when he had something to say. The summer sun poured its warmth over our heads like

135

heavy oil, but I resisted making small talk on the weather. Small talk, I suspected, might quickly grow into a long lecture on isobars, rainfall patterns, computer simulations of the El Nino effect.

Stella reappeared waving a boxed video-cassette.

'We shot this last night,' she said. 'If you are having doubts about being part of the project, I'm sure this will convince you.'

I felt no urgency to view the video. I doubted it would reveal anything I hadn't already seen; an extra circus trick or two perhaps. I spent the afternoon at the Institute, conquering a mountain of paperwork. At home, after dinner, I watched an ethnic telemovie with my parents, an Indian version of Romeo and Juliet, in Hindi. A Muslim Romeo, a Hindu Juliet, against a background of elephants and marble palaces, with English subtitles. I sat, as of old, on a cushion on the floor. My father's toes prodded my back from time to time, wanting to know who was speaking to whom, or what was happening off-camera. A happy ending, no one died, my parents went to bed smiling. As soon as their door was closed I slipped Stella's video into the machine and pressed Play, but without expectation.

I felt exhausted, ready for bed myself; I watched through heavy lids. It might have been shot by the same Hindi film-maker—there were no subtitles, but the jerky hand-held tracking and poorly focused images were characteristic. Stella's urging voice filled the soundtrack, as expected; her hands frequently appeared, close-up, in the corner of the screen, prompting, offering examples to be imitated.

136

Eliza was the central subject, crouched in her corner, offering vague, uninterested hand-shapes in reply. I wandered into the kitchen, set a saucepan of milk on the gas ring for cocoa, keeping half an eye on the television screen through the door. I almost missed it. There among the parrot-imitations, the indifferent shrugs and refusals, came a sign-series of sudden clarity, repeated several times, rapidly:

'S-T-E-L-L-A go. Me sleep. S-T-E-L-L-A go. Me sleep...'

Sleep: the universal sleep-mime, or sweet-dreams-mime; the head tilted slightly, pillowed by the Flat Hand.

I was instantly alert, roused, paradoxically, by that sign for sleep, a clearly intended message. I hurried back into the television room, eyes glued to the screen, and witnessed an even more startling message. Eliza pointed angrily to the camera, to Stella, then shaped a Spoon Hand and cupped it to her buttocks, an impromptu scoop. Her own invention, surely, but the meaning was clear:

'You—shit!'

137

I paused the tape, stunned; rewound, and replayed that sequence several times, disbelieving: *You—shit!*

There could be no mistake. Her black hands had shaped that insult with clear intent, had hurled it in Stella's direction as deliberately and accurately as her cousins in zoos might toss the substance itself through their bars.

After such excitement, what price sleep? I pulled on my wetsuit, and floated, mesmerised, in the sea for a good two hours, replaying that expression in my mind's eye. To the best of my knowledge Eliza had spoken the first symbolic utterance—the first poem—ever created by another species.

4

On a whim, I stopped the car at a shopping mall the next morning and bought a handful of fresh asparagus sticks. A nearby florist gift-wrapped the bunch, under sufferance, in a cone of green crepe paper, fastened with a dab of tape. Her sarcasm—'Who's the lucky lady?'—proved contagious; the bunch looked merely comical, sitting on the passenger seat as I drove up into the Hills. I ripped off the crepe sheath as I climbed from the car at the farm gate, and was tempted to bin the entire bunch.

But what gift do you offer to an eight-year-old gorilla? A banana? Asparagus was my only clue.

I pressed the intercom; Stella's voice crackled through the speaker, a sound that lifted, as always, the head of every animal within earshot.

'Push, J.J., it's open.'

I shoved the asparagus deep in my coat pocket and passed through the gate. The animals bent again to their dry stubble breakfast, ignoring me. I skirted the dam to the second gate, and entered amongst the trees. Magpies warbled, bees hummed, thick columns of sunlight fell between and through the foliage, another glorious morning.

Stella was sitting on the edge of the verandah, sandwiched between dogs. Her overalls and work boots were spattered with fresh mud; she had been working around the dam. The inevitable cigarette was jammed between her lips, her eyes were screwed half-shut against the smoke.

'Top of the morning to you, J.J.'

'And to you.'

'You watched the video?'

I nodded; she smiled confidently, sensing my change of heart, unlaced her boots, kicked them off, and led me inside.

'I have a good feeling about today,' she murmured.

Eliza was wedged in her favourite corner, waiting. I pulled the asparagus stalks from my pocket and offered them; she stared at the limp bunch for a long moment, then slowly toppled forward and rolled towards me—a single somersault. Upright again—there was something inherently stable, or self-righting, about that low centre-of-gravity shape—she took the bunch.

'Thank you,' she signed with her free hand, a clearly intended meaning.

Clive, watching, held out his own hand. 'Lunch,' he said to Eliza, and simultaneously shaped a simple sandwich mime, clearly well practised. The bunch was reluctantly handed over; he turned to me with a mild rebuke: 'She's just eaten breakfast, J.J. We don't encourage snacks between meals.'

Eliza was watching me, intently; I felt the need to defend myself, to defend both of us. Perhaps that rebuke could form the basis for some kind of alliance.

'I would have thought that gorillas would be snacking all the time in the wild. Constantly grazing.'

He nodded. 'A necessity when food-gathering is time and labour-intensive. It's a different matter in captivity—too often it leads to problems of obesity.'

He intended no slight; there wasn't a malicious bone in his body. At some later date I might suggest to him that the problems of abstinence and self-denial might be as great as the problems of obesity, but for now I bit my tongue. Eliza began signing again, in the corner of my eye. Her slurred, inexact hand movements were difficult to follow, moving too rapidly; her dark hands were still held shyly, close to her body, only partly visible.

The odd anatomy of those black hands also had a distracting effect, the message obscured by the medium.

'Slow down,' I suggested, right forefinger tracing left forearm, snail-pace.

She didn't recognise the sign. I showed her a see-through alternative: left palm an accelerator pedal, right fist a foot, lifted, slightly. Clearly she had driven in cars; the speed of her hands instantly slowed. The room seemed suddenly filled with her scent, a now-familiar mustiness, sweetly pungent, released, surely, by excitement.

I managed to read sense into her hands the third time: 'Sign me name you.'

141

The syntax was ponderous—mispronounced Sign grafted onto English word order, with finger-spelling thrown in. A faithful copy of something badly taught, or a spontaneous question?

'Sign your name, J-O-H-N J-A-M-E-S.'

More comprehensible the second time, but also more redundant—a question that contained its own answer. Did she have less understanding of these sign transactions than I was beginning to think, or hope?

'Short name,' she signed, clearly. 'Quick name.'

My pulse missed a beat. Short name I had shown her previously, but the jointing of quick and name was new, not copied from me. Here, without question, was proof that she was thinking as she signed. I turned to Stella. Smug triumph was written on her face, loudly. Even Clive's tight lips wore an expression of suppressed pride.

Eliza simplified the question further, as if speaking to a child, or someone too thick to understand: 'Me—E. You—J.?'

I finally found my hands: 'J.J.'

Her excitement was clear, though more in the jumpy restlessness of her body than in any facial expression. And in that scent, overwhelmingly pungent. Her gaze remained steady, as if she wanted to miss nothing, yet she still sat a little side-on in her corner, her hands difficult to read.

I showed her my sign-name: Sweet-Tooth. She copied, instantly. I told her that I was pleased to meet her—in sign, literally 'well met'.

She returned the pleasantry, several times, each time with increasing speed, and with perfect hand-shape.

'Sign more,' she demanded, with urgency. 'Sign more. You sign me!'

To me, these events still had a weird, dreamy feel. I was half stunned; nothing but the standard adult-to-child noises came to mind, or to hand. What's-your-name? Where-do-you-live?

'How old you?' I asked: literally how-many-you?

Did she understand the concept of age, of years? She held up eight fingers, and asked the question back.

I signed 'too old', using the eloquent shape for old age: the Two Hand sketching imaginary age-lines on the face, plus a mournful hang-dog expression. She laughed for the first time, a kind of soft, throaty cluck. From a human mouth it would have sounded forced and unnatural.

She signed: 'Too old—not.'

Her first grin was as disconcerting as her laughter, more a baring of teeth, unsmiling.

'A crowd of years,' I signed back; she seemed puzzled, I altered a word: 'A crowd of birthdays,' and she grinned again, understanding.

The smile might have looked inhuman, but there was human joy in the deep blackness of those eyes; they shone with the exhilaration of each new discovery.

'Show me your hands,' I signed.

She rested them gently in mine; I was able to inspect them closely for the first time. They were longer than human hands: a mix of soft hairless leather, and hair—*fur*—in all the wrong places. She could oppose the tiny thumb and thick forefinger, but I doubted the thumb would reach her little finger. Her hands were a different instrument, a different voice.

143

'Beautiful hands,' I signed.

'Too crowds of hair,' she signed, and improvised, or incorporated, another word by pointing at the thick shag-pile carpet on which we stood. 'Carpet-hands.'

I laughed, half-amused, half-astounded, at the joke, and signed back: 'Warm hands. Expressive hands.'

Then she did something even more astonishing. Both her hands were resting in mine, but another hand, a third hand—more elongated, differently shaped—appeared between the others, signing.

'Hello, Sweet-Tooth!'

I stepped back; she was standing on her left foot, laughing; her right foot was deftly tapping her front tooth with its big-toe-cum-thumb.

I dropped her hands and clapped.

'We don't like to clap her,' Clive said. 'Or reward her with food. She's not performing tricks.'

There was no rebuke in his tone, merely the usual matter-of-fact statement.

'But she's just a child,' I said. 'We reward children for learning. For innovation.'

'She's not strictly a child,' he said. 'She's eight. Sixteen or seventeen in human years. She menstruates. She comes into oestrus each month. She's a fully grown, mature female gorilla.'

Sweet sixteen. I looked at her; she watched me back, refusing to avert her eyes, waiting to see more, learn more.

'More signs,' she signed, and thumped her right foot, her third hand, impatiently against the carpet. 'More signs. Now!'

144

Clive said: 'I think perhaps that is enough for today.'

Stella added, on cue: 'She's easily overexcited, J.J. We were worried this might happen. She's such a quick learner—and she has such an appetite for learning. But she gets into a state. We've found it's best to take things slowly.'

I couldn't see why. Surely her excitement should be allowed full reign, used to fuel her learning. I kept my mouth shut. I was a newcomer, a guest. I didn't feel confident enough to argue the point.

'Sleep-time,' Stella signed at her foster-child: the same sleep-mime I had seen Eliza use on video.

Eliza shook her head, her eyes still fixed on me.

I showed her another version for 'sleep': thumb and forefinger, at eye-level, shutting together; the eyelids closing.

She copied, thrilled—a further discovery. Then shook her head, and grinned her weird grin, and performed the sign in reverse; the mime of eyes opening: 'wake-up'.

I laughed again. She had never seen the sign before, but had guessed that the hand-shapes, backwards, would mean exactly the opposite.

'This is wonderful,' I said. '*She* is wonderful. Can't we talk a little longer? You *can't* send her to bed.'

'I must insist,' Clive said. 'She's been up since dawn. She becomes unmanageable when she's too excited. She always has a morning nap.'

'Can I talk with her later? When she wakes?'

They glanced at each other. I sensed that Stella was wavering, caught up in the emotion of the moment.

'Trust us,' Clive said, standing firm. 'She's been with us for some time now. We think we know best.'

'Please, just an hour. It's so—fantastic. Miraculous. I've never seen anything like it.'

Clive shook his head, polite, even friendly: 'Tomorrow,' he said. 'Come at noon.'

'I can't come earlier?'

'I need to work on my manuscript. And Stella usually makes house calls in the morning.'

'Barn calls, mostly,' she said.

I turned back to Eliza, still watching intently. She couldn't speak English, but could she hear it? Did she understand?

'See you again,' I signed, a smooth blend of 'look again', or 'look twice'. Then added 'tomorrow'.

She looked puzzled. The 'tomorrow' sign is a little opaque, or symbolic, the Point Hand moving straight ahead, into the immediate future. How to make her understand? I was on familiar territory, classroom bread-and-butter for a teacher of Basic Auslan. I showed her the sign for 'Sun', a simple and beautiful hand-shape: the Round Hand bursting open, fingers spread; a sun and its rays of shining light.

146

I traced an imaginary path with my sun across the sky towards the west, then jerked to the east, the radiant sun rising, followed by the signs: 'You see me'.

She somersaulted forward across the carpet and hugged me round the waist, pressing her head hard against my chest. Her massive arms were a vice; I was fighting for breath.

Stella, alarmed, moved to separate us. 'She doesn't know her own strength, J.J.'

Eliza stepped back and repeated my shape for tomorrow, but with the Wish Hand, I saw, not the Point Hand: the first two fingers crossed in hope. It was a beautiful touch, an improvised variation, another poem which moved me as much as anything else I had seen during that extraordinary morning.

She watched me leave from the front window, her flat nose flattened further against the glass. I turned and waved from the tree line; she pressed her black palm hard against the glass. Clive and Stella escorted me through the trees, one walking each side of me; I had the feeling of being seen off the premises, politely bounced. The presence of their

Pied Piper caused the usual commotion among the animals in the outer field; various invalids which had been grazing, or sheltering from the summer heat in the shade of the trees, began to hobble towards Stella.

I unlocked the Fiat and climbed into its baking oven. Clive tapped on the window; I wound it down, he passed through a book. More required reading, it seemed. Another Set Text. I read the title: *The Education of Koko*.

'You might find this of interest,' he said. 'Much of Penny Patterson's work is twenty years old now, but still relevant.'

'I'll read it for my homework,' I murmured, but irony, as always, was beyond or far beneath him.

5

How many nights since I had last slept my full eight-hour quota, unbroken? I read *The Education of Koko* till one, slept only briefly, but woke, refreshed and recharged. Morning couldn't come soon enough; the remaining hours crawled past, less small hours than infinitely large. At five I jerked on my wetsuit, sneaked from the house, and floated in the dark ocean for an hour or so. Back in bed, temporarily calmed, I reread certain passages in the book, key Sign exchanges—American Sign—between the gorilla Koko and her human family.

How do gorillas feel when they die? Koko was asked. Her answer: 'Sleep.'

'Where do gorillas go when they die?'

Koko: 'Comfortable hole bye.'

'When do gorillas die?'

'Trouble old.'

149

I would have treated these transcriptions with extreme scepticism a day before. I would have criticised Patterson's methods, her statistics, data collection, lack of controls— but my third meeting with Eliza had made me become a convert, a believer. Contact with Eliza had also raised my expectations. I felt only impatience as I read of the crude pidgin-signings of Koko; I wanted to ask those same deep questions of Eliza.

At eight I teletyped a message to the Institute, claiming illness. My excitement was growing again; I couldn't face the tedium of work. I buried myself in breakfast, distracted, incommunicado. My father came and ate and read through the morning paper and left for work without a single sign. Without a textbook sign, at least. The righteous force with which he smeared his toast with anchovy paste was more than eloquent.

My mother finished her own breakfast shortly after-wards, rose from the table and routinely kissed the top of my head.

'Work,' she signed: the standard chop and saw carpentry-mime, always an odd description when applied to her work in the library. Even the most transparent signs often lose contact with their origins, become as stylised as words.

I signed back: 'Wait. I'll come too.'

She looked worried.

'Flexiday,' I lied, using my own invention, a sign I had been trying to sneak into the language, or at least into the next edition of my slim dictionary: simply the sign for day, bent.

I walked with her along the esplanade. Another fine warm morning, the sky pool-blue, unflawed by cloud. The usual steady westerly breeze was blowing in off the gulf, refreshing, invigorating. I had scarcely slept, but I felt no tiredness; I felt as high as the small red kite that floated in the breeze further along the beach. I felt far too exhilarated to concentrate on the small-talk signs my mother aimed my way from time to time.

She unlocked the library doors; I headed straight into the Natural Science section. Dewey Decimal 899.8846, G for Gorilla. Various titles caught my eye: *The Year of the Gorilla. The Natural History of the Gorilla. The Great Apes: A Study of Anthropoid Life.*

In three hours I was due at the farm; I wanted to cram as much knowledge as possible into that time. I sat and began to read, and, shortly, to scribble notes. Natural Habitat, Gestation Length, Brain Size, Behaviour, Social Structure.

There was much to absorb; far too much to swot in those swift-flying hours. At eleven, increasingly restless, wanting to be in the Hills as soon as permitted, I pocketed my notes, and lugged my stack of ape-books to the borrowing desk. My mother turned them this way and that, then signed, puzzled: 'Gorilla?'

Several readers glanced up at her, astonished; their demure, deaf librarian was beating her chest with clenched fists.

'Popular books,' I signed back. 'People like gorillas.'

She lifted the back cover of *The Natural History of the Gorilla* and stamped the due-date. The sticker was crammed with previous dates.

'See,' I signed.

I continued to read, on and off, at red lights as I drove, the book perched on the lectern of the steering wheel. A discrepancy still teased at me: the intelligence of adult gorillas was given as equivalent to a three or four-year-old human infant. The sign-speech of Koko was no exception, her conceptions of death, of heaven, her conception of self, all seemed roughly pitched at that level. Sophisticated, yes, even human—but a child-human. A three-year-old intelligence at best.

Which left Eliza where? Her intelligence, her creativity—above all her sense of humour—were light-years beyond this. As I left the city limits I cast the book aside and pressed my accelerator pedal hard against the floor. The tiny engine complained, the car shook and shuddered, but obediently climbed the long winding road to the ridge more quickly than ever before.

6

I was surprised to find Eliza waiting for me, alone, only partly screened by the trees behind the second gate.

'You see me?' I signed.

'I *hear* you,'—her hand cupped emphatically to her ear.

'Good ears.'

Stella appeared, approaching through the trees, a proud, beaming parent, followed by her small flock of dogs.

'We were sitting outside in the sun, J.J. Clive and I didn't hear a thing. Eliza pricked up her ears and headed off like a shot.'

'What's to stop her running away?'

'She never ventures beyond the trees. She hates open space—it seems to be some deep-seated instinct.'

Eliza, excluded from conversation, thrust a flurry of excited hand-shapes in my face. I'd seen that same excitement, that same joy before—in deaf children exposed to

Sign for the first time, discovering the existence of a new world.

'She's been impossible,' Stella said. 'I don't think she slept all night.'

I tried to read the fast-forward of those hands: Good Mornings and Beautiful Mornings and various quickfire questions scattered among the blur of shapes.

'Slow down,' I signed, pronouncing the deceleration-shape slowly and carefully.

'Sorry,' she signed, followed by the 'remember' shape, but using crossed fingers: an odd, improvised blend of Wish and Remember, her own quick shorthand, it seemed to me, for 'I'll try to remember'.

'Start again. Back to start.'

'Beautiful morning,' she signed.

'Perfect,' I signed back—the Okay Hand—then added: 'Later hot' and wiped my brow.

Did gorillas sweat? The sign might be meaningless to Eliza; I stuck out a panting tongue as well.

'Where would you like us all?' Stella asked. 'Inside the house?'

I hesitated, thrown momentarily by the phrase 'us all'. I had hoped to have Eliza to myself; to explore her world of signs free of parental interference, or interpretation.

Stella, always alert to body language, said: 'You don't mind us sitting in?'

'Of course not. You don't have work commitments?'

'Finished for the day. I'm trying to keep the afternoons free.'

'And Clive?'

His slightly stooped figure, in striped running shoes, was approaching more sedately through the trees.

'He's his own man these days. An apex without a pyramid. He needs one or two hours with his new book each morning—after that he's free. I think it's important we keep abreast of her progress, J.J. We need to learn the language that she learns. We don't want to lose touch with her.'

Clive raised his Good Hand, I returned the greeting, we walked through their small forest. Late morning, late summer, a clear enamel-blue sky, the sun in full flood pouring through the leaves. The day was hot already—the walk across the open paddock and up the hill had left me sweating—but the air beneath the trees was still cool and refreshing, even slightly knife-edged.

'Stay outside in sun,' Eliza signed.

She used the same shape for a radiant sun that I had taught her the day before, but added her signature-sign: 'Wish'.

The Wish Hand is not a common shape; the effect was distracting, once again I was reminded of someone speaking with a lisp. I asked to see her hands again—perhaps some deformity was responsible: a fracture incorrectly set, which caused the middle finger to ride over the index. She rested them gently in mine; I found nothing more than I had found the day before: eight thick fingers, two short, thin thumbs. Plus a slight greasiness of the skin on the backs of those fingers, a natural lubricant to aid in knuckle-walking. *The Natural History of the Gorilla*, chapter 3, Structure and Function.

I signed: 'Many wishes in these hands.'

'Crowds of wishes,' she signed back, then touched the tips of her fingers to her forehead: 'Here.'

An expression of great beauty, a Sign poem. I shivered suddenly, involuntarily; the shit-insult on video had astonished me, but the poetry of these shapes was exhilarating, magical. Goose bumps pricked my neck and back; it seemed, once again, an overturning of natural law, like being spoken to by a stone, a tree, a hill.

Or perhaps by a human in a gorilla-suit. A gap had opened between what the eye saw, and what the brain permitted itself to comprehend—between image and understanding. Things seen no longer matched things known. Watching Eliza I felt momentarily disorientated, even a little giddy. I half-expected, even half-hoped, that she might twist off her head, and reveal the whole thing to be an extended practical joke, a clown act, or gorilla-gram.

Stella spoke up: 'She wants to stay outside?'

'We'll sit in the arbour,' Clive decided.

We turned into a small rose-arbour before reaching the house. The morning papers were stacked on a wooden barbecue table; a silver coffee pot glinted in the sunlight. An ashtray was filled with butts. We sat among the roses: a profusion of half-wild blooms, small and unpruned. These feral flowers bore no resemblance to my mother's military roses; I felt I was sitting in the middle of an unroofed room, walled on all sides with a tangle of thorns.

I demonstrated the sign for rose; Eliza copied eagerly; I added the gardening sign, touching an imaginary flower to the nose, sniffing.

Stella and Clive sat together on a narrow garden bench behind the table, Stella leaning forward, legs apart, elbows on her knees, her dogs lying at her feet, Clive's posture more upright.

'Ignore us,' Stella said. 'Pretend we're not here.'

She shook a cigarette from a packet, lit it, inhaled. 'We'll be exemplary parents—seen and not heard.'

Easier said than done. I felt as if I were still auditioning, or worse, on trial. That barbecue table lacked only a gavel.

'More signs,' Eliza demanded. 'You sign me.'

Where to begin? She was more advanced than the beginners in my Basic class, but it seemed best to start from scratch, if only to measure exactly how much she did know. There was also a need to correct her mispronunciation. Misshapen—mishandled—signs were the norm.

A retreat into tried and tested teaching habits also had another advantage. I was on unfamiliar territory. I had taught Sign to children who could neither hear nor speak. I had taught Sign to adults, the parents of the deaf, who could both hear *and* speak.

I had never before taught a student who could hear but not speak.

I began with a test of common nouns, pointing out various familiar objects in our vicinity: flower, tree, hose, bush. It was soon evident that despite the occasional inspiration, and snatch of Sign poetry, Eliza's vocabulary was haphazard, a random patchwork. I could detect neither order nor method. She knew various obscure hand-shapes—'lawn-mower', 'snail-bait', even, memorably, 'venetian-blind'—but she didn't have a sign for 'cloud'. She could name every individual tree in sight—spotted gum, lemon-scented gum, blue gum, pointing to *her* gums, the gums of her mouth, each time—but she had no general sign for tree.

I demonstrated the hand-shape, another borrowing from American Sign. Auslan uses the Claw Hands to sketch a fluffy silhouette of foliage; I've reluctantly followed the

herd to the more see-through Ameslan:
Eliza's grammar was as unsystematic as her vocabulary, a pidgin application of English sign-order of the kind often seen in those who sign as a second language. Subject-verb-object is seldom necessary in Sign; who is doing what to whom is made clear from the position of the nouns in Signing Space, and the direction of the verbs.

Her grammar needed work, assuming that her ape-brain was capable of absorbing grammar. I knew of any number of linguists who would deny the possibility, utterly.

Another early discovery: she liked to hear language spoken.

'Talk *and* sign,' she demanded, then added her signature hand-shape: 'I wish.'

Those crossed fingers spiced her signing with a special flavour, a mix of hope and wistfulness, a subjunctive mood of ifs and coulds and shoulds not often found in Sign. Eccentric, perhaps, even ungrammatical—but always moving.

I turned to Clive and Stella: 'I'd like to suggest a name for her.'

They waited silently, an odd couple on a narrow bench, even now determined not to interfere.

'You—Wish,' I signed to Eliza, and to put it in context added, 'Me—Sweet-Tooth.'

I squirmed a little at the baby-talk feel of the signs, a Sign version of Motherese, the language parents speak to infants. Or perhaps not so much Motherese as Tarzanese. The name seemed to fit, however—she aimed her own Wish Hand at herself, repeatedly.

'Name that,' she signed, pointing to her foster-parents.

My turn to pass judgement. Clive first. The mime-sign for robot tempted me, briefly: two stiff, jerkily moving arms. The sign would be over Eliza's head, surely, a private joke; the connection of robot and cold intellect would mean nothing to her. A sudden inspiration: I circled my scalp with the Point Hand, tracing the imaginary halo: 'Saint'.

Wish copied, perfectly; Clive managed a tight smile; Stella laughed her husky infectious laugh. She proved easier to christen; a simple translation of her name. 'Star', a handful of twinkling fingers held high above the head.

'Thank you,' she signed, placed her palm over her heart, and added in English, 'that's very beautiful.'

Beautiful: a smooth blend of 'good' and 'face'; I demonstrated the hand-shapes.

'That sign is beautiful *too*,' she said.

Wish practised the new names, brow furrowed. I remembered something Jill had once told me—that we learn a new word every forty minutes from the age of one. Wish had a lot of catching up to do. I picked out other nearby objects, linked them into simple phrases—more word-strings than sentences—she handled these with ease. Her mind was a sponge; I supplied the flow of signs, she soaked them up, effortlessly. I was still guilty of speaking Motherese, a grammarless language. *See the bottle. Baby want drink?* Wish clearly deserved more than baby-talk. I introduced a simple subordinate clause, she grasped the concept instantly. I showed her several verb modifiers, building phrases from her existing vocabulary. I showed her the inflections that Sign uses to indicate tense, subtle forward movements into the future, backwards movements into the past.

Too much, too soon? I found it impossible to pace myself; her mind seemed to have been waiting for such knowledge.

Which meant what for the notion—a favourite of Jill's—that we humans have a unique grammatical structure wired into our brains, an inbuilt language machine, peculiar only to us? Were there also reserved parking spaces in the gorilla brain for these simple rules of grammar?

Time flew as swiftly as ever; the world about us baked in the summer sun. There *were* beads of sweat on Wish's black brow, charmingly human. The shadows of the trees moved across the grass; several times the sleeping dogs woke and struggled to their feet, and shifted, following the sun. After an hour or two Stella fetched a tray of cold drinks and sandwiches from the house; otherwise we sat impervious to the heat, insulated, or shaded, by our total absorption in Sign. The shadows were long, the sun almost gone when Clive's wristwatch bleeped, and he rose from his seat.

'Medicine time,' he announced.

Wish screwed up her face, clearly recognising the spoken word.

'What medicine?' I asked.

Clive explained: 'She takes various diet supplements. And a dose of cortisone each day. If she misses her dose it could be very dangerous.'

'Cortisone?'

'She was born with no adrenal glands,' Stella added, then changed the subject. 'Maybe you could teach us the sign for medicine, J.J.?'

A Bad Hand shape, the pestle of the little finger stirring an imaginary mortar. Wish mimicked my hands exactly, so enamoured with the symbol that she momentarily forgot her distaste for the thing itself.

'Bad medicine,' she signed, a visual pun with the Bad Hand, and laughed her odd purring laugh. Joy flared inside me again, a surge of pleasure and excitement.

Clive tapped his watch; a message aimed more at me than at Wish. Time to go. Time to take *my* medicine, the end of the lesson, and another afternoon's adventure.

'Tomorrow,' I signed to Wish. Then added in English, signing an exact word-by-word transcription of the phrase as I spoke: 'Same time, same place.'

I still wasn't sure how much speech she understood—a few words, certainly, probably even more. It seemed sensible to attempt to develop both senses, listening and signing.

Stella and Clive walked me to the gate; Wish, after a long farewell hug, a filibustering hug aimed at preventing my departure, remained reluctantly behind the tree line, out of sight.

Stella was gushing; too preoccupied with the subject of Wish to spare more than a passing glance at the animals clustering about her: 'An amazing transformation, J.J. Her whole attitude has changed overnight. I can tell you that these last few months haven't been easy. Her moods have been bleak, to say the least.'

Clive demurred. 'They haven't been *that* bad, my dear.'

'You wouldn't notice,' she told him, and turned to me: 'Clive tends not to see what she feels—only what she says. Signs.'

'I am always cautious about ascribing human emotions to her. She is an animal, after all.'

Stella, flushed with the success of the day, loose-tongued, laughed, mockingly. 'Clive doesn't believe in emotions.'

I sensed more than a hint of genuine grievance beneath the teasing banter.

'I believe in emotions,' he said, smoothly. 'I just don't trust them.'

'You're a cold fish,' she said. 'You've got a brain like a *squid*.'

Her face was still glowing with pleasure—but other, different emotions also seemed close to the surface. I hate marital discord, mine and others. Perhaps mine has sensitised me to others, perhaps oversensitised me—it was possible that this was still a joky, stylised game. Clive liked at times to play the role of pedant, sending himself up, forestalling criticism. But it felt more serious; it certainly made me feel uncomfortable. I tried to shift the focus back to Wish.

'She's been difficult to live with?'

Stella answered: 'Moody more than difficult. Up one minute, down the next. The first weeks were wonderful—there were so many new things to do, to see. She'd been cooped up in a laboratory all her life. After a few weeks she seemed to get bored. Or maybe just lonely. She'd sit up in the tree-house for hours. There was only so much that she could communicate to us.'

Clive intervened: 'We became bored too, Stell. I think she sensed that.'

Stella shrugged. 'Maybe. Whatever—now there's a new enthusiasm.'

The smaller of her ancient horses, frustrated by her lack of attention, gave her a sharp nip on the elbow. She turned, smiling, fossicking in her pocket for cubes of sugar.

'Mummy's been ignoring you, hasn't she? You were quite right to remind me.'

The animals, encouraged, jostled about, separating her from Clive and me. We reached the outer gate; with Wish out of sight, I could once again raise matters that were unmentionable in her presence.

'One thing puzzles me. All these great apes that were taught to sign—Washoe, Koko, Lucy, Nim Chimsky—none *remotely* approached what is happening here.'

163

'You've been doing your homework.'

'A little. Their vocabularies were a few hundred signs at most. Their grammar was minimal, almost non-existent. Sentences of no more than two, three words. And these were mostly repetitions of what a trainer would say.'

Stella called across the feeding multitude: 'Maybe Eliza—Wish—is a genius among gorillas.'

Clive added: 'There was enormous variation among those apes, J.J. Some couldn't manage to memorise a single sign.'

'Some couldn't sign boo to a goose.'

Stella laughed a little too loudly at her own joke. Clive kept the conversation moving under cover of that laughter, chatting about my plans for tomorrow as I climbed into the car. Their different body languages—her loud laughter and his tact—were telling me the same thing, that the high intellectual ability of Wish was a sensitive subject. I wondered, as I drove away, if I was getting the full story.

7

Unfamiliar smells saturated my mother's small kitchen; a new cookbook stood propped in a clear perspex stand on the bench. *Vegetarian Cookery.*

'I help?'

She shook her head: 'Too many cooks.'

I gathered together my library books and sat at the kitchen table, reading and jotting notes, as she worked. Her hands were busy with bowls and implements; conversation would come later, during dinner. I pored over the illustrations again; the sense that something was wrong with Wish still tugged at me, a sense of unease. The shape of her head seemed more human than those of her wild relatives, her forehead had greater depth, her brow was less protuberant. The juvenile gorillas in the photographs shared that same human look: larger head relative to body, higher brow, smaller jaw, bigger eyes —and more delicate features.

Wish, at eight years old, fully mature, weighing more than most adult humans—weighing almost as much as me—appeared to my untrained eye to be a much younger gorilla.

Another problem: I was studying photographs. Stills. They had been edited, carefully selected to illustrate certain traits, more or less human, such as ferocity, cuteness, curiosity, signs of intelligence. They surely bore as little relation to a living gorilla as the hand-shapes I have sketched on these pages bear to Sign. I needed to study apes in the flesh, moving, breathing, eating—even beating their chests, signing their own collective noun, introducing themselves, in a sense.

My mother leant over my shoulder to examine my books, set down her egg-whisk and beat her own fists against her small chest, amused.

'Research,' I tried to explain. 'Take Rosie to zoo Sunday-next.'

A plausible excuse. My daughter is a relentless source of questions, a machine that fires question after question. Tennis-Ball-Machine, I once nicknamed her.

'You visit zoo Sunday-past.'

'Saw apes not. Rosie wishes,'—I found myself, ungrammatically, using the Wish Hand—'to look apes.'

'You spoil Rosie.'

'School project.'

A bald lie, followed by an omission. I failed to tell her that the zoo I planned to visit with Rosie Sunday-next was seven hundred miles away, in Melbourne. There were chimps aplenty in Adelaide, and orang-utans—but no gorillas.

How to get there? Alone, I would have cheerfully driven, I love long-distance driving, but a day cooped in a car would stretch my daughter's patience. I rose from the table, riffled through the phone book, lifted the receiver and dialled. My mother watched, suspiciously; she has a nose for these things.

'Phone who?'

Another lie: 'Saint.'

I turned to the wall, shielding my lip movements from view. Even as I booked the seats—one adult, one child, return flight, Sunday morning—an easier alternative occurred to me: film footage. I cancelled the booking, recalling a movie I had watched, and translated for my parents, a few months before.

I hung up, turned and signed to my mother: 'Film with gorillas. Remember?'

She was seeding black olives; she set down the knife.

'Gorillas in fog,' she signed back.

'I borrow that movie tonight?'

'I see it—before.'

'See twice? See again?'

She shook her head: 'Too depressing.'

Depression: the Flat Hand pressing down on the Point Hand.

'Very important,' I signed back.

'Ask Father,' she signed, stalling. 'Maybe watch football tonight.'

I couldn't ask; he was working late. Miraculously, a teletype apology arrived mid-meal, announcing that he wouldn't be home for some hours. We ate dinner facing each other across the narrow table, but signing little. My mother was clearly on high alert, studying me intently, but trying to hide her concern.

'Yummy,' I signed, Flat Hand rubbing belly, circular motion, as if I hadn't a care in the world.

After washing the dishes I set out for the local video-shop. The evening was clear and mild, the sun about to dunk itself in the gulf to the west. Not a breath of wind stirred the air, the sea was smooth and flat and tea-milky, as far from the undulating wave-mime for 'sea' as it's possible to get. Sign also has a shape for calm seas, the same Flat Hand smoothing motion that is used for 'floor'. The sea that night was a grey flat floor, stretching to the far wall of the sky. I turned down the beach steps on impulse, sat on the bottom step, pulled off my shoes and socks and dabbled my bare toes in the cool sand. I felt another rush of contentment, a sweet exhaustion in the aftermath of the day's excitements.

A large warning sign was fixed to a pole set in the sand at the base of the steps; a dozen red, diagonally barred circles contained silhouettes of activities forbidden on the beach. The prohibition was comprehensive. No Dogs. No Motorbikes. No Alcohol—a stylised, slightly opaque beer bottle. I studied the list, diverted by its simple

Sign-Esperanto. Bicycles were forbidden. Littering—a hand casting away a scrunched food wrapping—was forbidden. Diving from the jetty was forbidden. Scattering burley from the jetty was forbidden. It seemed there wasn't much left to do on the Glenelg foreshore.

Gorillas were not specifically forbidden. I wondered, idly, if Wish had ever seen the sea, except in books, and what she would make of it. It warmed me in the cooling twilight to imagine her excitement, even though I knew, more deeply, that such a visit was impossible.

At length I pulled on my shoes and climbed the steps. The video-shop was empty, *Gorillas in the Mist* was sitting among the Recent Releases; I claimed it.

'You have anything else with gorillas in it?'

The manager, watching a new release on a monitor, resentful of the interruption, ran a scanner over my borrowing-card without looking. 'Tried *King Kong?*'

My father was eating dinner when I arrived home. The stench of grilled pork sausages filled my nose the moment I entered the house; nestled on his plate they looked like a litter of blind, newborn piglets. He watched me suspiciously from across his meat, he had clearly been discussing me with my mother, my new food fad, my gorilla obsession. I showed him the spine of the video-cassette; he scanned the title, briefly, gave me another odd look, then pointed to himself: 'Early bed.'

I watched the movie after my mother had also gone to bed, fast-forwarding the human-only scenes, freezing, frame by frame, the ape sequences. Was Wish the same species? She possessed the same nobility—the same presence—as the adult females and big silverback males on that small screen, but she lacked their fearsome appearance. She was unmistakably finer boned, less thickset, an overgrown child-ape. A thought: the apes in the movie were mountain gorillas, *Gorilla gorilla beringei*. Wish would surely come from the commoner western lowlands subspecies, *Gorilla gorilla gorilla*.

I had recently become expert in the classification of the species *Gorilla*.

I replayed certain crucial scenes again, and the more I watched, the more my suspicion became a certainty: the differences between Wish and her wild cousins were more than the subtle variations between subspecies.

8

'But we went to the zoo *last* Sunday, Pop.'

'We didn't see all the animals.'

'I saw all the animals I wanted to see.'

'We didn't see the monkeys, sweetheart.'

'I *hate* monkeys. I hate those red bits. They always look so *sore*.'

'You hate too many things, sweetheart. You should save your hate for more important things.'

My daughter looked up at me, incomprehendingly: 'Like what?'

'Oh—war. Pollution.'

I've never quite known how to talk to her. If I attempt to speak Child, she will invariably move into sophisticated mode, patronising me. If I speak to her as an adult, she will take refuge in Child; I find myself lecturing, talking down.

At times she still *is* a child. Beneath the smart talk, behind the precocious mouth, there are still glimpses of the little girl I loved inordinately as an infant.

'Racial prejudice,' I added. 'Poverty. Double-bacon cheeseburgers.'

'What?'

'Just joking, sweetheart.'

She shook her head, and looked up at me from under her brow with tolerant contempt: 'You're heaps weird, Pop.'

I steered her, still protesting, through the front gate of the zoo and followed the winding path to the Primate Section. An ice-cream from the adjacent kiosk helped keep her moving, acting as a kind of lubricant.

The great apes were housed in a row of pits that were more giant squash courts than cages. Enclosed on three sides by high stucco walls, each pit was open at the front, separated from the viewing public by a stagnant moat and a low wire fence. A dead tree was set in concrete in the centre of the chimpanzee enclosure, surrounded, or perhaps supported, by a network of wooden scaffolding. A thick hemp rope hung from the topmost branch of the tree, dangling a huge tractor tyre several feet from the ground.

The big adult chimps were slumped here and there in various postures of apathy. They bore little resemblance to Wish, seeming less noble and more clown-like with their jug-handle ears and smaller, flat-topped skulls. Cartoon apes. The mid-size chimps were more active, poking straw stems into an artificial termite mound, sucking whatever reward—honey? sugar water?—had been secreted inside. The infants of the colony came closest to establishing some sort of family connection with Wish; full of cheeky energy and curiosity, not yet bored by their tiny, cramped world. The smallest and most human of the faces peered at me intently; on impulse I waved hello, the simple Flat Hand salute. Of course there was no reply, not even monkey-see-monkey-do mimicry.

Rosie rolled her eyes, and took a step away, distancing herself.

An identical enclosure next door contained several orang-utans; a huge single male was housed in a third, separate pit. The orangs seemed even less interested in my sign-greetings that the chimps.

'Can I feed the monkeys, Pop?'

'Apes, not monkeys. Monkeys have tails. And no, you can't.'

Warning signs were posted everywhere: red-barred peanuts.

She tugged at my hand: 'I *hate* the zoo. I want to see the Children's Zoo.'

I resisted for a moment, studying the big orang-utan. A coat of orange-red matted dreadlocks covered his entire body; his eyes had a vacant drugged look. Rosie, still tugging at my hand, was chattering.

'You're not *listening,* Pop.'

'I was trying to listen, sweetheart.'

'Then what did I *say?*'

'Sorry, darling—I was thinking.'

'Your hands were moving,' she said. 'You were thinking out loud.'

'What were my hands saying?'

173

'Something about monkeys. And wishes.'

My own wish—for a visit to the zoo under different circumstances. With different company. I was imagining sharing those same sights and sounds and smells with Wish instead of with Rosie. What would she make of these great apes, her cousins, imprisoned in barren squash courts, bored out of their large brains?

'I'm hungry, Pop.'

'You've just had an ice-cream.'

'I'm hungry for *food*. Can we go to Hungry Jack's?'

'Grandma is making your favourite dessert tonight.'

'Not trifle *again*.'

'It's your favourite.'

'It *was* my favourite. Until I had to eat it every Sunday night.'

I followed her back through the zoo, past the flamingoes and armadillos, past the pygmy hippo and the yellow-footed rock wallaby—none of them apparently worth a glance. I followed helplessly, the exhausted partner of a tennis-machine. Exhaustion: a no-hands family sign, tongue lolling out, head flopped sideways.

'Dad, you're *embarrassing* me.'

I pulled in my tongue, jerked my head upright. 'Sorry, sweetheart.'

'You look like a *spaz*.'

She hurried ahead; I remembered with some poignancy those numerous times I had walked several paces behind or ahead of my own parents. A large Coke and regular fries kept her reasonably quiet until we reached home.

'Nice day?' my mother signed.

174

Rosie shaped the Good Hand automatically, without feeling. She replied in Sign to my father's standard Sunday questions about her progress at school—which to him meant school sport, scores and best player status—then headed for the television.

'Swim,' I shaped to my mother.

'Swim after,' she signed back. 'Dinner ready.'

I swam after dinner, in a tranquil twilight. Suspended in the still water, looking shorewards, I could see the front window of the house, a picture window, curtains drawn, lit from within. The television flickered against the moon-faces of the people inside: Rosie flopped in a bean-bag, my parents on the sofa behind her. I couldn't see, but I could feel, in sympathy, my father's toes poking the small of her back from time to time. Rosie signs slowly, but accurately— I taught her Sign in her first months of life, and sent her to Sign kindergarten in her infancy, before we travelled. She still signs with her grandparents; with me she thinks it pointless.

I floated, immobile, hypnotised by this scene of domesticity—a scene from my own childhood. A tiny car turned the corner, crawled along the esplanade and stopped outside the house, partly obscuring the window. The familiar figure of Jill emerged, stepped briskly through the neat garden, and pressed the door-button. The door-alarm could be seen flashing through every window, the door opened, my mother appeared, smiling. I was some distance off, but I could read Jill's Good Hand hello, and even, with the eye of faith, her plodding finger-spelling. My mother's conversation was also decipherable, her hands moving at snail-pace

175

and with great precision, as if speaking loudly and slowly to someone hard of hearing.

I first met Jill at a Sign class; she was my student for several months, dabbling in Auslan for a thesis she was writing. What little I know of linguistics I gleaned from Jill; she helped me organise my understanding of Sign, stretch it onto a rough theoretical framework. In turn, I taught her the basics. Her questions in those first classes intrigued me. She had been working in the desert, writing a dissertation on the Sign-language of Aboriginal widows. Forbidden to speak after the deaths of their husbands, the women had developed a complex Sign-language. Jill was interested in comparisons, in signs that might be seen as natural, or universal. The Two Hand shape for 'look', we soon discovered, was common to both languages, a simple representation of the eyes.

She was less interested in learning fluent Sign—she had no time, she told me, repeatedly. Her head was already crammed full of spoken languages. She was even less interested in the world of the Deaf. A 'ghetto', she once termed it, in an unguarded moment. The Deaf should be out in the larger world, assimilating, she told me on another occasion, digging herself in more deeply. Preserving their language, certainly—but also learning to lip-read, to speak, or at least finger-spell English, not hiving off into a private world of Sign.

She learnt to finger-spell—her minimal duty as a daughter-in-law—but she never grasped more than a handful of Auslan signs. *Hi, good, yes, no, look.*

At first my mother would finger-spell back to her, but the process proved arduous and exhausting. They soon found it more convenient to speak through me. This had an added advantage: I could filter out any misconceptions or unintended slights. And especially any intended slights; I could *improve* their conversations, grease the wheels, even sneak in little flatteries and courtesies that were never intended.

For a time each believed she was held in higher esteem by her in-law than she was.

Esteem had faded but civility remained, at least during the transfer of Rosie. I watched my mother's hands invite Jill in, a standard courtesy, I watched the polite refusal, a smiling headshake and tapping of her wristwatch. Rosie herself appeared in the door, always eager after an hour or two to escape the company of her grandparents.

Words were exchanged between mother and daughter, inaudible to me, and they both turned my way. Rosie raised a Point Hand, Jill waved, I lifted a dripping arm from the water and waved back, Rosie blew a kiss, then they climbed into their toy car and were gone.

9

'You walk-up-trees,' Wish demanded.

We sat in the garden at her request. March had arrived, but summer gave no sign that it was retreating; the day was hot, the blue sky completely free of cloud-lint.

Clive scribbled in his notebook; Stella watched, leaning back on the garden bench, hands behind her head, her dogs sleeping at her feet. Wish's hands were the usual blur.

'Sign again,' I requested. 'Slowly.'

'Walk-up-trees.'

I liked her improvisation—a smooth blend of the three separate signs—but felt it was a bit long-winded.

I showed her 'climb', two different versions. The Claw Hand mime, hand over hand.

And, more economically, two fingers walking up a vertical palm, a pair of little legs.

She preferred the first, repeating it with flourish. 'Climb trees—joy.'

'I believe you,' I signed back, with heavy irony.

She grinned broadly, pleased to have detected the nuance. 'Not true!'

I traced the shape of a long tongue between thumb and forefinger, the sign for fib.

She was puzzled. 'Long tongue?'

'Long-tongue equals not-true,' I signed back. 'But good not-true. Funny not-true.'

The concept seemed beyond her; she reverted to her original demand. 'Climb with me, Sweet-Tooth.'

'I climb trees—not!'

'I teach you.'

Her pronunciation of the teach-shape was slightly skewed; more 'forget' than 'teach', two signs that have an improbable similarity in Auslan.

I signed: 'You teach me to forget?'

This time she understood. She laughed her throaty chuckle, and pronounced 'teach' with perfect accuracy. Then abruptly she was gone, ascending the nearest tree trunk vertically, arm over arm, reaching the highest branches within seconds.

Stella spoke for the first time. 'Is that something, J.J.? Have you ever seen *anything* like it? Power and grace, like flying.'

We craned our heads, watching. Wish's face peeped over the edge of the tree-house platform, then her right hand appeared, beckoning.

'J.J. come.'

She was thirty feet up; a speaker would have needed to shout. It was no more than a whispered invitation, but clearly visible.

'Too fat,' I signed back, using our family see-through shape. 'Maybe fall.'

She didn't know the shape; I hammed up the panto-mime elements, trying to get through.

'Fall on fat,' she signed. 'Not hurt. Fall on—cushion.'

Or on pillow, or on mattress—the shape is interchange-able. She was teasing me about my weight, without doubt.

180

She laughed—but a breeze was stirring the leaves around her, carrying off any sound that might have reached us. She stretched out an impossibly long arm and jiggled the thick rope from which the tyre was suspended.

'Sit,' her free hand ordered. 'I swing you.'

Swing: a simple pendulum motion, an improvisation. I turned to Stella, she nodded encouragingly: 'You're quite safe.'

I squeezed my shoulders through the tyre, eased my backside into the seat, and clutched the rope with both hands. Almost immediately I began to rise smoothly through the air. I tightened my grip, white-knuckled, terrified. Wish was reeling me in, effortlessly; before I could gather my thoughts I was too high to consider escaping. It was an astonishing feat, requiring muscle strength far greater than even the strongest human male.

Suddenly we were face to face, she dangled me, one-handed, above thirty feet of empty air. With her free hand she tapped the platform next to her; I refused to release my tight grip on the tyre. Finally she swung the whole heavy pendulum onto the platform next to her; I tumbled free.

My hands were trembling, signing was difficult. 'Get down how?' I managed.

She held my eyes for a moment, a wicked glint in her own, then flapped her arms, bird-fashion.

I tried to smile; my face muscles were still paralysed.

She launched herself at a bough some distance off, and vanished, hooting with laughter, into the foliage.

I waited, stranded. The sound of human laughter also carried up, despite the breeze. I risked a peep over the edge of the platform. Clive had set down his notepad and was smiling as broadly as his prim preacher's mouth would permit. Stella was holding her sides, beside herself. I tried to fix on more distant points: Summertown nestling in the bowl of the valley a mile or so off; the triple television towers on Mt Lofty, high above the far wall of the valley.

My eyes came back to Wish, watching, amused, from the next treetop.

'Down now!' I begged. 'Please!'

She shook her head, grinning toothily. 'Climb trees— joy.'

The first Wednesday night class without Clive and Stella
lacked a certain spark. The class had shrunk to half its
original size; the survivors at least had clustered into the
front desks, making themselves at home. Sign, as always,
was bringing them out of themselves, turning introverts into
extroverts. They asked more questions, used their hands in
a more sensible fashion, but I missed the quick mind and
quick hands of Stella especially.

I found myself distracted, thinking mostly of Wish,
already planning the next day's lesson.

Miss-The-Point stuck his head through the door on
the half-hour, counted heads, a little theatrically, gave me
a fiercely concerned look, withdrew.

I wandered down to the common room after class, in
search of deaf friends. Two hours of exchanging pidgin Sign
with beginners always left me unsatisfied, an appetitiser

that stirred the juices without quenching them. I also felt restless and fidgety, I half-wanted to tell someone—anyone—about Wish, even though I had promised not to, and would keep that promise. I wanted to share my general excitement, if not its specific cause; I wanted somehow to *spend* that excitement.

Miss-The-Point was sitting at a far table; he beckoned before I could glance away and pretend not to have noticed him. His wife sat with him: Stilts, a native signer, profoundly deaf, profoundly tall. Even sitting, she towered above her squat husband.

I pecked her cheek, we small signed for a time. I hadn't seen her for years; there was news to exchange, new instalments in our life-histories to catch up on.

'You change—not,' I signed, and she returned the compliment.

'Children?' I asked.

She showed the Two Hand, I asked their ages and genders, the standard social questionnaire. As my hands moved I found the Wish Hand sneaking into my conversation, subliminally. Stilts smiled at the sight, and crossed her own fingers.

'Feeling lucky, Sweet-Tooth?'

'Always lucky,' I echoed, a Good Hand shape.

Miss-The-Point interrupted, in English: 'Your class seems a lot smaller this week, J.J.'

Stilts craned her head to read his lips; he repeated the words, patiently, with careful, exaggerated lip movements. My heart went out to her; she might not have changed, but neither had her life. Her marriage was still less a marriage than a charitable organisation; she was less a wife than a case. Am I too *un*charitable? Would Stilts have chosen Miss-The-Point if he didn't meet some corresponding need in her? If his self-love wasn't huge enough to somehow envelop and nourish them both? More likely, the dynamics of their relationship were another symptom of a larger problem. Miss-The-Point takes that same proprietorial, philanthropic tone with all the Deaf. He means well, he just misses the point.

'Some drop-outs always,' I signed.

Stilts smiled at the sight of 'drop-out', a see-through invention.

'I pride myself on my low drop-out rate,' he said, still in English, 'in these days of funding cuts we have to generate income, J.J. We *must* keep bums on seats.'

Stilts didn't seem to find it at all odd, or rude, that he chose to speak. I was tempted to translate his words into Sign—to translate, cheekily, between husband and wife.

'Fees paid already,' I signed, stubbornly. 'They absent—no problem.'

He smiled, indulgently. 'All the same—I'd like you to take a rollcall at the beginning of every lesson.'

Irritated, I spoke to him for the first time in English, excluding Stilts myself. Suddenly I didn't want to sign, the language seemed too good to waste on him, a string of pearls cast before a swine. I also didn't want to embarrass Stilts—someone I had always liked, despite her taste in husbands—by insulting him in her presence.

'You've got to be joking, Jeremy—it's not a bloody high school.'

185

He turned to Stilts and tapped his watch; the nearest he had come to Sign since I had joined them. He pushed his chair back, rose, and turned back to me.

'I have to insist, J.J.' he said. 'I want the attendance rolls on my desk first thing Thursday morning.'

Stilts sat for a moment, puzzled by the sudden chill in the air.

'Stay,' I signed. 'More coffee.'

She shook her head, signed 'late' and rose, towering above her husband on her long stilt-legs. He took her arm and gently guided her from the room as if she were blind. Perhaps it *was* love of a kind—each player wins a prize. I raised the Rude Hand after him, more in amusement than in anger. My mood was too good for Miss-The-Point to dent more than momentarily; I felt invulnerable to his carping. On the far side of night Wish was waiting for me, soon I would be driving back to my real work in the Hills.

11

There are mornings when your bedding falls away like softened eggshell, and you rise and walk out into the world as if newly hatched, as if for the first time. I hadn't felt so exultant since the first days of my marriage, and the birth of Rosie.

Those early weeks with Wish energised me in that same way. Her long black arms reached out to me each afternoon like a pair of jumper-leads, recharging my enthusiasm, forcing me to see afresh things I'd long forgotten to look at, or even to notice.

Her curiosity seemed inexhaustible, her infatuation with the world and its signs utterly engaging and infectious. We can't think about the world until we have named it, I'd always believed. We can't manipulate it, move it about in our minds until we have clothed it in language. We can't even *see* it, naked. Words provide the costumes, the labels, the categories—words permit us to divide the world, and rule.

I was wrong. As the days passed it became clear that the signs I taught to Wish were merely clothing things that she already knew, concepts she had thought about, grasped wordlessly, but could not communicate.

My own first lesson: we don't need words or signs to think with, merely to tell others what we already think.

How else to explain her instant absorption of Sign, except to conclude that she was ready for it? Each sign already had a pigeonhole—a think-slot—ready and waiting. My growing enthusiasm for the task alarmed Clive, who stressed, repeatedly, the need for objectivity, and caution. Among the required reading he sent home nightly were two accounts of the attempted education of feral children. Both were pessimistic in the extreme; neither Victor, the wild boy of Aveyron, or Kamala, a girl reared by wolves in Bengal, had been able to learn to speak more than a few words. Clive's attempts to pour cold water on my enthusiasm failed; Wish, I argued, had lived among humans since birth, her instinct for grammar had not atrophied through disuse.

I arrived on each of those first mornings with a firm agenda. Access days with Rosie were my model, the need for structure, for a schedule of activities to put spine in the day's jelly. The best laid plans! It soon became clear that structure was irrelevant, that the day's syllabus was being set by the student, not by the teacher. I learnt to follow where she led. I think, I hope, I was as much a companion as a teacher on those daily mystery tours. Where we finished each afternoon was rarely where I intended. Her endless questions, her thrilled inquisitiveness carried us off on strange tangents.

Clive and Stella watched over us patiently; Clive filling notepad after notepad, Stella's hands keeping pace as best they could, sometimes—rarely—interrupting to request that I repeat a sign, more slowly. Despite her skill, she would never learn to sign with fluency; adolescence sets the human brain in concrete, her capacity for Sign was nowhere near as large as her foster-child's.

I borrowed a small stack of library books for Wish each week, Clive added his own Set Texts to it, but there was seldom time for reading, or for translating text into Sign. A world of things surrounded us, numberless, infinitely varied. Even the small corner of that world, which was caged inside the inner-fence, could not be exhausted by mere words, or signs, in a few brief hours. We barely dabbled our toes—our fingers—in that rich, dense world.

A simple object—a leaf, a passing cloud, a stone— would lead Wish to other signs, chains of where and why and how that followed their own join-the-dots pathway through explanations, free associations, cause and effect. The limits of my own vocabulary were constantly tested and found wanting. Often I would surprise myself, remembering things that I no longer knew that I knew; equally often I would improvise, or be sent scurrying for help from dictionaries and encyclopaediae.

A frequent joy: Wish would shake her head from side to side after I had signed, and suggest a better alternative, or some new blend of old signs, a hybrid shape. Her inventiveness astonished me, her sense of humour, her playfulness, charmed me.

I still attempted, against the odds, to keep those lessons in some sort of order. I wanted to map her areas of understanding, find the gaps and weaknesses—the absences. She could read a little, she could comprehend at least some spoken words, she had a large, if eccentric, vocabulary of Sign. In the third week of lessons, or visits, I made another startling discovery: she had been taught to count. I stopped her rapid hand movement as she reached a hundred.

If she could count, could she add? Could she, say, add two and two?

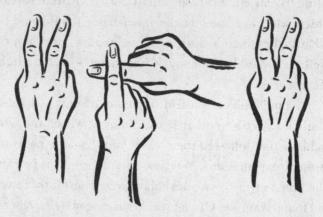

Answers to small problems of arithmetic are obvious in Sign. Sign *is* counting on your fingers. Wish instantly gave the correct answer:

Above five arithmetic becomes less obvious, the shape for six is not six fingers, spread across two hands.

'Three and three?' I asked.

Wish showed the six-shape. Opaque and arbitrary at first glance, it looks, with the eye of faith, a little like a stylised 6.

Clive said: 'We've taught her basic arithmetic.'

I wasn't fully convinced. 'Perhaps it's just a memory association.' He shook his head. 'I'm certain she think things through—logically. We taught her using fruit, individual grapes. Adding and subtracting to the pile.'

Stella grinned. 'She gets to *eat* the correct answers, J.J.'

I tested her again: subtraction, fifteen take away six. She was eager to show off her ability, glancing up for approval. I gave her answer the thumbs-up.

'Some believe that the ability to count is innate,' Clive said.

I smiled, politely sceptical: 'Surely mathematics is something that is taught.'

'There have been experiments done with babies,' he said, 'that seem to suggest the opposite.'

This was news to Stella; she screwed up her face: 'Experiments with *babies?*'

'Harmless enough. A familiar object—a bright toy, or rattle—is hidden behind a screen. Another identical object is brought into view, the baby watches the object placed behind the screen. When the screen is removed, and both objects are revealed, the baby shows no surprise.'

Stella, with sarcasm: 'Gee, that proves a lot.'

'I'm not finished. If when the screen is removed, there is only *one* object, the baby looks astonished.'

'What are you saying? Babies *know*, instinctively, that one plus one makes two?'

'They know that one and one don't make *one*, anyway.'

Wish was watching, intensely alert. How much was she taking in? Very little, surely. Clive pressed on, oblivious: 'Those results have been reproduced with subtraction, also. You can surprise a baby with the wrong answer to a subtraction.'

A confirmation of my own recent thoughts: 'So babies can think before they can speak?'

'Isn't that obvious?' Stella said.

'Not at all. Some claim that since animals, say, have no language, they have no thoughts. No mind.'

She bent and fondled the ears of the nearest sleeping dog. 'Anyone who has a dog knows otherwise.'

We were outside, among the roses. Most of those first afternoons were spent outside, at Wish's insistence, soaking up the late summer-cum-early autumn sun. Having spent her early life imprisoned in a laboratory, she clearly hungered for the open air.

Clive was watching Wish. 'My point is that we have an immense opportunity here. Wish can allow us to re-examine some of the standard linguistic pieties.'

Stella said: 'Let's not lose sight of our goal, Clive. We mustn't find ourselves at cross-purposes. Wish is above all an animal.'

I was still watching Clive watching Wish. I sensed, suddenly, that all *three* of us were at cross-purposes. Stella wanted a spokes-ape for Animal Rights; Clive wanted, at least in part, a guinea pig to test certain theories of language acquisition; I wanted a single, happy student.

The obvious question: what did Wish want?

'She's not a guinea pig,' I said.

Wish picked up the last word, and signed, clowning, the snout of a pig, her fist clenched over her nose.

How perfectly that simple comic gesture suited the moment, deftly sabotaging our disagreement and joining us together in laughter. She was laughing herself, baring her teeth, sharing our pleasure. Sitting there with my new friends I was struck by a bizarre realisation: the friend whose company I enjoyed above all others was an eight-year-old gorilla. I felt a little giddy at the thought, and reached out a hand to grip the edge of the barbecue table; not so much to steady myself, or to touch wood, but to re-establish contact with something suburban and mundane, that lay squarely within the realm of everyday experience.

12

The long Indian summer ended, finally, in late April. The week had been hot, the hottest of the year—and it was humid-hot, last-gasp hot, the heat harvesting cloud from the gulf, stacking it in high thunderclouds. I spent the morning in my cubicle in the Institute, catching up on paperwork, maintaining the pretence of full-time employment. The gloom of the sky surprised me when I emerged at noon. I drove up into the Hills beneath gathering clouds. Towering high and loose above, their dark undersides seemed sheared off, or ironed flat. I parked at the outer gate of the farm and looked back towards the city. Beyond the ridge, the flickering of lightning could be seen, connecting cloud to ground.

Thunder rumbled, distantly, felt rather than heard. As I crossed the field and skirted the near-empty dam the first rain of autumn began to plop onto the dirt track: big round single drops, as warm and heavy as pigeons' eggs.

195

Wish was waiting at the tree line, behind the second gate, untroubled by the rain. Her coat seemed waterproof; the drops that splattered against her head and shoulders ran from her fur as if from oil-cloth. We walked hand in hand to the house through rain drops that were almost big enough and sparse enough to dodge, individually.

Stella stood on the verandah, eyeing the weather; I followed her into the lounge. A flash of light outside, a deafening thunder-crack directly overhead. Wish clutched Stella's hand, agitated by the sound effects; I took advantage of the opportunity for a quick Sign lesson. The vibrating, ground-shaking Spread Hands of thunder:

The downward zig-zag of the Point Hand, a lightning strike:

196

She mimicked my movements, and to name those fierce elements seemed to calm her. And also, magically, to calm the storm: the thunder rolled again, but more distantly, as if driven off by the power of language.

Wish tugged me towards the stairs, signing, one-handed: 'Show my room Sweet-Tooth.'

Weeks had passed, but I had not yet been permitted, or invited, upstairs. Did some sort of house-rule operate: upstairs was for sleeping, out-of-bounds during the day? Rules of such rigidity might be expected from Clive. I glanced to Stella; she glanced to Clive. He nodded to her; she nodded in turn to me—then grinned, self-consciously, at this absurd chain of command.

Wish beckoned me up the narrow stairwell; I followed close on her heels. Or were they wrists, hind-wrists?

The room might have belonged to any human child, if more spartan in style. The bed was uncovered; Wish, after all, carried her own quilt on her back. Several soft toys sat on the bare mattress: a small blue elephant, a mid-size tiger, an enormous green frog. There were no toy primates. I found it curious that despite the mature age of Wish, the decor of her bedroom was that of a small child. It seemed an inconsistency, at least on Clive's part. Shelves lined one wall, crammed with wide, flat picture books. A small plastic radio sat at one end of a shelf, playing music that was middle-of-the-road, soothing and melodic, barely audible above the drumming of rain on the roof. Elevator music. A glass aquarium stood on another shelf, a stream of rising air bubbles at one end, two plump goldfish at the other. A low desk was covered by thick stacks of drawing paper and a miscellany of crayons and paintbrushes. Drawings and paintings created, apparently, from these materials were taped to the walls. Clive and Stella watched from the door as I examined the artworks. Wish squatted at her desk and pretended to sketch a new drawing—but I knew her better, she also was watching out of the corner of her eye, intensely interested in my reactions.

The artworks seemed arranged in a rough chronology, the earliest pieces taped low on the the walls, the later, more sophisticated pieces higher up. An abundance of green crayon had been splashed about on the paper, a jungle of lushly leafed trees. The house featured in several pictures, the uncrossable 'moat' of empty stubble that surrounded it, the tree-house. The animal figures—horses, kangaroos, the three-legged deer—had a childishly naive quality. There were also representations of human figures which although schematic were quite obviously portraits of Stella and Clive. Their sign-names—recent additions—had been sketched above them: a small star for Stella, a halo for Clive. Highest on the wall—the most recent drawings—was a sketch of another figure, a pale fat man, as wide as he was tall, waiting at the front gate.

I examined this for a time, puzzled—blind to the most obvious portrait of all, my own. Even the unmistakable bubble-car sketched in the background failed to register. Only when I read the letters scrawled at the top did the penny drop: J.J.

Highest on that first wall was a sketch of the same tubby figure—mine—swinging through trees, flying between branches, airborne, with wings of crayon sprouted from my back; and Wish herself waiting, hands outstretched, to catch me.

I covered my eyes in mock terror; Wish, still pretending not to watch, couldn't prevent herself gurgling, amused.

The next wall displayed several crayon-sketches of another figure I didn't recognise, male, bearded, stick-thin. Vegetarian-thin.

'His name what?'

Wish finger-spelt the name, the first finger-spelling I'd seen on her hands for some days: 'T-E-R-R-Y.'

'Who T?'

'Friend,' she signed, her right hand shaking her left.

I looked to Stella, surprised.

'Terry Wallace,' she said, as if that were sufficient.

I stared meaningfully at her, she smiled and added: 'Terry is the friend who rescued Wish. Who first brought her to us. Terry is Clive's, ah, *protégé.*'

I turned back to the artworks. The self-portraits interested me most. The human figures were close simulacra of their subjects, but the self-portraits seemed at first glance more fanciful and impressionistic. The subject was Wish, clearly, but the legs were longer, the stance more upright, the face paler—and each figure was hairless. The irony took my breath away—was the gorilla herself guilty of the sin of anthropomorphism? In several she was even wearing human clothing, although I had not yet seen her in those forbidden items. I made a mental note to study the self-portraits more closely later. Clues to the workings of her mind could surely be discovered there by even the most amateur psychologist.

'Beautiful drawings,' I signed—the shape for paint, or sketch, given emphasis by a sudden intake of breath; more literally: paintings which fill the viewer with awe.

She continued scrawling large shapes on her sketchpad, feigning indifference.

Clive said: 'She's very talented.'

Stella added: 'It's a kind of language itself, don't you think? You draw the signs instead of shaping them.'

I had other things on my mind. 'Could she learn to write, I wonder? Or even read?'

'She recognises some words,' Clive said. 'We have a number of word-cards. Flash-cards. She can match the word with the thing, although we're not exactly sure what kind of understanding she has of the process.'

Wish clearly understood the spoken word 'card'. She somersaulted to the bookshelves—two easy rolls, her preferred method of travelling small distances—tugged down a small shoe-box, and lifted the lid. She rolled back to my side, and scattered the cards at my feet: an alphabet of animals, pictures on one set of cards, names on another. Aardvark, Buffalo, Cheetah...

I pointed to a name at random: Kangaroo. She scrabbled briefly among the picture cards, producing the correct match.

I brandished the sign: a pair of kangaroo-paws, hopping. She smiled and copied, exactly. More cards, more pictures, and more signs, followed. Aardvark was beyond me, but zoo visits with Rosie had nourished my menagerie of animal-shapes. Lion, tiger. The double-handed antler-shape of antelope.

The curved beak of eagle, a sign made with the rare Hook Hand.

Wish absorbed the new shapes, twenty or so simple animal representations, with ease. Clive sat on the edge of the bed, making notes, Stella practised the signs herself.

A more difficult test: I chose a name-card—Owl—and asked her to shape the matching Auslan sign with only the clue of the written word. A leap forward—a cognitive shift, once removed, from the simple memory-association of sign and picture.

Wish responded, almost immediately tracing large owl-eye circles around her own eyes.

I shook my hands high above my head, surprised that she knew the shape, amazed that she had made the connection. She nodded, a token bow.

She seemed ready for another quantum jump. I spoke the names of the animals, in English—in several cases she responded by pointing to the correct picture, or shaping the correct sign.

A thought: why limit her to the words printed on those cards? I handed her the sketchpad and crayons and began to name, aloud, other random objects. I was careful not to offer cues by looking at the object, or equally, by looking everywhere *but* the object.

'Tree,' I said, staring at a blank wall—she sketched a quick, deft cartoon-tree. Then showed me the hand-shape, distorted a little by her grip on the green crayon.

'I can't see why she shouldn't be taught to read and write,' I said.

'We've always thought it possible,' Clive said. 'What we needed was some sort of intermediate language—a language we could teach reading and writing *in*—a language we could resort to when reading and writing failed.'

'That's where I came in?'

'That's where you *also* come in. We see Sign-language, above all, as her primary means of communication—as I'm sure you do.'

I suddenly wasn't so sure: 'There is another possibility. You say apes lack the anatomy to make speech—they lack a human larynx?'

Clive nodded; I finally put words to an idea which had been crystallising, slowly, for some weeks. 'Perhaps they could be taught to speak *un*-voiced speech.'

Stella looked at me, puzzled; Clive also watched, more interested. Wish turned back to her sketchpad, bored by our talk; a few spoken words were within her grasp, but complex sentences were clearly not.

'Why couldn't she be taught *whispered* speech, using tongue and lip movements only? She obviously has the brain for it.'

Stella was still puzzled. 'I don't follow.'

I took her hand in mine, gently bunched her fingertips and pressed them to her own larynx.

'Say sss...Now zzz...Feel the difference? Same lip and tongue positions, but one unvoiced, one voiced.'

In my early twenties I had helped teach speech to deaf children. It's a specialist's job; I was more a go-between, a translator, but I picked up a smattering of anatomy from those endless hours of manhandling little mouths and lips, moulding chubby faces into correct shapes, even at times reaching inside their mouths and sculpting their tongues. Then having them press their fingers to their voice-boxes and generate vibrations that they were able to feel but not hear. Such programmes have fallen out of fashion, washed away, not before time, by the high tide of Sign—but I remembered the techniques.

'The rain in Spain,' Stella said aloud, then repeated the words in a whisper, fingertips still pressed to her throat.

'The larynx isn't used in whispering,' I said, unnecessarily.

Clive tried the same trick, fascinated. His judgement, delivered after a brief deliberation: 'You're welcome to try to teach her to whisper.'

'I teach Sign. For speech you'd need a professional. A speech therapist.'

'Surely you could make a start,' Stella suggested. 'See how it goes—if it looks promising...'

The rain was still falling when I left, a constant, steady downpour. Stella pulled on a Driza-Bone and a wide-brimmed hat, Clive unfurled an umbrella and took my arm, sheltering me through the dripping trees and across the outer field. The dirt track had turned to slippery mud, his steps were slow and painstaking. He placed his words as carefully as his feet, clearly he had something he wanted to get off his chest. He was pleased with Wish's progress, he said, but he wanted to stress again the need for caution, for objectivity, the need to avoid getting carried away by enthusiasm.

'I think we need more structure in the lessons, J.J.'

So did I, but I resented being told so.

'I think it important we become friends first,' I said.

He nodded, conceding the point, but added, 'If you aren't her friend already, I don't know who is.'

'I'd prefer to do things in my own way. Softly, softly.'

The reference went over his head; Stella, following behind, retarded by the animals and the mud, missed it altogether.

'Of course. You're the boss. But I think we should cover *some* of the reading list.'

He was overstepping the mark—my job description had been Sign teacher, not translator. I have trouble criticising people directly—as always, it took a bent form, a circuitous route.

'I thought you wanted her animal mind to develop free of cultural prejudices.'

His eyes held mine; the point was taken. 'Perhaps. But there are some things she should know about. A little history, a little science. Some grounding in basic logic might not go astray.'

He tugged a closely typed list of book titles from his coat pocket; I scanned it briefly. One or two were familiar; most I hadn't read. I was more than happy to study them—as much for my further education as for Wish's.

'I want you to know we're pleased with her progress, J.J.,' he repeated.

Meaning we're pleased with *your* progress, an oblique compliment which I saw more as a kind of mid-term report.

Stella extracted herself from the huddle of wet animals, and wrapped a wet arm around me. 'You're very good, J.J.,' she said, reassuringly.

I tried to be objective. If Wish spent those first few weeks studying my hands, I spent them studying her. Her hands, her dark eyes, the glossy pelt that covered much of her body. The black-crepe skin of her bare breasts and armpits. Her small, fine elf ears.

The acuity of her ears was disproportionate to their size. Several times, sitting outside in the sunshine, she paused mid-conversation and cocked her head towards the house. I could hear nothing, but on each occasion Wish signed 'telephone' to Stella. She used an archaic sign—a forefinger dialling mime—rather than the receiver-on-ear Ambivalent Hand of official Sign.

Lizard-rustle in a bush, a favourite song playing upstairs on the radio, a plane, fire-spotting beyond the ridge out of sight—her head often turned to catch sounds that were below, or beyond, the threshold of human hearing.

The approach of a rare passing car on the distant dirt road would send her high into the trees, craving a look, long before the rest of us could hear the noise of the engine.

She clearly hungered for the world beyond the trees.

Her sight was less acute than her hearing. I was always able to read her hands at a greater distance than she could read mine. Eyes are possibly less important than ears as survival aids in the dense rainforest of the native habitat of her species.

Watching Wish pore over her books, I liked to imagine her in reading-glasses, but in fact her near-vision was fine. Longer distances were the problem. This deficiency meant that she had the ability to make sense of the images on a television screen. Animals with acute vision—dogs, say—find television meaningless, Stella claimed; they are in effect watching too closely, unable to separate the coarse pattern from the fine weave of 500-odd scanning lines.

Wish's television viewing was rigorously censored. She knew the sign: T-V, two letters, finger-spelt.

But my suggestion one afternoon that we watch an educational programme was met with blank incomprehension.

'We don't watch a lot of television,' Stella explained, apologetically.

'We watched Clive's interview the first night I came here.'

'The second night,' he corrected.

Stella ignored his pedantry. 'We watch the news,' she said. 'And sometimes, rarely, current affairs. We *never* watch daytime television.'

'Movies?'

She shook her head. 'But I suppose an educational programme might be permitted.'

Clive didn't agree. 'Thin end of the wedge.'

An argument followed, although the pro and con were oddly parallel. Stella thought programming was the problem, that the programmes were uniformly idiotic; Clive thought that all programmes were beyond salvation, by definition—that the nature of the medium determined the stupidity of the programmes.

She demurred: '*Some* programmes are worth watching.'

'I've never seen any.'

'I have,' she said. 'From time to time.'

'When?'

She turned to me, and winked. 'Sometimes I watch a little television after Clive goes to bed. Secretly.'

His surprise deepened. 'You never told me that.'

He was sitting on the sofa, she was standing behind him; she leant down and kissed him affectionately on the toupée, a favourite gesture. 'There are a lot of things I don't tell you.'

'I watched a lot of television in childhood,' I put in. 'It didn't do me any harm.'

Stella spluttered, suppressing her amusement; Clive scrutinised me as if he could see the evidence of harm, clearly written. I scrabbled about for arguments that sounded less banal.

'It was my best friend. It was *many* friends.'

'Any friend of yours, J.J.,' Stella said.

'I'm serious. Television showed me the world outside the world of the Deaf. Wish is in a similar predicament. It seems unfair—cruel—to keep that from her.'

'We can show her the world in books,' Clive said.

'She can't read.'

'Yet. She can recognise a few words. Besides, there are picture books. She can see the world in books.'

'That's like trying to *read* Sign,' I said. 'It's inert. Lifeless.'

'We're trying to teach her to think critically, J.J.—not lie on a couch, hypnotised.'

'We could still censor what she sees,' Stella suggested. 'J.J. can translate the programmes into Sign for her.'

I said: 'It's a much richer medium than you seem to think. The opportunities for education are too great to ignore.'

Clive watched us, considering. An advantage of that cool mind—it had no emotional prejudices. Its beliefs were never more than provisional hypotheses; they were always open to reason, to disproof.

'We must be careful,' he finally pronounced. 'There is an immense bath of rubbish out there. An *ocean*. We swim in it without even noticing. It determines the limits of our thinking—allows us to think only certain things. Feel certain things.'

The last phrase brought another amused splutter from Stella. He pressed on, regardless. 'All of us live within that system of beliefs. We breathe it like air—we don't even notice it. I want Wish to stand outside of all that, looking back in.'

The subject under discussion squatted on her haunches on the carpet between us, hugging herself, watching intently. And, apparently, listening, her black head tilted to one side. I wondered again how much she understood.

Clive continued, still in lecture mode. 'Wish is the first animal mind that can tell us what it sees.'

'It?' I said, hoisting him on his own petard.

He smiled, grateful, if anything, to be corrected: '*She* is outside human culture, looking in—free from the preconceptions, the acculturation. We can learn much by looking at ourselves through her eyes.'

'Her mind seems mostly human to me,' I said.

'What do you mean?'

'I mean that by teaching her a human language surely we are setting limits to what she can think. We are supplying the frame. Perhaps she can only see what language permits her to see...'

He nodded, waving away my arguments a little wearily—one of the few times I had seen any trace of impatience in him.

'Of course, J.J. Of course. We've all read Whorf. She can't avoid some contamination. But that's the advantage of Sign—it's a young language, still evolving. It's open to improvisation. Wish is free to invent as much as she learns—she can mould the language to *her* consciousness,

210

rather than have her mind trapped by the language. I think we see the evidence of that already.'

Wish waved her signature hand in front of us, then, holding our attention, pronounced a smooth sequence of hand-shapes: 'Change-speech-into-Sign'.

I considered demonstrating the Auslan 'interpret', but the sign is opaque, and lacks the simple bluntness of her own invention.

'We speak about speech,' I explained, in Sign.

She shook her head. 'I hear name Wish. Saint speaks name Wish.'

Sign permits different word orders: subject-object-verb, even object-subject-verb. The signing of Wish was less flexible—she showed a marked preference for the subject-verb-object order of standard English. I wondered again how much she could hear, and comprehend; how much her signing had been affected—*in*fected—by the patterns of spoken English. Or was the word order natural? Creole languages the world over, I knew, fell, as if by instinct, into subject-verb-object as they developed.

I signed: 'Saint say Wish very clever. Very—inventive.'

The strangeness of this new sign confused her; I tried to explain it in terms of the more familiar shapes of 'new', and 'making', and 'find.'

'I don't think we should talk about a particular person in front of that particular person,' I said aloud. 'I think a particular person understands far more English than we realise.'

Wish grinned, toothily, as if on cue. The effect was unsettling; I had to persuade myself the timing was a mere coincidence.

Stella rose and switched on the television; the picture slowly formed. Wish watched, amazed; having trouble grasping the notion that she might choose to watch something other than the National News. Or perhaps grasping the notion that there *was* anything other than the news on television.

Cartoons were screening: Daffy Duck and some droll ironic dog whose name I didn't know were taking turns battering each other senseless. Wish watched, fascinated. A small bleat of terror escaped her open mouth as a falling anvil shattered Daffy into a thousand shards; she turned her face up to me, worried.

A milestone—she had turned to me for help, rather than to her foster-parents.

'Not hurt,' I signed. 'Pretend.'

Pretend: literally 'true-not'. I wondered if crayons and paper would help, a demonstration of the principles of cartooning, even a riffling of pictures scribbled in page corners.

But for now reassurance was unnecessary; the duck had already reconstituted his separate pieces. Resurrected from the dead, he was rushing towards the next catastrophe. Wish sank back onto the carpet, mesmerised.

'I don't know if this is a good idea,' Clive said. 'Cartoons can't be good for her.'

'Nonsense,' Stella said, and gave me a teasing look. 'J.J. has watched cartoons all his life.'

14

'You live alone, Sweet-Tooth?'

Her phrase was literally 'house-you-one-you?' I shook my head and held up three fingers. 'With my mother my father.'

'Me meet those?'

'Future day.'

For the first time we were alone together. Clive was working in his study downstairs, correcting the proofs of *Primate Suffrage*; Stella had taken her black bag of vet tools and headed out into the rain to answer a distress call in one of the nearby towns.

A new daily schedule had been negotiated. I had asked for more time with Wish; Clive and Stella had agreed, with certain stipulations. I was to brief them on my plans each morning; in the late afternoon we would lunch together and review the day's progress. The hours between were mine and Wish's. Their consent had been given with surprising quickness. Had I bored them into submission, or were they merely grateful for the baby-sitting? Clive claimed to need time with his book, Stella with her veterinary work—'I've been neglecting my practice.'

A new intimacy was apparent between us from the moment I shut the door of her room and sealed us in—a feeling that was somehow awkward and liberating at the same time. Wish's first tentative probings about my personal life, delivered shyly, avoiding eye contact, were clearly questions she had been desperate to ask.

She signed again: 'You own children—not?'

'I own children—yes. I own daughter—one.'

I set aside the implications of that word 'own'. It intrigued me, I planned to come back to it, to explore the implicit sense of her own self, and her place in the world.

'Her name what?'

'Rose.'

The familiar flower-shape caused no problem.

'Rose where?'

'Rose lives with mother.'

She waited, quizzical, I fingerspelt J-I-L-L. 'Rose lives with me—Sunday.' The shape for Sunday: flat palms together, a simple prayer mime.

'You live with Jill—not?'

She squatted on her bed, watching intently, waiting. I was momentarily lost for signs. I could teach her the simple shapes for 'daughter' and 'wife'. I could teach her to count. I could teach her the annual rainfall of the Congo—but how to explain my complicated family life? And what mind was

I trying to explain it *to:* human or gorilla? What family-norm would she measure my answers against? Nature-norm, or nurture-norm? The norm of a troop of promiscuous gorillas with a single dominant and various sub-dominant males— the norm whose imperatives were surely in her blood? Or the norm of Clive and Stella, a married couple, mono- gamous as far as I could tell—the norm of human culture?

Food for thought: if she had seen more television, daytime television especially, might she have a better grasp of the variety of domestic living arrangements, my own in particular?

I signed: 'Tell me your mother.'

I too had been hoarding questions for these first moments alone with her—questions which Clive and Stella had always managed to deflect.

'Star?'

Did she believe that Star was her mother? If so, exactly what did the word mean to her?

'Before Star. Sign me your people.'

'Forget,' she signed, her fist exploding out from her temple, knowledge, escaping.

The sign was fluid, unhesitating, but her eyes avoided mine.

'Long-tongue,' I signed.

She shook her head, pressed a closed fist against her chest, and shielded it, protectively, behind her Flat Hand. 'Secret.'

Clive arrived with the midday sandwiches, asparagus, interrupting our mutual interrogation. One thing at least had been learnt: we each wanted to know much more about the other than we were prepared to reveal about ourselves. After Clive had left, we steered clear of the subject for the remainder of the afternoon. I kept her hard at work reading flash-cards, but there was probably no need. She seemed to respect my reticence.

I arrived in rain again the next day. Delayed by a lengthy summer, the normal scattered showers of autumn had been concentrated into the last days before winter, as if required to meet some sort of statistical rainfall quota. Several days of steady rain had transformed the unsealed roads of the Hills into long shallow lakes, the gullies were raging torrents. I parked outside the first gate, trudged past the rapidly filling dam and up the hill. The second gate was open, Wish was standing in the gap, offering me Clive's umbrella.

'Outside today?' she asked with her free hand.

'Too cold,' I signed, two tight, shivering fists. A smile spread slowly across her wet face; I realised, belatedly, that she had been joking.

I left my muddy shoes on the verandah and reported to Clive and Stella in the lounge. The day's agenda was discussed—arithmetic, vocabulary. Clive suggested one or two amendments, Wish tugged me upstairs, closed her bedroom door, thrust sketchpad and crayons into my hands, and the agenda was instantly forgotten.

'Draw Rose.'

'I can't.'

'Please.'

I sketched, reluctantly, a stylised stick-figure, person-alised by a pony-tail. I considered adding purple lipstick, but put an ice-cream in her hands instead.

'Rose likes ice-cream,' I signed.

'Me too.'

Wish took the paper from me and examined it. An odd sensation: of tables turned, of *my* artwork being scru-tinised, searched for psychological clues. I extracted my wallet from a coat pocket, and offered her a more objective, less self-revealing portrait of my daughter.

'Photograph,' I signed: the Good Hand a camera held at eye-level, the thumb pressing down, a shutter button.

She studied the snap, then handed it back.

'Photograph J-I-L-L?'

I shook my head: 'J. likes camera—not.'

I reached for the sketchpad and scratched a few aimless strokes. She was still watching me—my face, not my hands. She signed, 'You sad inside?'

I forced a smile, irritated. 'Happy inside.'

She was my pupil, not my confidante. I loved being with her, loved exploring the language of Sign with her, but to cry on her furry shoulder seemed beyond the pale.

Her hands moved again. 'Sign me about Jill.'

'Forget,' I signed.

She caught the irony, her own answer of the day before thrown back at her.

'Long-tongue,' she signed, and bared her teeth, grinning. Those powerful canines were always a startling sight, and a reminder of her animal status.

A stand-off; we watched each other for a long moment. Finally she signed: 'You show secret, I show secret.'

'You first.'

She jabbed the finger-pronoun. 'You. You!'

I shook my head, holding firm. 'I ask before. I ask yesterday.'

The smile faded from her mouth, a slow unstretching of those wide lips that made my scalp tingle. Clive might argue against ascribing human emotions to the expressions of a non-human face, but to me there was no mistaking the signs of sadness.

'My mother—dead.'

Sign offers a choice of shapes for death, possibly even more than the numerous euphemisms of English. They range from the evasive—gone-to-sleep, passed-on—to the laconic: waving bye-bye to an imaginary hole in the ground, or simply two stiff forefingers, legs in rigor mortis, lying parallel. Wish used her own version: the hand keeling over, belly-up, stiff-legged.

A joke in the hands of humans, its terseness seemed poignant in hers.

There is a third category of shapes for death, more hopeful, and full of promise. I think above all of the Point Hands, aimed heavenward, a sign that is half flight and half pointing the way. I performed the shapes; she wrinkled her black nose, puzzled.

'Sign again. Sign twice.'

I repeated the shape; she copied slowly, clearly unable to make sense of it.

I tried to explain: 'People think—after die—go to heaven.'

Heaven above, a sky-variant that only added to her puzzlement:

'*You* think, Sweet-Tooth?'

'I know—not. Not yes. Not no. Maybe.'

There was more I could have shown, the standard theological vocabulary of resurrection and damnation, punishment and reward. I knew the hand-shapes backwards; I had been dragged to Sign Church at the Institute every Sunday as a child. The concepts seemed too cumbersome to foist on Wish; I might as well have tried to explain the Tooth Fairy.

'Heaven—where?'

'Know not. Learn after dead.'

I used her own blunt shape for death.

'Long-tongue,' she signed, with an impatient stamp of her feet, and thrust both her hands forcefully downwards, in the opposite direction to heaven.

'Die in *ground*. Like B-I-L-L.'

My turn for puzzlement: 'B?'

'Dog,' she signed, the Here-boy slap of Flat Hand against thigh.

She took me by the hand, and tugged me to the window. Her first-floor room looked down onto the back garden, a patch of grassy lawn, several beds of vegetables, and a rotary clothes hoist, enclosed by the circle of surrounding trees.

'B,' she finger-spelt again, and pointed.

I followed the direction of her finger. At the edge of the trees, a small patch of grass had been enclosed by a picket fence. At first glance I thought it another vegetable bed, more careful inspection revealed five or six small earth-mounds of various lengths and widths, arranged in two unequal rows. At the head of each mound a length of wood had been stuck, upright, in the earth. Grave markers, unmistakably. I was surely looking at the final resting place of the ex-members of Stella's flock.

Wish mimed the act of digging, then pinched her nose between thumb and finger, and averted her face. She shivered slightly, and squeezed my hand—clearly uncomfortable with the bald facts of decomposition, even though they issued from her hands. I also sensed, as her eyes scrutinised mine, that she was crushing my hand as much for my comfort as for hers. *She* was giving the lesson, teaching me a tough truth of which she felt me ignorant, which I had clearly hidden from myself behind sentimental euphemisms.

'I sign secret. Now *you* sign secret.'

A day has passed, but our informal contract had not been forgotten. Once again we were alone, shut inside her room.

'What secret?'

'J-I-L-L.'

She squatted, waiting. The door was closed, lunch still some hours away. There could be no escape.

'I love Jill before. She love me. Now—not.'

A minimal version of the events of the last seven years of my life. Even so, I had said far more than I wanted to. I always say either too much, or too little. Even the simple shape for love I found enormously painful, and difficult:

'Why? Why love—not?'

'Love gone.'

'Where?'

'Vanish,' I signed, a shape I call the reverse-rabbit, the right hand disappearing into the makeshift magician's hat of the left hand.

It's also the sign for drown, and, poignantly, for extinct. I had discussed these events with no one, especially not with my parents. Wish's blunt, naive questions, free from expectation or assumption, were more difficult to evade. I averted my face, unable to sign further, then rose, and made the sign for 'piss', a stylised letter 'p', and excused myself. I hid in the locked bathroom across the hall, trying to recover composure.

After some minutes I returned to the bedroom, and my original schedule. Once again Wish seemed sensitive to my needs, and tactfully avoided the subjects of love, and family. We spent the rest of the afternoon in the practise of whispered speech.

This was to prove a losing battle in the coming weeks, not so much beyond my powers, as beyond hers—beyond the anatomy of that too-wide mouth, those sharp canines and thick pink ox-tongue.

She had mastered, quickly, a serviceable plosive 'p' of the lips parting. More slowly came the fricative 'f', a release of air between the lips, under restraint. Sounds produced further back in the mouth caused greater problems. Even the simple hiss of an 's' between her gleaming teeth, or the tip of her tongue tapping 't' against the palate proved non-negotiable, or uncontrollable. I spent some time with my fingers inside her mouth, moulding her big, clumsy tongue. I guided her thumbish fingers into my mouth, to feel my tongue and teeth positions. My efforts were largely wasted. The difficulties were not entirely mechanical; other objections began to surface. For one: the few sounds she did manage to whisper could have been produced by anyone. All whisperers sound the same, a shared, universal whisper-voice, incapable of drama or inflexion.

Why squander valuable time teaching her to whisper English if she could Sign, loudly, in her own unique 'voice'?

I abandoned the project after several weeks of shrinking returns. I had no regrets, the idea had always smacked of the whimsical. Its cleverness had appealed more to me than its practicality. Clive and Stella were disappointed; a whispering gorilla would have more force, more shock value, than a signer—it would have more *use*.

'We *could* try a speech therapist,' Stella suggested.

'How to find someone reliable?' Clive said. 'Someone... discreet?'

'We found J.J.'

They both turned towards me, inviting me to enter the discussion. I had stayed for dinner, an occasional invitation which I never declined. Rain was falling in the darkness outside, Eliza was upstairs in bed, asleep, as always, the moment the sun set. My mouth was crammed full of beancurd; my friends waited, politely, while I chewed and swallowed.

'I think you're missing the point,' I said. 'We don't have time to devote to whispering. We don't have enough time for Sign as is.'

My protests won the day even though I was dissembling. For I had another, unstated objection. I was increasingly possessive of my star pupil, and unwilling to share her with anyone.

16

Longer nights, shorter days. The world was turning, yes—but in part the shrinking hours of daylight were also a matter of perception. My days with Wish passed all too quickly, my nights and weekends without her dragged by.

I spent less time at the Institute, I arrived earlier at the farm each day, sneakily increasing my contact hours. I had been rostered on the Sign translators' panel, but the work was largely piece-work. If I didn't work, I wasn't paid. I felt no guilt. Access visits with Rosie caused me far more heart-ache. I was increasingly resentful of those endless Sundays of ice-creams and burgers and teenage movies and game parlours and ice-skating and zoo visits, and increasingly guilty that I felt such resentment.

Each Sunday night I spent long hours immersed in the sea, meditating, relaxing. And allowing the promise of

Monday's lessons, held in abeyance through the weekend tedium, to rekindle inside me, a glow of pure pleasure.

Those lessons still followed their own meandering path, unstructured—but I tried to keep an overview, a large-scale mental map of the regions we had visited, and those still to visit. Her introduction to music came in our second month together.

As usual she was waiting at the second gate; I arrived carrying a bulky, awkwardly wrapped package.

'That what?'

'Gift,' I signed, a palms-up offering.

She followed, excited, into the house, gesturing to Clive and Stella. The four of us climbed the stairs to her bedroom; I handed over the package with due ceremony. Stella watched, curious; Clive's expression was more cautious.

Wish ripped open the paper and extracted the guitar that I had bought for myself as an adolescent, and rarely used since. I tuned the strings, and strummed the first bars of 'Blowin' in the Wind', a three-chord kindergarten version from *The Bob Dylan Songbook*.

'Me?'

I nodded; she took the guitar, carefully, and propped it in approximate position on her thigh. I sat behind her, one hand reaching round her broad back to grasp her strumming hand, the other guiding her fingers into a basic G-chord. She strummed, clumsily, but enjoying the sound. I showed her a C-chord, an F7; we strummed the first bars of the song. I sang, she strummed; after a short time I released her hands, her fat thumb-fingers made the chord-changes

227

slowly, but accurately, demonstrating a tactile memory, a position sense, far ahead of mine.

Shortly after that she began to croon along, tunelessly. The words were beyond her; it was more a form of scat-singing, a throaty woofly chuckle, rhythmic, but without melody.

'I don't know that I approve,' Clive said.

Stella murmured to me: 'Don't mind him, he's tone-deaf.'

He smiled, patiently.

'Music doesn't compute,' she added, teasing him.

He held up a quibbling finger. 'I beg to differ,' he said. 'Music *does* compute. The musical scale is nothing if not a table of logarithms.'

Stella laughed; a cue that he was joking, sending himself up.

'I want Wish to develop an appreciation of music,' he said. 'But this is just tricks on a guitar. An organ-grinder's monkey.'

Stella hustled him, still protesting, from the bedroom, following him out and closing the door.

I gently took the guitar from Wish.

'Play too much,' I said. 'Fingertips—bleed.'

She showed me her fingertips, human fingerprints embossed on inhuman skin, as thick as calf leather. She could have played all night without damaging those tough pads.

She handed the guitar back, I strummed through another song from the same book: 'Mr Tambourine Man'.

'Your music sad,' she signed. 'Cry-hurt here,' she tapped her chest, 'wants out.'

She listened a little longer. I could only remember the words of the chorus, I hummed through the verses. Perhaps some plaintive quality in my singing touched her, when I finished she returned again to the personal questions that had been suspended some weeks before.

'You not live J-I-L-L—why?'

As with the signing of my parents, it seems inadequate to represent Wish's language as a kind of pidgin English. It was not fluent Auslan—but neither was it simple Koko-speak, or Washoe-speak. It was a hybrid: her own improvisations, her own inventions, grafted onto an Auslan frame. And it was always quick and intelligent—often far quicker than I could cope with. To recreate it in a richer, more poetic English would be no less false than my terse pidgin, but there was a gentleness in her movements and her tone that day to which I cannot do justice. 'Would you like to tell me about it?' is perhaps the closest I can get.

What to tell her? When I remember my years of marriage I remember only stupid things. Trivial things.

'J. make me eat less,' I signed.

'You eat *more*,' she signed, and tumbled her own stout frame forward across the floor, surfacing from the somersault at my side, and hugging me gently around the shoulders, her face buried in my shoulder.

'Cuddly,' she signed. 'Tickle good.'

She held my hand as Clive and Stella walked me to my car later that evening. For the first time, instead of a farewell hug at the tree line, she followed me through the inner gate and into the field, still clutching my hand. I could

229

sense anxiety, even terror, in her tight grip as she stepped into the open—but she refused to release my hand.

Clive stopped, and peered towards the road. No passing cars were in sight, none could be heard approaching, but her exposure, standing in the stubble, clearly concerned him.

'I come,' Wish signed.

'You stay,' I said.

'*You* stay. You sleep here.'

I hugged her, squeezed breathless by those massive arms. At last I extracted myself and left her squatting, a forlorn figure at the edge of the trees. At the outer gate I turned and waved; she stared back impassively, refusing to acknowledge the gesture.

'I think she's got a crush on you,' Stella said, and chuckled.

A weakish pun, but also an articulation of something I had been half-denying: Wish's growing puppy-love, adoring even when she was teasing me, added immensely to the pleasure of those days.

17

Attendance at my night classes was in steep decline, a reflection, surely, of my distracted state of mind. On one of the last and wettest nights of autumn I arrived to find a completely empty classroom. The rain seemed a legitimate excuse for the absentees. I sat at the desk, twiddling my thumbs, an unofficial sign of boredom, as if telling myself how I felt. I yawned once or twice—the textbook sign.

After half an hour, when no one had appeared, I began packing my books. Miss-The-Point poked his head through the door.

'Where the hell is everyone, J.J.?'

I offered a weather-mime, ten fingers of rain, a two-handed downpour.

He wasn't impressed. 'You don't think it a little convenient to blame the weather?'

I continued packing my books, irritated. A lecture was clearly in the offing.

'I have to say, J.J., I'm not surprised that no one has shown. I've had one or two complaints of late. Students say that your lessons are too complex.'

'Which students?'

'I can hardly mention names, not without their consent.'

My indignation rose even further. Wish needed my company, night and day. Why was I wasting my time in an empty classroom? I *should* have been living in that house in the Hills.

'They want to be spoon-fed, Jeremy. They dabble their toes, learn a few signs—and they think they're doing their deaf relatives a huge favour.'

The criticism was aimed at him, obliquely. It went over his head.

'J.J., we can't afford to alienate the wider community.'

'Fuck the wider community.'

He took a step back, feigning shock—as much perhaps at the vulgarity of the accompanying sign as at the words.

'Is it Jill?' he said. 'Want to talk about it?'

'It isn't—and even if it was, not with you.'

The directness of the insult surprised both of us—but the process of saying what I thought I found therapeutic, the verbal equivalent of poking a garden sprinkler through a bedroom window and turning on the tap. Uttering the thoughts also clarified what those thoughts actually were. I realised that I didn't give a fig for his job.

'Keep your shirt on, J.J., I was only trying to help.'

'My private life is none of your business.'

'It is when it begins to affect your work.'

'If my work isn't up to scratch, I'd better resign.'

I could see the idea appealed to him.

'Ah...Let's not rush into things. But it might be best if you took the rest of the term off. Have a bit of time to yourself. Sort out your life. There seems to be a lot of anger there, J.J.—a lot of unresolved feelings you need to deal with. I'm more than happy to cover for you here.'

Miss-The-Point could even make a sacking sound a philanthropic act.

'No, I've had enough. It wasn't a good idea—it was never going to work out.'

He waited, hiding behind his mask of smug concern again.

'I don't think we can work together, Jeremy.'

'Why not?'

'Because you're up yourself,' I signed—literally 'you-up-you', an improvisation, but clearly, for once, not over his head.

Exhilarated by my new-found sense of freedom, I felt I could say anything.

'Take job and *shove* job,' I added.

There could be no mistaking that eloquent gesture either, the same 'fuck' hand-shape, re-orientated, literally shove-it-up-your-arse.

'Teaching tonight—not?'

'Class cancelled.'

Had my mother heard something on the grapevine—
seen something on the grapevine? We sat at the kitchen
table eating dinner. I busied my hands with knife and fork,
not wanting to discuss the matter further; my father chewed
his meat steadily, his gaze tigerish, waiting to pounce. My
mother picked at her food with suppressed agitation. Always
diplomatic, she wouldn't raise the subject till I was ready,
instead she gave me cues, provided conversational openings
into which I might choose to insert the news myself.

'Holiday?' she signed.

Holiday is a Rude Hand variant on the shape for lazy—
literally, a lazy time in which you do bugger-all.

My father's impatience with her approach was clear,
despite her pleading glances. After some minutes he threw

down his own knife and fork, unable to contain his frustration any longer.

'Beat around bush—not! Sacked why?'

Sacked: the brush-off mime of dismissal, made with terse force.

I set down my own cutlery more carefully. 'Sacked—not. Resigned.'

The opaque, emotionless shape failed to soothe him. He repeated the interrogative: 'Why?'

'Miss-The-Point.'

He rolled his eyes; shook his head. 'Beggars can't be choosers,' he signed—literally, beggars not allowed to make a choice.

'Me beggar—*not*!'

My protest went ignored. 'Your mother did huge work,' he signed. 'Find job. Bend *backwards* to help.' He almost fell backwards himself, emphasising the point. 'You throw job in face. You live here, our house, you eat here, our food.'

'I pay rent.'

'You pay nothing else. Nothing important. You here never. You give company—not. Use home like hotel. Now you throw away good job.'

He shaped a good job with his hands, and tossed it towards the door with derision.

'I *have* good job—teaching private student.'

'If you not beggar—maybe choose another hotel to live.'

'You kick me out?'

'Not kick. Give you time—to choose another hotel.'

My mother seemed to agree with the message, if not the harshness of the signing. 'We love you—but you need to stand on your feet.'

A lull, then she added: 'J. is right—maybe. You never grow up.'

To quote Jill at me I found infuriating—the first time, ever, that I could recall my mother taking the side of my ex-wife. I stood and leaned across the table, reaching my hands into their Signing Spaces, shouting in their faces, so to speak. If the truth was to be uttered, then I could utter it with the best of them.

'What I think—I think you forgive my ears—never. You love me—not. Because I'm deaf—not.'

They looked at me, then at each other, shocked. My mother began to sign, sadly, but her message was swamped by my father's anger.

'Get out,' he signed, enraged. 'Now—tonight.'

He rose and shoved me hard in the chest, but only succeeded in pushing himself backwards. He might as well have tried to toss a Sumo wrestler.

'I go next week,' I signed. 'I go when *I* choose. I pay rent already.'

I fled through the kitchen door. My wetsuit was pegged on the clothes line; I plucked it angrily, sending the pegs spinning onto the lawn. I gathered my seal-flippers from my room, and headed for the beach.

Food for thought as I floated in the dark ocean, seething inside: my ex-wife refused to have me in her house, now my parents had kicked me out. Was there an ounce of truth in their common complaint—I had never grown up?

Immersion gradually calmed me; I flippered slowly past the broken piles of the old jetty, then turned and let the rising tide lift me and carry me back towards the shore. Along the length of the esplanade only the window of my parents' bedroom was still lit, a dull, curtained beacon in the night. Soothed by my own weightlessness, by the rhythmic rise and fall of the swell, I tried to imagine the argument of hands that must be taking place, in furious silence, inside. My dismissal, or resignation, would be discussed at length; tempers would slowly settle; Miss-The-Point would be reappointed scapegoat for my failings, at least by my mother. She would always finally find it easier to blame someone other than her own son.

The porch light flared, a much brighter beacon; the front door opened; her slight dark figure appeared. She was carrying a torch; she followed its weak dancing beam across the esplanade and down the beach steps.

She was waiting when I emerged from the mild surf, dripping, a few minutes later. I glomped awkwardly out of the shallows and sank into the dry sand next to her, struggling to remove my flippers.

The torch was embedded in the sand between her legs, beam-up.

'Sorry,' she signed, her hands held, illuminated, in the narrow cone of light. 'Your father sorry.'

'No,' I signed back. 'Both—correct.'

I sensed rather than saw the surprise in her features, obscured in the darkness.

'I must stand on these feet,' I added, and jerked a flipper off with difficulty, and overbalanced backwards, sprawling in the sand.

I drove over the last rise before the farm and spotted her immediately, squatting beside the outer gate. Stella and Clive were nowhere in sight. Had she crossed the open stubble field, alone, to wait at the gate? Her back was jammed hard against the gatepost, she was glancing warily about, some ancient instinct keeping her head and eyes moving.

I stopped the car, climbed out, scanned the surrounding ridges for any witnesses to this strange sight.

'Star know you here?'

She leapt the fence without answering, and knuckle-loped towards me in the manner of her wild cousins, her normal attempt to mimic human walking forgotten. She hugged me, nuzzling her nose against my face. My reservations melted; I knew that for the love of me she had exposed herself to open savannah for the first time, overcoming her terror of whatever leopards or hyenas inhabited her deepest race-memory.

I also realised, with a recurrence of giddiness, that it was one of the most perfect expressions of love I had ever received, a gift, with no strings attached.

At length I pulled myself free and pressed the intercom buzzer; Stella's voice crackled from the speaker after a few seconds. 'It's open, J.J.'

She clearly had no idea of the whereabouts of her charge.

'Tell Saint-Star—not,' Wish signed.

'Staint' might be a better transcription than Saint-Star. The two sign-names had merged into a single fluid abbreviation in recent weeks—more evidence, it seemed to me, of the diminishing importance of Clive and Stella in her life.

'I tell not,' I signed, 'if you stay trees tomorrow.'

She nodded, reluctantly.

'Come here alone—never,' I signed.

She stared up at me, rebuked—but more with a residual stubbornness than with guilt.

'I tell Staint—not,' I signed.

We crossed the field hand in hand, her head swivelling about, watching again for predators. Her tight grip loosened a little as we passed through the second gate and into the safety of the trees. Clive was waiting in the lounge for the morning briefing, Stella joined us from upstairs. Wish clutched my hand, watching my face anxiously, but I kept my promise. I had other matters to discuss.

'I need even more time with Wish,' I announced. 'I'd like to stay every evening—until her bedtime.'

'What about your duties at the Institute?' Clive asked. 'I've resigned.'

Something passed between them, subtle eye contact, a current of apprehension. 'Uh…J.J. You're a very important part of the team. But it might be a good idea not to put all your eggs in one basket.'

His words surprised me. I'd assumed he would be pleased.

'I wouldn't like to think you had given up other opportunities for what is a rather insecure, possibly short-term, job.'

'It had nothing to do with Wish. A clash of personalities—that's all.'

A partial truth, but reassuring to Clive, whose tense body language relaxed considerably. I felt less comfortable. It had been spelt out, for the first time, that my presence in their house was regarded as provisional. I remembered again those first tentative questions of Wish about my family life—did I 'own' any children? The usage, her own invention, now had an added poignancy. I had become the most important person in her life, but they retained sole ownership. Not for the first time I sensed a different set of priorities. They enjoyed her company, Stella surely even loved her, as she loved all her animals, but to both of them, Project Wish came first, even at the expense of Wish's happiness.

'Serendipity?' Stella said, enigmatically, to Clive.

I waited; he explained. 'My publisher wants me in the States for several weeks. Publicity for the new book.'

'It would be good to have an extra pair of hands around the house,' Stella said. 'So to speak.'

'I would be happy to move in,' I said, hesitantly.

Another meeting of their eyes, the transmitted message inscrutable to me. They both spoke, in turn.

'It's a lot to ask, J.J.'

'Your help has been invaluable but we can't expect to monopolise your time.'

I ignored the unintended slight. In my mind, they had been helping me.

'How long do you plan to be away?'

'*If* I go.'

'If you go.'

'Two weeks. Perhaps three. It's a huge nuisance. A contractual obligation. The terms of my contract—signed in the days before I became father to a gorilla—compel me, at the discretion of my publisher, to make myself available for interviews.'

Stella laughed, loudly. 'Poor Clive! His publisher is *forcing* him to be famous.'

Clive ignored her. 'It would be a considerable help, J.J. Even if you only stay a few nights. And not just for Stella. Wish will need extra affection.'

Stella leant forward on the sofa, her body language alert, interested. 'You think she'll *miss* you?'

'There is a precedent. After Terry went back to Melbourne—when she first came to us—she missed him terribly.'

'What you are really saying,' she said, 'is that you'll miss *her*.'

He smiled, then said, with exaggerated pedantry: 'That's not what I'm saying at all, my dear. I'm merely saying that we should try to learn from our past mistakes.'

They were playing their favourite game again: spot an emotion. Clive enjoyed the contest as much as Stella, slipping into self-parody, erecting ever-higher barriers.

'Of course I'll stay,' I intervened. 'I'd *love* to stay.'

'I may not need you for the entire three weeks,' Stella added, quickly, as if to remind me again that the arrangement was merely temporary.

20

On the afternoon of Clive's departure I filled the Fiat
with winter clothes and books and set out for the Hills.
The weight of my baggage was minimal but sufficient
to slow my progress. My little car struggled; I arrived
late. Stella had planned to drive Clive to the airport,
leaving Wish in my care; she had obviously given up
on me, a cab was already waiting at the outer gate.
The face of the cabbie behind the wheel was familiar, the
same giant who had ferried me home from my first visit to
the farm. Perhaps he lived nearby. He failed to recognise
me; his window was wound down, he was peering intently
at the tree line.

'Tell me, squire,' he said. 'Can you see something
moving in the trees over there? Something big.'

'A koala?'

'Bigger.'

He was curious, but not curious enough to heave his great bulk from the cab and take a closer look. Stella's jeep appeared from between the trees, canvas roof up, and churned slowly down the muddy track towards us, followed by the usual herd of animals.

'Who's in that?' the cabbie asked. 'The pied piper?'

'The poet,' I said, but he still didn't remember.

The jeep halted at the gate; Clive climbed down, reached back inside, and tugged out a large suitcase. I pushed open the gate, and went to help.

'Nice of you to join us, J.J.,' Stella said.

'Sorry. Car trouble.'

She ignored my excuse and turned to her husband. 'Now that J.J.'s finally here I could follow you down.'

The suggestion puzzled him; he seemed unable to understand why his wife might want to see him off at the airport, a waste of her valuable time. He shook my hand, and was about—or so it seemed to me—to reach up and shake Stella's, but she slid from the jeep, stepped inside his extended arm and hugged him, warmly.

She watched the cab over the rise, but her husband didn't look back. I climbed into my Fiat, and drove through the gate, following her jeep up the track. Wish was waiting at the second gate, out of sight of the road. Any sorrow she might have felt at the departure of Clive was swamped by pleasure at the sight of me. She scooped my bags from the car with one long all-encompassing arm, and tugged me through the trees and into the house. Her big bare feet were covered in mud; well trained, despite her excitement, she paused to scrape them hard against the verandah steps in the manner of boots. I wondered if she had ever worn shoes. My room was the guest room upstairs; she tossed my bags onto the bed and watched, curious, excited, as I began to unpack. My wetsuit was the first item to come to light; she fingered it, bemused. The black flippers caused a bigger reaction; she took a step back, concern written on her face.

I sat on the side of the bed, pulled off my shoes and socks, and demonstrated their use—which caused even more astonishment.

'Walk on water?'

'*Under* water—like fish.'

Prepositions in Auslan have an immediate, natural clarity. On: the back of one hand slapping the palm of the other.

Under: one Flat Hand passing beneath the other.

I pulled off the left flipper and knelt at her feet, cupping her heel in my hand like a prince trying to locate some aquatic Cinderella. Her odd-shaped appendage, more hand than foot, had no chance of squeezing into my rubber slipper.

'Swim in dam,' I signed.

In: the forefinger inserted into the hole of a partly closed fist, an old family sign.

She grimaced, horrified. 'I hate water.'

She fished in my bags for more treasures: music cassettes which she insisted on hearing, picture books, and a few of Rosie's discarded toys that I had salvaged. Late in the afternoon, Stella appeared in the door carrying a tray.

'Come and get it.'

She set down the tray on my bedside table and passed a huge bowl of steaming greens to Wish, who crossed her legs, set the bowl on her lap, and began to shovel food into her mouth, using the fingers of her right hand. An open bottle of champagne also stood on the tray; Stella filled two slender glasses and passed one to me.

'Welcome, J.J.'

'Thank you.'

We clinked glasses. I offered Wish a sip; she shook her head violently, Bad Hand circling her lips, the sign for bitterness, or bad taste. Stella drained her own glass, poured out another, climbed onto my bed and lit a cigarette, settling in, it seemed, for the evening. I found her presence inhibiting; the easy intimacy I shared with Wish vanished. She examined my wetsuit, sceptically.

'Planning on doing some swimming, J.J.?'

'It's how I relax.'

'We're a long way from the coast.'

'I thought I might use the dam.'

She laughed. 'Jesus, J.J.—we *drink* that water.'

I continued to unpack items from my second suitcase; she provided a running commentary. The unpacking took time; I only had one free hand. Wish kept a tight grip on the other; sitting on the bed next to Stella, peering into the suitcase, but without her former enthusiasm. Like me, seemed to feel that three was a crowd.

'What time do *we* eat?' I finally asked.

'Hungry, J.J.?'

'Starving!'

Stella rose and gathered the various bits of glassware, and the empty bowl.

'I've made something special for dinner.'

'Asparagus?'

An old joke, more a ritual response than an attempt to be funny—but she managed to find a smile.

'I thought—maybe you could sign Wish a bedtime story as a special treat. Then you and I can have a little privacy.'

247

She turned to Wish, shaped a tooth-cleaning mime, and opened her arms for a goodnight hug. Wish was still holding my hand; she enfolded Stella briefly, with her free arm, then tugged me into the bathroom. Now that she had me living in the house, she wasn't about to let go. One-handed, she balanced her toothbrush carefully on the basin, bristles up, picked up the toothpaste and squeezed out a dollop. She cleaned her powerful teeth vigorously, and swallowed the foaming lather with clear pleasure. Task complete, she plonked herself, without warning, on the toilet seat, still gripping my hand tightly. A stream of piss spurted immediately, resonantly, into that porcelain tuba, the room filled with the rank scent of urine flavoured, I now recognised, by the distinctive tang of asparagus. I looked away, then back. She grinned toothily at me as if pissing in public were the most ordinary thing in the world. Or was she teasing me, enjoying the spectacle of human embarrassment?

Still in tow, I was pulled into her bedroom. She tugged a clutch of books from her shelves and climbed onto her bed; I sat on the edge and began to translate the topmost book with my free hand, the story of a happy lion in a zoo in France.

'Speak too,' she signed.

I propped the open book on my lap and read the story aloud as I signed, never an easy feat. After a few minutes her eyes slid shut. I wondered what sort of sense she made of my voice alone. Perhaps the soothing music of it was sufficient, a background murmur. When I finished the book, she lifted her hands and signed, drowsily, her eyes still closed: 'More book.'

There seemed little point, but I obliged, reading in English, without moving my hands, until Stella's voice called up the stairs: 'It's getting cold, J.J.'

Even asleep, Wish's grip was a vice. I reclaimed my hand with difficulty and headed downstairs, ravenous. An astonishing sight greeted me: a large cooked fish, wrapped in palm leaves, doused in spice, was sitting in the centre of the table.

'Isn't this illegal?' I said.

Stella was watching me with an expression of great anticipation, enjoying the shock value.

'The fish is for you, J.J. I'll stick to the salads.'

'I've become a vegetarian too,' I protested.

She made the long-tongue sign, and added, aloud: 'Don't tell fibs. I can smell a carnivore a mile off.'

'Do we smell that badly?'

'Rancid.'

She trowelled a thick flake of white flesh onto a plate, and passed it across. Her nose was accurate: my vegetarian zeal had lasted no more than a month. Shellfish had first forced the door open—then finned fish, thicker end of the same marine wedge. Fish didn't have feelings, I managed to persuade myself. Free-range meat soon followed, in small doses. I still held the line at pork and bacon—the images of suffering, self-aware pigs painted in Clive's book had been the most vivid, and durable.

'I don't want you to break house rules just for me, Stella.'

'Nonsense. You're doing us a big favour. I want you to be happy here. I want it to feel like home.'

249

'Please. Anything but that.'

She laughed, obligingly; I forked a fragment of the white flesh to my mouth.

'Delicious.'

'I'd better check to see that it's properly cooked,' she said, and with a cheerfully wicked wink reached her own fork across the table, and lifted a tiny flake from my plate, an intimacy I found exciting, like sharing her cigarettes.

She chewed, and swallowed.

'I love cooking, J.J. I just don't have much of a chance to let my hair down in the kitchen.'

'When the cat's away,' I said.

'The cat's still here,' she said. 'It's the *mouse* that's gone away.'

She laughed loudly, hugely amused at her own joke. I laughed with her, but felt a small prickle of surprise. Such irreverence at her husband's expense, so soon after he had left, seemed disloyal.

'I love him dearly,' she said, as if reading my thoughts. 'But he's such a fucking fundamentalist.'

She reached across the table, took another forkful of fish and ate it.

'Clive believes fishing is torture, but I'm not so sure. Do fish feel pain, J.J.?'

'They wriggle on the hook.'

'Linguistically,' she said, 'I think we find it more natural, more acceptable, to eat fish.'

I wasn't with her; she expanded. 'Cow becomes beef, pig becomes pork. Deer becomes venison—anything to hide

250

the truth, to pretend we picked it off a tree, like fruit. But fish stays fish. We feel we don't *need* a euphemism. We're comfortable with the bald fact.'

I had read Clive on this same subject. Part of the fight for Animal Rights, he had written somewhere, was the fight to call a spade a spade.

'We seem able to accept it, emotionally,' Stella said, increasingly prolix. 'We don't need to distance ourselves. We can *cope*.'

She sipped at her wine, then burbled on, thinking aloud. 'Or is it because fish is the only meat we still routinely kill ourselves? In person. What's the point in pretending fish-meat is something else—giving it a new name—if you yanked the hook out of its mouth with your own hands and watched it flop to death on the jetty?'

'You mean there might be *limits* to our capacity for self-deception?'

Stella chuckled. 'You and I are going to get on famously.'

The phone rang in the next room, she rose, a little unsteadily, and answered it. I couldn't catch the sense of her words, but her tone was playful, intimate. Clive was reporting from a transit-lounge somewhere, I guessed. I refilled both our glasses with wine, then carefully separated another thick flake of fish from the spine.

'Clive sends his best wishes,' Stella said, returning to the room.

'How is he?'

'Clive is always fine.'

This time it wasn't so much the hint of mockery that I found disconcerting, it was the dislocation in tone. Only a few moments ago she had been chatting to him fondly. I fumbled for small talk.

'No jet lag?'

'Clive doesn't believe in jet lag. He believes it's all in the mind.'

She drained her wine, shook out another cigarette and bent to light it. Her personality seemed to hang on her as loosely as her generous flesh: a mix of thick skin and soft heart, joky irreverence and puppy-eyed sentimentality. I watched her refill her glass for the fourth or fifth time and suspected that all of these disparate selves were equally soluble in alcohol.

Yet another self revealed itself as we parted for the night, in the hall outside the bathroom. She leaned her face into mine without warning, and kissed me wetly and drunkenly on the mouth.

'Sweet dreams, Sweet-Tooth,' she said, and wobbled away in the direction of her own bedroom.

Wish woke me at first light; I surfaced through a thick hangover to find her fingers wrapped about mine, moulding them like puppets, putting words in my pliant hands, Sign ventriloquism.

'Up time,' I found myself signing. 'Tickle Wish.'

I tickled; she hooted, rolling on the bed with me. My head ached; my bladder was about to burst. Outside, rain was falling again; liquid gurglings on the roof and in the gutters. I rose, and headed for the bathroom, locking Wish outside the door with difficulty. An absurd coyness? My feelings were not the issue. To feel shame or embarrassment in her presence, even a pretence of embarrassment, was to grant her a certain status and dignity. I might appear happily naked before a dog, or a cat—but not before Wish. I showered, towelled myself dry, and poked my head through Stella's half-open door. She was snoring gently somewhere in the darkness.

Wish was waiting in my bedroom, turning my wetsuit inside-out, absorbed.

'Look wall,' I signed.

She seemed puzzled, but complied; I dropped the towel and pulled on fresh clothes. I made the porridge-spooning sign for breakfast; she signed back, insisting: '*I* cook breakfast.'

We walked down the stairs, hand in hand, but as we reached the ground she dropped my hand and sniffed the air, suddenly alert. I followed her into the kitchen; even I could now smell the lingering stench of last night's fish. Wish sniffed her way about the kitchen, dog-fashion. She rapidly located the scraps bucket and stared intently into its depths. Finally she reached in, and gingerly lifted out the fish-skeleton by the tail.

The head came last, intact, soft-eyed; she stared at the final piece in the puzzle, horrified, then dropped it back into the bucket.

'You eat fish?' she signed, urgently.

'Most people eat fish.'

She knew this, surely—but seemed unable to comprehend the simple fact; I realised again how sheltered her life had been.

'*Fish* eat fish,' I signed. 'Big fish eat little fish.'

At this she fled from the room. I heard the front door open, and slam shut; I opened it again, and stepped out onto the verandah. Wish was already halfway up the nearest tree, and was soon sitting on the platform of her tree-house, a bleak black bundle, her long arms wrapped protectively around herself. She stared down at me from across those arms; I stood at the edge of the verandah, and held my hands out into the rain, trying to explain.

'Fish eat people,' I signed. 'Sharks eat people.'

No response; the Flat Hand dorsal fin was probably unfamiliar. I used something more immediate: big-fish-with-teeth.

She stared down, immobile. For a moment I considered climbing the tree myself, then finally those long arms unwrapped themselves and reached out into Signing Space.

'Bad fish eat fish.'

'All fish eat fish,' I signed, emphatically. 'Big fish eat little fish. If not—they die.'

I used her own terse sign, the hand gone belly-up.

'You eat animals?'

'Sometimes.'

'Which animals?'

'Cow. Sheep.' I signed slowly, trying to avoid the shapes of any of the animals that were grazing in the outer paddock, in full view of the treetops.

'You eat me?'

'Never!'

'Why eat those?'

What could I say? There was no simple answer to her simple logic. Except that it was a learnt logic, a human logic—it had nothing to do with the natural law of the rainforests of central Africa. I tried to appeal to her emotions instead, to that part of her, that part of all of us, which is more purely animal, and pre-rational.

'Come down. Hug me.'

She shook her wet head. 'Sad thoughts. Me sad inside.'

Stella appeared at the door, blear-eyed, tousle-haired, wrapped in her quilt.

'What's all the commotion? What's the matter, J.J.?'

'Wish found the fish bones.'

She smacked her forehead. 'Shit! I knew I should have buried them.'

'I tell Saint,' Wish was signing, high up in the drizzling rain. 'Saint eat fish—not.'

'What's the sign for fink?' Stella asked, amused.

I suspected that Clive would be less upset, than thrilled. Or perhaps that's not quite the right word for the emotional range of the man. He would at least have been gratified. Pleased. Wish was speaking on behalf of animals, even speaking on behalf of fish. Her reaction also offered new insight into her perception of self. Either she regarded herself as animal rather than human, or she regarded *all* animals as human. In this she clearly differed from other apes raised in human families, all of which—all of *whom*—believed themselves human.

'Does she know the sign for promise?' I said.

'Cross your heart?'

I nodded, and stepped further out into the falling rain: 'I promise,' I signed. 'I will eat animals again—never. I promise.'

I repeated the shape pleadingly, until, at last, she began to descend, crossed the grass between us, and hugged me, soaking me even more than the rain.

She was almost herself for the remainder of the afternoon, cooperative, alert, interested in the day's lessons. Only the sight of her evening meal, the sight of food, reminded her of the previous night's crime.

'Not hungry,' she signed, abruptly.

For the first time we sat at the table with her, something I had long been urging, and to which Stella, prodded by the fish episode, had finally agreed. We both made a great show of relishing our own vegetables; still she refused to touch hers. She went to bed early, refused also to hear—and watch—a bedtime story. Her aquarium bubbled steadily on its shelf; her accusing glance in that direction reminded me how stupid we had been.

'Too sad,' she signed. 'Crowds of thinking.'

She hugged me but refused to hug Stella, who, unfairly, was taking the bulk of the blame. A fine moral distinction: was preparing meat a greater crime than eating it? I finally left her lying in the darkness, listening to her favourite middle-of-the-road music on the radio, soothing movie themes, slow sad ballads.

Downstairs, Stella was pulling on her overalls. Calving problems at a local dairy, she told me. She apologised for leaving me alone—there was no alternative. If she didn't attend, some butcher-cum-midwife would botch the job. I made myself a toasted cheese sandwich after she had left, and retreated upstairs to an early bed, grateful for the reprieve from another night's drinking.

2 2

A different Wish woke me the next morning, again at
first light. One hand held a tray of breakfast, the knuckles
of the other were pressed against the carpet, balancing
herself. She set the tray in front of me: orange juice,
cereal, bun, jam. Plus a single rose standing in a slender
vase—a setting she must have seen in a book. My canni-
balism was forgiven; she sat on my bed, helping herself,
clearly hungry, to the food as I ate, tickling me from time
to time.

Stella poked her head in the door, relief written on her
face. Wish acknowledged her presence, if without enthusiasm. Things were almost back to normal; the holiday
mood created by Clive's absence was restored. I rose and
tugged back the curtains. The rain had finally ceased, the
sky had cleared, the early sun was shining above the eastern
edge of the valley.

Stella, wedged into overalls and rubber boots, clomped off into the fields to check her flock after breakfast, followed by her dogs; I sat outside in the rose garden with Wish. Back to basics: reading, writing, arithmetic. In the afternoon the three of us, and the three dogs, watched a movie, a 1950s musical, soaked in the sugary kind of music that Wish preferred. As she closed her eyes and rocked her head in time, I realised that the main sense of those sweet songs was in the melodies; the words needed no translation.

As the final credits screened, Wish asked to watch the movie again, using her signature sign of crossed-fingers, the shape of hope.

Stella shook her head and signed: 'Supper time.'

We ate together, sitting at the dining table, Wish requesting three extra helpings of fruit. I recalled once more the lines of Clive's: that a visit to the abattoirs might put most people off their dinner, but they will usually manage a hearty breakfast.

After dinner, I shared again her one-handed teeth-clean, and another unembarrassed piss. I sign-read her a sequence of stories, and sat with her till her eyes closed and I could detach my wrist from her tight grip.

Stella was sprawled on the sofa downstairs, watching the news on television, putting the last lick to a lumpy, hand-rolled cigarette. She mostly smoked tailor-mades; this was cannabis, at a guess. Clive's absence seemed to have magnified her excesses: the late rising, the drinking, the television. The fish. Perhaps it was merely holiday spirit, a moral equivalent of wearing thongs and shorts and not bothering to shave.

'Come and sit here,' she said, patting the sofa.

She gently pushed her dogs aside, making space; I eased my bulk between them. We drank wine and talked of Wish for a time; I allowed the cigarette she forced on me to smoulder between my fingers, before passing it back.

Clive rang from New York at nine; after that we talked of him.

'He's a very special kind of person,' Stella said. 'He's a living national *treasure*, for Christ's sake. But sometimes it's nice to have a little private space.'

She settled her head comfortably against my shoulder. The three dogs watched, jealously; Binky, the smallest, growled, softly, and inserted herself between us.

'You're very warm, J.J. You *glow*.'

There's a lot of me. Lots of metabolism. I make a lot of warmth.'

'Clive's not a warm person,' she said.

I felt uncomfortable discussing her husband in his absence, it seemed a breach of trust.

'Of course I miss him when he's away.'

I waited for the implicit 'but'.

'But he sucks it out of me, J.J. He's not warm. Not— demonstrative.'

Again I said nothing. She eased Binky off the sofa between us, swung her legs over the end of the sofa, and rested the back of her head in my lap.

'Do you mind, J.J.?'

I was too surprised to answer. The heavy pressure of her head aroused me, my first erection for some time. The feeling was unexpected and exciting, I had been dead from the waist down for several years.

'You pleased to see me?' she asked, and laughed.

My pulse flared, my cock shrank instantly, scared off, just as it had hidden too often from Jill in the last years of our marriage.

Oblivious, she returned to the subject of Clive. 'He's no good at Sign, is he?'

'He's okay.'

She repositioned her head. I half-expected her to turn and plump my belly like a pillow.

She said, jokily: 'Cuddle Stella, Sweet-Tooth?'

I draped one arm awkwardly around her.

'I get so lonely when Clive's away,' she said. 'I *need* human contact.'

Her big loose body had been loosened even further by alcohol and cannabis, made pliant—but the eyes that stared up at mine had a residual hardness that alcohol had not yet dissolved.

'You know what I *really* need, J.J.?'

My heart lurched—pure anxiety now, not a trace of sexual excitement.

'I need relief,' she said. 'All this pelvic congestion. Here—see.'

She took my hand and planted it between her thighs. I felt myself shrivelling, growing ever smaller. There is an awkward English verb, to detumesce. The sense is much more economical in Sign, and much more eloquent: a droop of a stiff arm.

The bleating of the phone saved me, miraculously. Stella rose and answered it, a veterinary colleague, apparently, seeking advice. Despite her drunkenness she managed

261

to give it, or at least fake it. I sneaked off up the stairs under cover of shop-talk: heartworm, active and passive vaccines, immune proteins.

I peeked through Wish's bedroom door as I passed: she lay sleeping on her back, splay-limbed, open to the world, trusting.

I closed my own bedroom door. There was no lock. Stella knocked and entered as soon as I had climbed into bed. She came and sat on the edge of my bed, and rested her hand on my thigh. My cock shrank even smaller, retreating from her fingers.

She laughed, and withdrew her hand as if it were all too much trouble.

'It's only sex, J.J. It's not as if I'm asking you to *kiss* me.'

'I haven't made love since Jill and I split up,' I said, apologetically. 'I haven't even had the interest.'

'It's just habit, J.J. The less you have the less you want.'

'I'm *very* tired.'

She smiled, drunkenly tolerant. 'We don't have to make love. Just cuddle me. I need a little affection. A little tenderness. Is that too much to ask?'

'I can manage that.'

She deftly peeled off her clothes and was naked within seconds. I tried not to stare as she climbed into bed but her breasts were huge, stretched pendulous by their own weight, semi-autonomous in their movements. I had seen nothing like them in the world of small dainty women I had grown up in, and married into.

The polite sign for breasts is opaque, made with a single Flat Hand. Size can be indicated, tactfully, with two

Good Hands—but when I think of Stella I think solely in the vernacular, an extravagant double-handed cupping, considered vulgar among the Deaf.

'Let's modify the rules, J.J. We can cuddle, we can play with each other, but no actual penetration.'

Her speech was slurred, but her words sounded oddly logical, carefully thought-out. My cock retracted completely, on the verge of becoming a vagina. Then, miraculously, I was rescued again: Stella fell asleep without warning, mid-sentence, draped half across me, snoring slightly. I eased my leg from beneath her heavy thigh, and lay sleepless at her side, thoughts tumbling. The situation was too familiar, the last months of my failed marriage too immediately past. Tears seeped into my eyes, threatened to clog my throat. The puzzled questions of Wish came back to me, fingers probing a tender wound. I *had* loved Jill enormously. Where had that love vanished?

Stella stirred around midnight, reached into my groin, and murmured, mostly to herself: 'I don't think it was meant to happen, J.J.'

'Sorry.'

'Not your fault.'

I turned my back to her, facing the wall. I sensed that she was still awake, and screwed my eyes shut, but I couldn't shut out her movements: the rhythmic shifting of her weight, then the quickening jiggle of the mattress and of her breathing—and, finally, the small, suppressed, plosive gasp of air between her lips.

She lay still after this self-release; soon she was snoring gently. I must have joined her in sleep, when I next opened my eyes, light was filtering through the window; a glow of red digits in the far corner of the room read, blurrily, 5.55. I slipped from the bed, careful not to disturb my companion. I pulled on my clothes, hoping desperately that Wish had not yet risen. Too late; her room at the end of the passage was empty. There was still a slight possibility that she hadn't peeped through my bedroom door, and a marginally smaller possibility that she had, but made nothing of it: two adults enjoying a friendly consenting cuddle, even if one of them was naked. I searched the rooms downstairs, then poked my head out through the front door, screwing my eyes up against the morning glare. No sign of her in the treetops.

I turned inside, and mounted the stairs. Stella was still asleep, snoring softly, unrousable.

My bladder was making the usual morning demands; I headed for the bathroom—and stepped back again at the door, dumbfounded. Wish was squatting on the tiles in front of the full-length wall-mirror, her arms and shoulders lathered with shaving cream. A pair of scissors sat open-jawed on the tiles; scissored hair had been shed onto the floor all around. My disposable razor was gripped tightly in her right hand; she was in the process of shaving her left shoulder.

A comical sight, even ludicrous, but I sensed the terrible seriousness of purpose.

She hadn't noticed me. She leant to one side; now I saw, horrified, that she had already shaved, or scissored, most of the hair from her legs. I also saw the blood; the black skin of her thigh was a mess of cuts and lacerations.

I stepped forward into the bathroom; she turned to me, startled, then quickly turned her back again, crouched forward, hiding her injuries. I remembered our first meeting, months before—how she had slunk sideways, crab-wise, into the room, embarrassed, it seemed to me at the time, by her nakedness.

My hands moved: 'Why?'

She stared at me in the mirror, reflected. There was something new in that look—a hardness, or directness, which I hadn't noted before. The room was suddenly drenched in her characteristic musk, but more rank than usual. Then she backed into me, suddenly, reached one elongated arm behind her to grip my thighs, and leaning forward, her weight resting on her other elbow, pressed my groin against her backside. Startled, I pulled free as quickly as I could. A sticky wetness stained the front of my jeans; I realised, shocked, that she was in oestrus.

She was presenting to me, a word that doesn't exist in any dictionary of Sign.

'Wrong,' I signed, frantically. 'Bad.'

She half-turned to me, puzzled. 'Why?'

265

No immediate answer came to hand; she reached for me again, and tugged me towards her. Her grip was gentle, but inexorable; her wet hind-parts pressed hard against me—and now I panicked, flailing at her with both fists, striking her thick-furred back several times, as hard as I could. Her astonishment gave me time to break free.

I fled downstairs to the laundry, ran the hot tap over a damp cloth, and wiped, *scrubbed*, at those stains on the front of my jeans. The heat of the cloth seemed to release, or heighten, a new, volatile odour: rank, fish-like, identical to the smell of a woman. I rubbed frantically at the denim, aware of the growing stiffness of my cramped cock beneath. Horrified, I peeled off the jeans, dropped them into the sink and ran the hot tap, at maximum gush, over them. My own stiffness remained, straining inside my flimsy jocks. A reflex, surely—the effect of that universal female-smell. Or was it a residual waking erection? Even as I pleaded with myself—*please* let it be that—another, more disturbing thought refused to let me off the hook so leniently. If it were a reflex, where had that reflex been last night? Stella had also been on heat. 'I'm the sort who needs it every day,' she had murmured, drunkenly, during the night. My hard cock still refused to sag; I felt harder than I had felt for many years. Given back to me also was the urgency of old; an urgency that demanded to be addressed, immediately. I pressed my thighs hard against the edge of the laundry sink, gripped my cock, a rigid faucet jutting over the lip of the sink, and squeezed. Already balanced on the edge of coming, I was pushed instantly over the last threshold. A groan-shout escaped my lips, helplessly, I ejaculated. And the image that filled my mind as I came—as much, still panicking, as I tried to suppress it—was of Wish presenting, her swollen hindparts pressed hard against me, her long arm gripping my buttocks, my face buried into the warm, thick fur of her shoulders.

I slumped over the sink, wobble-kneed, paralysed. Horror at my actions filled me, the hands of sign-shame rose to hide my face. The noise of my coming would surely bring Wish down the stairs. I couldn't face her; I could barely face myself. I managed to tug on my jeans, soaked through, still steaming, and escape from the house through the laundry door.

I hurried through the trees and across the outer field. Stella's flock watched me, incuriously; my hands rose again to hide my face, automatically. I needed to drive, and think, safe in my Fiat tortoise-shell. I needed to drive to the nearest beach, and immerse myself in the salt water, and float, cleansed, far out to sea.

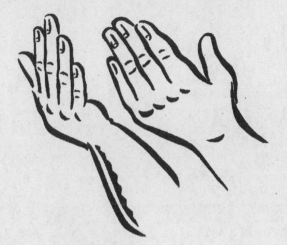

BOOK

THREE

The polite sign for sex, a throat-cutting mime, but made with the Good Hand; a weird mix of the sweet and the sour. The little death of orgasm: the surrender of the self? Or something deeper and weirder: sex equals danger, sex is a kind of suicide.

A see-through sign, certainly; a bifocal lens that first shows this, then that, a different focus, a further meaning.

The sign was a favourite of Jill's. The same contradiction is buried in English, she once told me—always keen to find patterns and make connections between languages. To fight and to fuck have the same ancient root: *ficken*, to strike.

I'm no fighter. I'll run a mile to avoid conflict. And no one, least of all Jill, would describe me as oversexed, the kind of man who thinks with his cock. A crude expression?

On the contrary. English at its best, at its closest to the simple poetry of Sign.

I drove up out of the bowl of the valley, crossed the western rim, and rolled at speed down Greenhill Road and through the city to the waiting surf.

The sea was grey and choppy, white-flecked by a strong westerly. My wetsuit was still hanging in the guest-room wardrobe in the Hills; I had nothing but my own thick seal blubber for insulation. Sand and frigid salt-spray whipped my face and skin as I stripped to my jocks and waded in. The first heart-stopping shock of cold quickly faded, and I felt only a warm glow as I floated beyond the surf line, sole swimmer as far as the eye could see. Less buoyant without my rubber suit, I was still unsinkable, more walrus than man.

The shock of Wish presenting to me was also fading. I felt again a tremble of excitement as I remembered that bathroom scene, a pilot-flame had been lit somewhere inside me, and was growing, surely and steadily. Gratitude for that excitement nourished the flame even further. Guilt, shame, gratitude, relief—a sweet-and-sour mix, definitely. I floated with my eyes closed, limbs flaccid, a buoyant cork at the whim of the sea. I wanted to feel my way to some sort of resolution, rather than merely think—but self-justifications were also easy to find, or invent. A small, logical voice nagged at me: if Wish deserved human rights, she deserved human pleasures.

Excuses, excuses? Her face came to me clearly as the swell lifted and lowered me. Her wide nose, her dark, mischievous eyes. Her thick 'mink' coat. The warmth of her

272

big body. Above all I remembered her hands, her bare black fingers emerging from thick fur as if from fingerless mittens.

Clive would have condemned these comparisons: I was committing the sin of anthropomorphism. But such scruples had come to seem petty, and irrelevant. As I floated, glowing, one single, overriding need shouldered through the jostle of contradictory feelings: I missed her.

Should I feel guilty if I preferred her company to others, if I loved being with her?

Loved. The word had sneaked into the open indirectly, under subterfuge of that innocent sentence. It now insisted on being spoken more clearly: I realised that I loved more than merely 'being with' her.

I loved *her*.

The classification of that love, its type, its specifications, refused to wait. A tutor's love for a gifted pupil? A foster-parent's love? These, certainly. These at the least. Sign is less ambiguous than English on the subject of love, less able to hide its feelings and hedge its bets behind the euphemisms of infatuation, bewitchment, temporary insanity. The shape is clear, powerful, undeniable:

I knew also, equally clearly, that those feelings were returned. Wish loved me, I loved her. Armed with this knowledge, armoured by it against guilt and doubt, I kicked back towards the shore, and the neat pile of clothes waiting in the dry sand above the tidemark.

2

Stella opened the door, agitated, dishevelled, restlessly shifting her weight. Her hair was a matted nocturnal tangle, but she had pulled on some clothes. A stethoscope dangled about her neck.

'Where have you *been*, J.J.? I found Wish in the bathroom. Shaving herself with your razor. Where *were* you?'

'I'm sorry—I had things to do.'

'She's in a terrible state. She might have bled to death.'

She stood blocking my path; I wanted to push past her and up the stairs. What was the significance of the stethoscope?

'Is she alright?'

'No thanks to you. I've patched her up as best I could.'

She ran the fingers of both hands through her tangled hair, distraught.

'You shouldn't have left her *alone*, J.J.'

She seemed to think I had left the house before the shaving disaster. I wasn't about to tell her otherwise.

'I didn't leave her alone. You were in the house.'

'I slept in because I thought you were *here*. You should have woken me. You shouldn't have left your razor lying about.'

Her voice trailed off as if she had realised the absurdity of the accusation, an attempt to find anyone, or anything, to blame.

'I want to see her.'

She stood aside and followed me up the stairs, her tone more conciliatory. 'I'm sorry, J.J. I went off half-cocked. I don't want to point the finger. Wish is the one we have to worry about. It's *very* disturbing.'

The bedroom door was deadlocked, a security measure that had been neglected in Clive's absence. Stella turned the key and pushed. Wish was lying on her bed, facing the wall. Her back, once thickly coated with fur, was now a kind of savannah: bare shorn skin, with just a few central tufts of hair, out of reach of the razor. Adhesive plasters had been stuck here and there, flesh-pink against the underlying blackness. Her neck and arms were more smoothly shaven; a hacked thatch of hair perched on top of her head. I was reminded, absurdly, of Clive's ill-fitting toupée.

I sat on the edge of the bed and touched my fingertips, gingerly, to her damaged skin. She was trembling slightly, sobbing, perhaps. She refused to turn and face me; she failed even to acknowledge my presence. Her mattress was smeared with stains, the brick-reds and red-browns of dried blood.

'I couldn't get through to Clive,' Stella was babbling somewhere in the background. 'I left a message—in Chicago. I was desperate.'

I wrapped my left arm across Wish, my hand in the Signing Space between her chest and the wall, hidden from Stella. 'Mink grow again.'

No response.

'Me sorry,' I signed.

She shivered violently, a small convulsion—I realised that her trembling was more physical than emotional. Black goose bumps, human goose bumps, pimpled her damaged skin. I turtled my head towards Stella. 'She'll freeze to death. Get some clothes.'

'I've turned up the heating, J.J. It's *hot* in here.'

'She can't sit in front of a heater till her hair grows back.'

'We can't reward this behaviour with clothes.'

'You sound like some fucking *animal* trainer! I thought you believed she was human.'

I was shouting, the first time my voice had been raised in that house. The fact that someone else was doing the worrying, expending the emotion, seemed to permit Stella to relax slightly.

'Not human, J.J. *Obviously* she's not human. I just believe she should have human rights.'

'Humans are usually allowed to wear clothes. And shave themselves, for that matter.'

There was a Clive-logic in this that seemed to flummox her; she glanced sharply to one side as if half-expecting to find him nearby.

'I'll get a quilt,' she said, a reasonable compromise, and left the room.

'You sick?' I signed, my hands still reaching across Wish's broad back, into Signing Space.

'Cold,' she shaped, tersely, one-handedly—her first acknowledgement of my presence.

I lifted my legs onto the bed and pressed myself full length against her. Footsteps approached; a thick quilt was shaken out above us, momentarily suspended, it descended slowly and gently, settling across the bed.

Stella was right: the room was hot, the quilt unnecessary. I was soon sweating profusely—but Wish was shivering again, uncontrollably. Her breathing seemed laboured; was she feverish?

'She's ill. She might have pneumonia.'

'She's fine, J.J. I've been over her with a fine-tooth comb.'

'Are you sure? You're only a vet.'

Not the most tactful choice of words; and not at all what I meant to say.

'I'm sorry, Stella. All I meant was—she's not a dog, or a horse. Her anatomy is human, surely. Perhaps we need a real doctor.'

Another bad choice. I regretted the word 'real' as soon as it left my mouth.

'A specialist,' I corrected myself, more diplomatically. 'A chest specialist.'

'J.J., she is an animal and I am a vet. Believe me, I know more about primate physiology than any doctor in this city. The problem is not in her body—it's in her head.'

'What are you saying—she needs a *psychiatrist*?'

My voice was raised again; Wish shifted her weight on the bed and cupped her hands over her ears, a clear rebuke. She might have done better to cover her eyes; as always at times of stress, my hands signed, involuntarily. The shape for 'mind'.

Then 'doctor', two fingers, taking a pulse.

Mind-doctor. I wrapped my arms around her again; she shrugged them off with a twitch of her powerful shoulders, then rolled onto her back and held her hands high above her, in full view.

'You go,' she signed. 'Me wish alone.'

'Alone' was all her own work, but instantly readable: the Point Hand personal pronoun—me, Number One—sheltered inside the curved Flat Hand.

I had never seen that hand-shape before, but it seemed far more heartfelt than the official sign for aloneness, or loneliness, an opaque borrowing from British Sign.

'Go!' her hands repeated, more forcefully. 'Me—alone!'

I looked over my shoulder at Stella; she stared back, guilty, silenced. Finally she shrugged and nodded towards the door; I reluctantly eased myself from beneath the quilt and followed her out.

3

We faced each other across the cluttered living room, bewildered. I lay slumped on the couch; Stella sat on the floor, leaning against a bookcase, surrounded by her dogs. I remembered an Aboriginal term Jill had brought back from a field trip to the desert, the description of a very cold night: a three-dog night. Stella seemed in need of similar protection, or comfort.

'Should we leave her alone, J.J.?'

'She wants to be alone.'

'All the same...'

She pressed the side of her face into Binky, sitting astride her lap, but the presence she most needed was Clive's, I saw. She might mock his calm rationality, she might even spend odd nights with other men, but without that bedrock, she was lost.

'Perhaps I should sit with her all the same, J.J.'

'She'll order you to leave.'

'Then I'll sit outside the door where I can keep an eye on things. Until Terry gets here.'

This was news; she tossed me another scrap as she detached herself from her quilt of dogs. 'I'm sorry, in all the fuss I forgot to tell you. I rang Terry in Melbourne when I couldn't reach Clive. He's flying over on the first plane. Sometime late this afternoon.'

I called up after her: 'What did you tell him?'

'That Wish had mutilated herself.'

'You told him the reason?'

Her tone was impatient. 'We don't *know* the reason—that's the point.'

I was speechless for a moment, surprised. The connection seemed obvious: Stella had spent the night in my bed, naked; Wish had shaved off her fur.

I said, carefully: 'It might be best not to tell Wish that Terry is coming.'

She paused on the stairs, puzzled. 'I think we should play the whole thing down,' I added. 'It's a bit out of control. It's possible that your own reactions have just added fuel to the fire—just reinforced it. I'm beginning to think we should treat it as a...bit of a joke.'

'It's hardly a joke, J.J.'

'I said *treat* it as a joke.'

She moved a step back down the stairs, watching me. 'If you have any theories, please share them with me.'

A small turning-point had been reached, a moment of truth. To tell, or not to tell? The question could no longer be evaded, or postponed.

I said, limiting myself: 'Perhaps she wants to be more human.'

More impatience from Stella. 'Obviously. But it's such a *neurotic* gesture.'

I decided I wasn't ready to share my theory with her. She waited; when nothing more was forthcoming, she turned again and climbed the narrow stairs, followed, laboriously, by her dogs.

I lay on the couch, thinking. Rain was falling again outside, drumming against the roof, spilling from the gutters—soothing water-noise. I had no proof that Wish had seen us in bed together. Was the connection entirely mine, the product of a guilty imagination? The possibility was seductive, a three-dog fantasy it would have been easy to clutch at for comfort. But I *knew* that Wish had shaved herself out of sexual jealousy.

Mid-afternoon, I made some salad sandwiches and carried them upstairs. Stella was sitting on the floor outside the locked door, surrounded by her dogs.

'Any sign?'

'I've looked in once or twice. She hasn't moved.'

She passed a sandwich-half to each dog, I returned downstairs to the couch, and my thoughts. The gate intercom buzzed as the afternoon light began to fade. Stella's voice carried down the stairs. 'Could you get that, J.J.? I don't want to leave her alone.'

I pressed the intercom but received no response. I forced my big feet into a pair of Stella's gumboots, opened an umbrella, and picked my way through the rain and slippery mud to the outer gate. A taxi waited on the far side of the road, exhaust smoking; as I approached, a tall bearded figure, carrying a rucksack, emerged into the rain. Terry, surely—recognisable, in essence, from the crayon sketch taped to Wish's bedroom wall. He signed a one-handed hello, then dropped his rucksack to the ground, freeing his other arm, and finger-spelt his name: T-E-R-R-Y.

He wasn't deaf. It would have been far easier and quicker to speak the word, especially standing in the rain, but perhaps he wanted to prove something. I stepped closer, sharing the umbrella.

His hands moved again. 'Your name Sweet-Tooth?'

The attempted familiarity irritated me, but his use of Sign irritated me more—an attempt to establish a professional intimacy which had not been earnt. There seemed a selfishness in it, a self-absorption. He had flown from Melbourne for Wish, but was more interested in impressing me with his grasp of Sign than asking how she was. I watched his hands, critically. He was self-taught, clearly, his signing cluttered with ingrained bad habits. The hint of a beginner's course of Auslan, half-digested, could also be detected. His movements were slow, with too much emphasis on finger-spelling; there was no flow. The same mispronunciations and errors of grammar I had corrected in Wish some months before were evident even in those first greetings.

'Let's get out of the rain,' I said aloud. 'You take the brolly.'

He waved it away. 'No point in both of us getting wet.'

He shouldered his rucksack and strode, lopsided, ahead of me across the mud and through the inner gate into the trees. His soaked shirt clung to his bony back; a rat-tail of long wet hair hung behind his head, stiff and shining, like a length of electric flex. When we reached the verandah he dumped his rucksack and shook himself in the manner of a wet dog.

'Wish—how?' he finally asked, in Sign.

The choice of medium still seemed more important to him than the message.

'I think she has a fever,' I said aloud.

Further sign-language seemed beyond him; he reverted to speech. 'What does Stella think?'

'She doesn't think it's serious.'

Stella's voice carried to us, vaguely, from upstairs, a book-reading monotone. We climbed the stairs to find the door open, and Stella sitting in a bedside chair, reading to Wish, reading at her *back*, trying without success to rouse her from her torpor.

Terry walked to Stella's side and squeezed her shoulder. He stared silently at Wish for some time, at her hacked head of hair and damaged back. He managed to hide any distress he felt. Water dripped from his hair; Stella rose and left the room, returning with a towel; he rubbed his wet head, gratefully, squeezing his rat-tail in a milking fashion.

'You need to get out of those clothes, Terry.'

'I'm fine.'

His first words in Wish's hearing; she lifted her head slightly at the sound—then returned it to the pillow, still facing the wall, determined not to acknowledge our presence.

Terry watched her intently. 'If you don't mind I'd like to be alone with her. It's been a while, we need to get reacquainted.'

Stella's eyes met mine, I reluctantly followed her out. Terry closed the door behind us; excluded, we retreated downstairs. Stella uncorked a bottle of wine and we sat at the kitchen bench, sipping, saying little. Her three dogs flattened themselves against the floor at her feet, staring up, not taking their eyes from her face, alert to her unease. Rain fell steadily, cigarette butts accumulated, the big hand of the kitchen clock counted out the minutes, in small jerks, inexorably. Thirty, at least, had passed and Stella had uncorked a second bottle, before Terry descended with news.

'She held my hand.'

Stella's relief was brief, subsumed by other concerns. 'Did she sign to you? Did she say what's troubling her?'

He shook his head. 'I think she just wants to be left alone.'

He sank into an armchair; I joined Stella on the couch opposite, waiting for more information.

'In retrospect I think it was a mistake for me to fly over.'

'What do you mean?'

'I mean we're making a mountain out of a molehill, Stella. What happened, after all? Wish tried to change her appearance—tried to make herself more human.'

'She *mutilated* herself.'

A smile fought its way out through his beard. 'Hardly. Let's keep it in perspective. The hair will grow back.'

His low-key approach, eroding the mountain back into a molehill, had a calming effect on Stella; his professional assurances—as zoologist, primatologist—clearly carried more weight than mine. Her dogs, sensitive to human body language, also relaxed. Binky struggled to her feet, waddled to her water bowl and lapped, briefly.

Terry's voice murmured on, soothingly, a resonant bass, surprising in one so thin and flat-chested. 'She just wants to fit in. I suppose you could even argue that it's reassuring. She obviously thinks deeply about who she is, and where she belongs. I've seen similar behaviour in other orphan apes.'

I was beginning, despite myself, to warm to him. His English was far more fluent, and less pretentious, than his Sign.

Stella quibbled: 'Even apes brought up in human families?'

'*Especially* apes brought up in human families. And perhaps especially apes with enhanced intelligence.'

I almost let this pass; said matter-of-factly, in that soothing tone of voice, it didn't obtrude. Stella's stifled half-glance in my direction alerted me.

'I don't follow. What do you mean, enhanced intelligence?'

Terry glanced towards Stella, surprised. 'He doesn't know?'

'Clive thought it best—given the legal situation. The *ill*egal situation.' She turned my way and placed her hand over her heart.

'I'm sorry, J.J.—believe me, we were going to tell you. But you must have had an inkling. You've said yourself,

Wish is *much* smarter than the Washoes and Kokoes of the world. And she looks different.'

'What *are* you talking about?'

'I'm talking about why Wish is such a special—person.'

I sat, suspended in ignorance, more curious than annoyed. The wine had loosened Stella's tongue; even if Terry hadn't leaked a hint, she would have told me sooner or later.

'Wish is smarter than the average ape, J.J.'

I watched her, uncomprehending. She added, realising that she hadn't made herself clear: 'She has been *given* a bigger brain.'

The words were breathtaking, heart-stopping, the shock of a first plunge into a frigid sea. My startled hands moved in time with my mouth, saying the first thing that came into my head, a Claw Hand cauliflower-brain at the temple. 'She hasn't got a *human* brain?'

Terry, mildly amused, shook his head. 'We can't transplant brains yet, John.'

We? There was something boastful in his use of the first-person plural pronoun, arrogating the miracles of science to himself. I felt myself harden a little towards him again.

They both watched me; it seemed I was required to keep guessing. 'Genetic engineering?'

'Something much simpler. We remove the embryonic adrenal glands, *in utero*.'

'You operate on a gorilla foetus?'

He nodded; I pressed on. 'I don't follow. How does that affect the brain?'

'The theory is a little skimpy. It works—we're not entirely sure why. You possibly know that the adrenal glands produce cortisone. Hormones. It would seem—I stress seem—that these hormones are involved in switching off the growth of the infant brain. The early work was done on rats—take out their adrenal glands, their brain cells proliferate.'

'Don't tell me, they can run a maze more quickly?'

His eyes widened, surprised and impressed; perhaps I had shaded my sarcasm too subtly. 'You've read the early work, J.J.? Rachel Yehuda, the University of Massachusetts?'

Stella intervened: 'I think J.J. was joking, Terry.'

His tone turned cautious. 'The laboratory rats *did* solve problems more easily. The rat cortex, at post-mortem, was found to have grown bigger, more dense with cells.'

'It's a big jump from rats to gorillas.'

'We duplicated Yehuda's work with smaller primates first. *Rhesus macaques.* We have some pretty smart monkeys in Melbourne.'

Once again, there was an odd relish, or pride, in his tone. No vegetarian, this, surely. A protégé of Clive's, perhaps, but no Animal Libber. So why exactly had he rescued Wish from the laboratory? He ploughed on, in lecture-mode, his resonant voice filling the room.

'Human brains and gorilla brains are comparable in size in the embryonic stage. The difference is that a child's brain keeps growing after birth, a gorilla's stops. Remove the adrenal glands, it doesn't. The brain continues to grow—much as a human child's brain continues to grow through the first years of life.'

Wish was temporarily forgotten; I found myself side-tracked by absurd particulars. 'But if the brain continues to grow, how does it fit inside the skull?'

'Increased density, in part. The skull capacity is there. The brain-cases of humans are often no bigger than the average gorilla.'

Stella, calmer now, fortified by more wine, managed a weak joke. 'It's not how big it is, J.J.'

'Of course it's not *just* density,' Terry said. 'As the brain grew, we found the skull also grew—responded to the pressure. Wish *has* got a bigger head. Higher brow.'

'I thought it was just a juvenile head.'

Terry shook his own head. 'She has an IQ of 110 on the Stanford-Binet.' He added, unnecessarily: 'Well above the human average.'

This was all too sudden to assimilate. I said: 'There must be problems.'

The faint pride in his voice vanished. I had reminded him of the seriousness of the issues, or perhaps reminded him of a different source of pride: that it was he who had stolen—rescued—Wish.

'There are technical problems. The animals can't survive without replacement medication. A daily dose of corticosteroids. They have sacrificed a lot of animals in Melbourne.'

They? Could We so easily vanish, without responsibility, or apology?

'Shit! With all the fuss I forgot her medication.' Stella jerked up out of her seat and headed for the stairs.

I was pleased to see her leave; I felt I could criticise Terry, a guest in her house, more easily behind her back.

290

'What was it all *for?*'

The question seemed painful; his tone of voice became less resonant. 'Pure research, originally. But we live in the real world—a world of compromise. Money was needed.'

By whom, I wanted to ask: You or They? *Money was needed.* Here was a third category of grammatical responsibility, a sentence free of human agency completely, the buck stopping nowhere, batted between transitive verbs and disappearing subjects.

'The money came with strings attached. The goal was to produce primates that could perform a range of intelligent tasks.'

I saw it, suddenly, through his fog of euphemisms. 'Slaves for the assembly line! You bastards.'

'Hey, don't shoot the messenger, Sweet-Tooth. I'm on your side. What do you think I'm doing here?'

We watched each other for a moment; he finally averted his eyes.

'Sweet-Tooth is a family name,' I told him coldly.

The extended family of the Deaf, perhaps—but excluding him.

He shrugged, taking the rebuke in stride. 'There *is* an argument for such animals, John, even if it's not a particularly good one. You can't get humans to do certain jobs anymore. Domestic help, for instance. Look around you; we've educated ourselves out of the workforce.'

He was speaking generally, intending no irony, but I couldn't help glancing over the cluttered squalor of that living room; the books and papers heaped on the floor, the unwashed coffee mugs and wineglasses and dog-bowls, the discarded shoes.

'We can't all be brain surgeons and film directors, maybe, but we won't spot-weld on an assembly line anymore. We think the world owes us a living—plus happiness, fulfilment, a career path...At least that's the theory.'

He tried once again to distance himself from the notion, but this part of it—the theory—obviously appealed to him. I wondered again when he had first turned against his own project.

'What happened after Wish vanished? There must have been a witch-hunt.'

'The shit hit the fan for a few weeks. But apparently I was a citizen above suspicion.'

'Gee, I wonder why.'

This time my sarcasm found its mark, too easily. His eyes slid away from mine again, he smiled, wistfully. 'I stayed with the project. It seemed best to work on the inside. They managed to get hold of some gibbons. Siamangs. I can live with that—it's a matter of damage control. A pragmatic decision. I'm only a small cog in the machine, John. I do some of the surgery. If I don't do the work, someone else will.'

Once again my hands moved with an urgency of their own, saying the same thing as my mouth. 'That's bullshit.'

He looked me directly in the eye. 'Maybe. I wouldn't tell Stella this, let alone Clive, but half my life is bound up in this project. It's asking too much to throw that away.'

Logic had failed to convince me, now he was trying to woo me with intimacy. Sensing only hostility in return, he came back to more general arguments: 'I still *believe* in it—it's important work. Think of the implications for human intelligence. These issues are always more complex than they seem to outsiders.'

All of which still didn't explain his rescue of Wish. I took an inspired guess: 'But you got emotionally attached to one animal?'

He smiled weakly, caught out. I felt a small surge of sympathy; for the first time I had a handle on his confusion. Sentimentality, not moral principle, was his guide.

'They wanted frozen sections of her brain,' he said. 'I couldn't possibly agree to that.'

Other apes, yes, gibbons, *rhesus macaques*—but not his favourite. Stella returned before I could put the question. She seemed fraught.

'She won't take her cortisone. She threw it all against the wall.'

Terry's tone of voice was warm, buttery, calming. 'That might be a good sign. She's reacting again.'

'She's communicating,' I said. 'It's a well-known Auslan sign.'

He obligingly asked the obvious: 'What does it mean?'

'It means I don't want to take my medicine.'

He chuckled; even Stella managed a small smile.

'I'd better go back up,' Stella said.

Terry shook his head. 'I think you should give her time. She's an adolescent—a teenager, in human years. She doesn't want her mother prying in her room. She needs a little headspace.'

'I'll take her some food.'

'Later. Relax, Stella.'

'No, I'll take it up now.'

'If you must, but I suggest you merely knock, and leave the tray outside the door.'

4

Stella carried down the tray an hour later; Wish's bowl was empty.

'Sign for—I'm feeling a bit better,' Terry joked.

His boots were elastic-sided, he eased each off with the toe of the opposite foot, and settled himself lengthways on the sofa. Stella began fishing vegetables from the fridge, whatever came to hand; I joined her behind the bench, peeling and chopping as she heated oil in a wok. The problems of the present receded somewhat; I was keen to hear more of Wish's early infancy. This made for problems of priority; Terry was as desperate for news of the previous months as I was for news of the previous years. A kind of tacit trade-off, or pattern of exchange, emerged. Tit-for-tat.

'I've been in phone contact with Clive and Stella of course. They've told me of her progress. I have to congratulate you, John—it's remarkable what you've achieved.'

'*She* deserves the congratulations. I can't recall a single human student of Sign with anything like her aptitude.'

Stella tossed a handful of chopped fresh chillies and garlic into the hissing oil; a pungent, eye-stinging aroma instantly filled the room. The world outside was wet and cold, the downstairs rooms unheated, but the smell of her cooking warmed and comforted me, nourished me even before the food it promised had arrived. The wine also helped. I answered Terry's questions freely and expansively, even set down my chopping knife to demonstrate a few of Wish's own sign-inventions. Later, as we ate, it was my turn to ask the questions. The first received a blunt answer.

'Her father was a test-tube of frozen sperm, John.'

'And her mother?'

'Dead.'

'Old age?'

He shook his head. 'Childbirth. They had to sacrifice the mother. Transverse arrest.'

I looked from the primatologist to the vet, puzzled.

'The head got stuck, J.J.,' she said.

'Couldn't you have used forceps? Or done a caesarean?'

Terry ignored the implications of 'you', a nuance I couldn't resist. 'Not my field of expertise. You have to understand, this was a new area for all of us.'

'I assumed you'd been working with primates for years.'

'Ordinary primates—yes. Not primates with extra neurones. The average gorilla neonate weighs a couple of kilos at most; they squeeze out with ease.'

Another clue to digest. 'Let me get this clear in my mind. The mother died because Wish's head was too *big* to squeeze out?'

'The price of intelligence, John. Man is the only species which experiences pain during childbirth.'

Stella reached across and rested her hand lightly on his. 'Woman,' she corrected.

There was something in that touch that alerted me; I began to watch for other signs of intimacy.

Terry said: 'A design fault, you might argue. Our brains have grown too big for our pelvic outlets.'

'Sounds like some kind of moral fable.'

Stella chimed in. 'It's already been written, J.J. It's called the Book of Genesis. Eve's punishment after eating from the tree of knowledge.'

I looked at her blankly, she intoned: '*I will greatly multiply your pain in childbearing; in pain you shall bring forth children...*'

Terry chuckled, and refilled her wineglass, encouraging her.

'Surely you must have known the baby had a big head,' I said.

'A caesarean *was* planned. The mother went into premature labour: it was suddenly too late. The head got stuck. The foetal monitors were going haywire—we...' there was a slight flicker in his gaze, a near-seamless correction '...*they* thought they might lose the baby. It came down to a simple choice, but everything happened in a hurry.'

'The dumb mother was sacrificed for the smart child?'

'Not deliberately. Fertile mature gorillas don't grow on trees.'

I opened my mouth to ask another question but he held up his hand, smiling.

'My turn, John. Fair's fair.'

I nodded, granting the point, reluctantly.

'Stella mentioned your experiments with music,' he said. 'I'd like to hear more.'

'She strummed my guitar a few times. I wouldn't call it an experiment...'

I sketched an outline of the guitar episode; Stella, more talkative as she drank more wine, coloured in the spaces. Later, still drinking steadily, she became suddenly less talkative, as if her blood alcohol had crossed some hair-trigger threshold from stimulation to sedation. After draining the last of the wine, she climbed the stairs, yawning, returning shortly with a pillow and folded quilt, and the news that our joint charge was sleeping peacefully.

'I'm for bed,' she said. She dumped the bedding on the couch, and turned to Terry. 'The sofa okay?'

'Fine. But I'm not tired. I'll sit up for a few minutes.'

I watched this transaction, eagle-eyed, but could detect no hidden messages, or invitations—no cues for me to make myself scarce. I also wanted to sit and talk a little more. The day had been spent rolling in a heavy surf of emotions and ideas; I was exhausted, but not unpleasantly, beached in a tranquil aftermath.

Stella seemed reluctant to leave us alone, unchaperoned, as if fearing that more secrets might be shared. She urged us both again in the direction of bed, but finally trudged up the stairs alone. I made no move to follow. Bed seemed impossibly distant, the reward at the end of a long journey strewn with Herculean tasks: the climbing of stairs, the removal of heavy clothing, the emptying of a bladder, the brushing of too many teeth. Water-music carried down to us; the gurgling of bathroom pipes of various pitch, amplified by the drumskin of the ceiling; then, after some minutes, silence.

We faced each other, sunk deeply in ersatz-leather armchairs. The room, walled by bookshelves, had a distinctly clubbish atmosphere in the half-darkness—if I had known where Stella kept the port I would have filled two glasses. I was drawn again to the question of Terry's motivation, his frank confession of amorality, a charge mitigated only partially by his admission of the lesser charge of sentimentality. He answered my questions, but briefly, wanting to take turns again, more interested in asking than answering.

'I've told you enough of my secrets, John. Perhaps it's time for you to tell me some of yours.'

My pulse lurched: did he suspect?

'Wish is in oestrus,' he said, bluntly. 'I could smell it as soon as I walked into the house.'

He waited; finally I said: 'I think you can guess.'

'I'd rather hear it from you.' His tone was neutral, uncritical—the tone, exactly, of his teacher and mentor, Clive.

'It's extremely embarrassing to talk about.'

'Try me.'

A hesitation, a deep inhalation. 'She...presented to me.'

The zoological term seemed safest; keeping the events in textbook discussion mode, positioning myself at a distance, less participant than observer. I restrained my hands, itching to provide illustrations.

Terry shrugged, unimpressed. 'Haven't you ever had your leg mounted by an aroused dog?'

'I'm afraid it was more than that. This was specific to *me*.'

'And you rebuffed her?'

'Of course!'

He watched me, sceptically. Had there been too much protest in my 'of course'? Was his eye trained at least partially by the study of Sign, made sensitive to the revelations of body language? His pronouncement came after several long seconds. 'It's happened before in primate institutions. It's no big deal. Think of it as—a student crush.'

'Is it normal for the student to shave off all her hair afterwards?'

He leant back in his chair, hands tucked behind his head. His pony-tail jutted between his clasped fingers, he toyed with it as he spoke, thinking aloud. 'A student crush is not the best analogy. Clive would tell me I'm thinking too much in human terms. It's probably more some sort of ritual thing—submission to the dominant male.'

I laughed, relieved. The notion was absurd.

'*I'm* the dominant male?'

'You *are* the biggest. No offence.'

'None taken.'

'You're the silverback in this troop, John.'

He grinned, taken with the idea. I tried to joke my way free. 'I know I've got a few grey hairs…'

'It's all a matter of size in the wild. Survival of the strongest genes. A female must always choose the strongest partner.'

'Somebody should tell my ex-wife.'

Now I was getting close to secrets, to True Confessions— but he wasn't listening, wasn't remotely interested in Life-Before-Wish. He was already following another train of thought. 'Adolescence is hard enough for humans—trying to reconcile thinking and feeling. Instinct versus social constraint. Imagine what it's like for Wish—with a whole different set of instincts.'

'What are you saying? Apes will be apes?'

'The interesting thing about Wish presenting to you,' he said, 'is that gorillas are not a tournament species.'

'What do you mean?'

A look half-mischievous, half-curious was written on his face. 'Gorillas mate for life, John. The silverback has several females in his harem, but they are his and his alone. The males are not all in competition for one female, which is what I mean by a tournament species. Female gorillas are not promiscuous—like, say, chimps. Or humans.'

He smiled again.

'I still don't follow.'

'If Wish has decided on you she may be heading for spinsterhood.'

I was silenced, half-convinced; he pressed on: 'It might be best if you kept your distance, just for the time being. And maybe we should suspend your lessons.'

Antagonism, dormant since earlier in the day, flared in me again. 'You want to suspend the teacher?'

'We have to think this through very carefully. I was a little flippant at first—but it does have ramifications.'

'*I'll* need to think it through,' I said. 'The project means a lot to me.'

Wish means a lot to me, I wanted to say—but perhaps I had said it, implicitly.

'Fine,' he said. 'I'm just an outsider now, looking in. I realise it would be a big sacrifice if you left the project. But we wouldn't want this situation to get out of hand.'

I looked across the small room at him, his hands clasped behind his head, flipping his pony-tail up and down. It seemed he could read my thoughts.

'Goodnight,' he signed, then added in slow finger-spelling, a wry smile on his face: 'S-I-L-V-E-R-B-A-C-K.'

I retreated into teacher-mode, showing him the quick way, the sign for 'silver'—an elaborate ornamentation of the letter 's' followed by a simple pat on the back. My own broad back.

Silverback. I repressed the deeper implications; there was something in the nickname that I liked, some implication of greybeard wisdom that appealed to vain parts of me.

'Think of it as a kind of title,' Terry said. 'Like Duke. Or King.'

So much for wisdom. As I mounted the stairs to bed this last word resonated in my mind, mockingly: King of the Apes.

5

Not even the most fluent hands could properly describe the events of the night that followed. As for words, I can only promise this: not to gloss over those events or smother them with euphemisms. What follows is central to this story—what follows *is* the story, in essence.

I lay in my bed, brooding. Terry's words faded from notice, I could think of nothing but Wish, lying in the next room. Was she sleeping, as Stella had claimed? Her proximity excited me against my will; I felt again the tremble of arousal.

I rose and tugged on my wetsuit, refusing to accept the physiological fact. Shouldering my flippers, I tiptoed down the stairs. Terry was audible if not visible—a vague pale bundle on the couch, purring rhythmically. I slipped out of the house and through the trees. Three horses were drinking from the edges of the dam, they scattered before the lumbering creature that appeared from the trees, clad in black rubber, heading for the lagoon. I waded through the shallows with difficulty, my flippers retarded by the suck of soft mud; finally I was out of my depth, floating freely. Freshwater is less buoyant than brine; I floated, sunk to my top lip, breathing with difficulty, my nostrils barely millimetres above the mirror-smooth surface. The frigid water shrank my half-erection, but my thoughts remained aroused. With that name Silverback—that title—went certain duties, I argued with, and against, myself. Wish was, finally, my responsibility. We shared more than language; we also shared the nearest thing to a natural relationship in her life. It was to me that she must finally turn for advice, and leadership.

Not to mention love.

Swimming failed to relax me, there was something too yielding and unsupportive about the water. I waded from the dam after half an hour, leaving my right flipper stuck fast in the sludge, irretrievable. I sluiced my muddy feet beneath the garden hose, hung my wetsuit over the verandah rail, and sneaked into the house, shivering. The rhythm of Terry's breathing didn't falter as I crept upstairs. Stella's door was shut; I towelled myself dry, pulled on a loose tracksuit, then unlocked and pushed open the door to Wish's room. She was sleeping on her stomach, head facing the wall, arms folded beneath, haunches raised. Clive believed that her rhythms should be attuned to the natural cycle of light and dark; her windows were curtain-less, her black-crepe skin silvered by moonlight. She had become a silverback herself, at least until the moon set. Her smell—that familiar sweet rankness—grew overwhelming as I approached.

As I knelt at the side of her bed she turned her head abruptly to face me, startling me; she had not been sleeping. Her broad head watched, waiting; it was my turn to act—to prove something.

'Me sad. Come back. I miss you.'

Words, or signs, were not enough, it seemed. She turned her head back to the wall.

I reached out tentatively, and lightly stroked the dark scabbed mound of her shoulder; she shrugged off my hand, effortlessly.

It occurred to me that she was still embarrassed by her hairlessness—her nakedness. I stood and peeled off my tracksuit top, then my pants, balancing with difficulty on one foot, trying to pull off my jocks, feeling suddenly ridiculous. She turned her head again at the sound of my struggle in moonlight, and this time did not turn away. I stood bathed in moonlight; her eyes travelled over my naked body, pausing here and there, curiosity overcoming reticence. After a few moments she reached up a long arm and lightly brushed the hair on my chest. She seemed reassured to find a different kind of human surface, a surface that had more in common with hers, if only a few token body hairs. She gripped my shoulder and looked directly at me; I felt a rush of love.

She shifted her haunches a little, raised them higher, and a gust of her smell came to me; not her usual asparagus-musk, but the raw smell of heat, a hot universal woman-smell. I began to harden again. Her eyes left mine, moving down to watch this strange growth. This time I didn't turn away. I stood by the bed, facing the curtainless window, clothed only in moonlight, fully aroused. I felt, for once in my life, beautiful: a giant of a man, a human silverback, in full sexual rut.

6

A childhood memory: emerging from bed one morning to find my parents huddled at the breakfast table, heads together, chortling over some newspaper article. I pushed my own head between theirs, curious, but my father quickly turned the page, and changed the subject. The newspaper vanished after breakfast and was never seen again—'Sorry, Sweet-Tooth—wrap rubbish.'

I bought a copy from the newsagent en route to school, and spent the morning sitting in the sand on a windy beach, searching those big, fluttering pages for clues. I found only a brief mention of a court case involving a lonely farmer and his favourite ewe. It seemed more pitiful than obscene. The ewe had not been his first. He complained that he had been 'widowed' several times. Surely, he argued, the laws of bestiality should take this into account—the fate of all those who choose short-lived animals as their lovers. Multiple bereavement, he seemed to be arguing, was punishment enough. Years later, in the pages of some trashy men's magazine, flipped through in a barbershop, I read of another case. This time the gender roles were reversed, female stripper and male Great Dane. The tone of both reports was more amused than serious—which is, Clive would surely argue, unfair to the animals. They are as much victims as any human victim, a crime against them is as serious as any human crime.

I lay down on the bed and wrapped my arms about Wish, but awkwardly, trying to keep the lower half of my body out of actual contact. She rolled suddenly onto her back and pulled me on top of her, the force of her great arms gentle, but irresistible. For the first time our lower halves came in contact, which meant the end of my resistance. I wanted suddenly to be inside her—not because of the thrill of a forbidden sexual act, but simply because I loved her. And yet somehow I couldn't enter her in that position; our limbs did not seem to fit together, our body shapes were mismatched.

Perhaps it was my ineptitude; perhaps it had been too long. With Jill such hesitations would have caused instant deflation, but here, glowing with the warmth of Wish's presence, her scent of her arousal filling my nose, I remained hard. She rolled onto her stomach again, raising her hindquarters.

The English word is 'to mount', ugly, loveless—veterinarian. 'To cover', likewise. Even Sign offers no help. I was slitting my throat certainly—but the shape is imprecise, non-specific. I need to be *exact*. The various permutations of the sexual act in Auslan are merely two-handed mimes of whatever position is used. The left hand plays the part

308

of one partner, the right hand the other. Index and middle-finger become a pair of legs, the left hand can 'mount' the right from behind, or face to face, or inverted head between legs. A beautiful language at times, certainly; at others, blunt and economical. Modifications of position, speed, and tension can add further nuances—but here I can illustrate only the bare mechanics.

Afterwards she turned to face me, we lay in the bright moonlight holding each other. The Deaf will sometimes shape a one-handed sign using both hands as an added emphasis, a kind of shout, in stereo. As we lay on the bed Wish went further, gently lifting her two feet—those longer, flatter hands—into the Signing Space between us. All four Flat Hands moved outward in turn from her chin, folding into the you-shapes of the Point Hand.

Thank you. Thank you, thank you, thank you.

I watched, stunned—*deafened*—as those four limbs moved repeatedly and silently in the moonlit room. I had seen nothing like it before: an expression of love and gratitude, bizarre and thrilling. The stirrings of guilt were stilled, temporarily. Her four hands, waving like those of some dark Hindu goddess, seemed at that moment the most beautiful thing I had ever seen.

7

I lay with her, cradling her, till her rapid breathing slowed into the rhythms of sleep, then slipped off the bed and out of her room. I should have spent the night with her, my limbs tangled in hers, loving her in the wider sense—but I felt I needed to be alone, to examine my feelings, increasingly dissonant. I still felt, in part, exultant—but a residue of other, messier feelings remained. Given four hands, each would surely have signed a different emotion: joy and gratitude, yes—but also guilt and shame.

Sign does not separate this last pair; for once, the discrimination of English is superior. But having named them, which is worse? Guilt or shame? The inability to face ourselves, or to face others? Self-contempt, or the contempt of the world?

Other body parts also still had things to say. Back in my own bed I found myself aroused again, surprisingly.

My skin tingled as if with some static sexual charge, the bedsheets clung to my body, adherent, magnetised. Years had passed since I had felt such rapture.

I rose and shut my bedroom door, if only to keep out whatever subliminal woman-scent might still be wafting from her room, then stood at the window, staring out. The dam glinted, moonlit, through the trees; I pulled open the door again, and tiptoed downstairs. Terry was still asleep on the couch, wrapped in the quilt, oblivious. Stella's cigarettes sat on the coffee table; I pocketed the pack and her disposable lighter. My wetsuit was draped on the verandah rail; for the second time that night I pulled it on, never an easy task when damp. I hurried through the trees and waded into the water barefoot, holding a single lit cigarette high above my head. And there I floated, smoking, my legs slowly pedalling.

Neither water nor nicotine could soothe me, and the tight pressure of the wetsuit only seemed to heighten my excitement. I tried to summon images that might provide an antidote: memories of lovemaking with Jill, human fashion, face to face. It seemed a useful test, a measure of the present against the past. I had treasured these memories of Jill once. I had loved the way lust changed her expression completely, her calm, cool face became the mask of someone else, someone far more—ugly. I loved the way her dimples and laugh-lines vanished, her wide smile narrowed into a painful hole, her face became first humourless, then distorted.

At first, I was in awe of these changes. And flattered. I felt that I was special, that the two of us were special

311

together. As time passed, I began to wonder if it was merely Jill who was special, if perhaps I didn't even need to *be* there. All too quickly she reached a point where she was on her own, her eyes turning upwards and inwards, her shudders synchronised to the beat of a deeper, slower pacemaker, unrelated to mine.

Towards the end of our marriage these changes merely left me feeling alone. Familiarity breeds contempt? It was more than that, surely. I lost Jill each night just when we should have been closest; for a few moments only, perhaps, but enough to leave me dissatisfied as she slowly returned from whichever zone of bliss she had been to, alone, without me.

Those images from the past had long lost their power to stir me. Jill certainly provided no protection from the immediate presence of Wish.

Our encounter had not been over-successful, physically. Yet the realisation was growing inside me: there had been more intimacy, more love, in that brief 'mounting', than in the numerous prolonged occasions on which Jill and I had made so-called love.

A realisation: my deepest need was for tenderness, for intimacy. Stella's drunken words from the previous night came back to me, powerfully: *It's only sex, J.J.—it's not as if I want to kiss you.* They might have been spoken equally by Jill.

As I floated in the cold muddy water my guilt vanished. As for shame: did I care for the opinion of others? I waded out and strode back through the trees and into the house, willing to look anyone in the eye.

312

Wish was either already awake, or woke at my entry; she assumed that same position of natural submission, or invitation. I peeled off my wetsuit and mounted her immediately, as if it were the most natural thing in the world. I came immediately, with more relief than pleasure, and toppled sideways and lay against her rough back.

We nestled together like broad tablespoons. Nothing specific needed to be said, or shaped. Her long arm reached behind her, clasping me gently to her, the glow of her shaved body returned my own warmth, magnified, her sweet musk filled my nostrils.

I had intended to return to my room before dawn, but I slept the sleep of the contented, the deep dreamless sleep of a sated lover. Her huge presence blanketed me, quilted me, sealed me from contact with the outside world.

I slept through the buzz of the gate intercom, just after dawn. I failed to hear the footsteps which mounted the stairs, slowly and sedately, shortly after.

I woke, squinting, against a dazzle of light. Clive was standing in the doorway, his hand frozen on the light switch, staring in, amazed. For a moment there was silence, then Stella appeared behind him, less amazed than enraged.

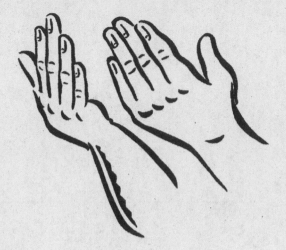

BOOK

FOUR

1

If Terry had switched on the light that morning, he might have merely switched it off and returned to bed. If Clive's flight from America had been delayed, Stella might have slept soundly till mid-morning, I might have crept back to my own bed before she woke.

If.

The word is less a shape in Sign than an intonation: a raised eyebrow, a shrugged shoulder, a tilt of the head. An accompaniment. Sign subjunctive offers the Good Hand shape for 'pretend' as an added emphasis. *Pretend* Terry discovered us, then perhaps...

The time for pretending, for the make-believe of ifs and buts and might-bes, was past. I pulled on the nearest clothes in my bedroom as an argument raged downstairs. Rain was beating against the roof, drowning the sense of that argument. Only the general melody, the gusts of pro and con, carried to me. I could hear Stella's raised voice, the steady background murmur of Clive's, Terry's occasional intercessions.

To run the gauntlet of those voices—Stella's sandpaper rasp especially—was beyond me. I crept from my room and tried Wish's door; it was locked, the key nowhere in sight. I sank to the floor, leaning against the door, and tried to speak to her through that inch of wood. Unable to use Sign, I could only murmur, reassuringly. That she was listening I was certain; I could sense the pressure of her weight against the far side of the door, opposing and returning mine.

Time passed. Rain fell. The murmuring of voices downstairs stopped, started, then stopped again. Mid-morning, footsteps mounted the stairs, a slow metronome tread that preceded the appearance of Clive. He stood for a moment above me, then folded himself onto the floor opposite, his thin mantis-legs bent about him.

'Stella can't bring herself to speak to you at present, J.J.'

He spoke without rancour or recrimination.

'Hell hath no fury,' I murmured.

No reaction. The slander, as transparent I would have thought as any sign-mime, went not so much over his head as beneath his notice, too trivial to acknowledge.

'Well,' he finally said, 'what a mess.'

He clasped his knees to his chest. He seemed in some discomfort, an elderly man with stiff joints trying too hard to be informal. Despite my predicament, I felt a small surge of pity. The ginger toupée and white running shoes enclosed his body at each end like parentheses, as if to protect what they contained from the ravages of time—but the wig was slightly askew, and one of the shoes unlaced. He was showing his age, the years were leaking through, not to be denied.

'I want the key, Clive. We have a lesson today.'

'You can't seriously expect to go on teaching her.'

'Why not?'

He looked away and back, considering.

'There would seem to be several ethical reasons. First, you have exploited a student for your own sexual pleasure.'

This sounded half-hearted; a quote from a campus behaviour manual.

'*She* presented to *me*.'

'A moot point. You would argue that she gave consent?'

Only Clive could sit on a floor and discuss such matters, at zero degrees emotional weather, in the aftermath of that morning. His academic steadiness might have offered a life-line, a buffer against the high feelings downstairs, but part of me wanted to reject that lifeline on the grounds of inhumanity. He reminded me too much of Jill, of her irritating insistence on the power of words, and discussion, to 'work' things through. I almost preferred to take my chances with the unpredictable Stella downstairs. Hypocrisy, at least, was human.

'I would have thought that presenting her swollen vulva was a sign of consent in any language.'

I sought to shock him, to jolt out of him what he felt, not what he thought. He merely shrugged.

I tried harder. 'If she is entitled to human rights, those rights should, I would have thought, include the right to *fuck*.'

319

He opened his mouth to speak, then turned towards the stairs, distracted by a raised voice. Somewhere below us Terry was trying to restrain, or comfort, Stella. The interruption derailed Clive's train of thought; instead of addressing the point, he moved on to another.

'Secondly, there is the question of her age. As Stella points out—she *is* a minor. At least in legal terms.'

'She is fully mature. And Stella is jealous.'

He looked at me, surprised; I told him, abruptly, bluntly: 'We went to bed while you were away.'

If his thoughts were ruffled, he disguised it well. 'Stella occasionally goes to bed with other friends while I'm away. It's an arrangement we have.'

'Bullshit.'

He was staring past me now, unfocused.

'Adultery is written in our genes, J.J. It's nothing to become unduly concerned about. Remind me to show you the statistics sometime. There are some nice mathematical models using game theory. What the sociobiologists call pursuing a mixed reproductive strategy.'

'We're not talking game theory. We're talking about Stella.'

His gaze returned to me. 'I'm not the possessive type, J.J. And I'm not a young man. It's perfectly natural that her appetites don't entirely coincide with mine.'

His tone was benevolent, paternal—irritatingly *helpful*.

'I came to terms with this some time back. One of the mercies of old age, J.J.—to be freed from the dictates of your balls.'

He smiled slightly, amused by the sound of the unchar-acteristic word in his mouth.

'Perhaps you should try monkey glands injections.'

'Sarcasm doesn't become you, J.J. I'm truly thankful for the serenity of age.'

'Is that why you wear a wig?'

His smile widened, acknowledging the point. 'My halo is slipping?' he said, and stirred his forefinger vaguely above his head.

I waited, impassively; his smile faded.

'No one's perfect, J.J.—but I suspect that sainthood is less of a struggle in old age. The emotions loosen their grip—we operate on a narrower bandwidth. Perhaps the alleged wisdom of the old is nothing more than that—the mind finally shaking free of the flesh.'

Reason without emotion. His own continued to provoke me. 'Then you understand that Wish might have similar needs.'

'Perhaps. I don't judge you, J.J. I wouldn't dream of judging you.'

He added his own sign shape, two Cup Hands, palms up, balancing each other, a weighing of judgement.

This also irritated me, as if he were speaking down to me, offering pidgin Sign as if that were the only way he could make himself understood.

'Well, I judge you! I think you're a fucking *machine*!'

Did I speak the insult, or speechless, only sign it? I cant remember; certainly my hands moved, with or without my redundant tongue. Machine: two Spread Hands, a furious meshing of cogs.

His tone remained mild: 'I suggest we discuss these matters later, J.J. When the dust has settled. For now, it might be best for all concerned if you left.'

The pressure of weight against the far side of the door shifted slightly, a barely perceptible bulge, a shutting of the tiny air-gap between door and frame.

'I refuse to leave until I've seen Wish.'

'I think that would create too many difficulties.'

'She must be very upset. She needs to see me.'

'We're quite capable of looking after Wish. Terry is here. His ties with her antedate yours.'

I sat, pressed against the door, impervious to reason. He sounded like a lawyer. He unfolded his uncomfortable stick-legs, and rose from the floor:

'I'm sorry, J.J.—I can't permit you to stay. We all need time to think. Stella is very upset. She wants to involve the police. If you won't leave voluntarily I can see no other course.'

'It's raining,' I said, absurdly.

'You can take the umbrella.'

2

My parents' house was empty. I fell onto my bed, face-down. Outside the rain fell steadily and soothingly, a percussion played on the tin roof with soft brushes. Its music reminded me of the tranquillising power of immersion, the curative powers of taking the waters. I rose, dug my second-skin from my bag, rolled it on, and headed outside. The cold rain on my face was less tranquillising than invigorating. The surface of the sea seemed flattened, made smooth, by the pressure of falling water. After wading beyond my depth I was lost; visibility shrank within arms' length, a rain-dimpled foreground against a background of featureless grey. I floated aimlessly, encased and insulated. Frigid rain thumped against my head but the sensation was not unpleasant; a sensation, more importantly, that drove out other sensations, that was a kind of forgetfulness.

When the rain thinned I found that I had drifted no distance at all; the world that reformed was identical to the world I had left. Nothing was missing. The doll's house faced me from the esplanade, exactly abreast; even the blurred outline of the Hills was emerging from behind a further, more distant, veil of rain.

I clambered up the beach steps to find my mother in the kitchen, unpacking a small bag of groceries. If she was surprised to see me back from my new home in the Hills so soon, she managed to hide it. Or perhaps her surprise was merely swamped by the usual maternal concern. The day was cold, I was soaked and dripping.

'You crazy,' she signed, Point Hand version.

'For swim—perfect,' I signed, an emphatic Okay Hand. 'You catch cold.'

'Warm inside,' I signed, then added, teasing: 'You borrow wetsuit?'

Literally, wet-clothes. She laughed, a brief, raucous explosion. Having won her over, I asked the question that needed to be asked.

'I come home?'

'This home or that other home?'

Despite this reminder that she was not to be taken for granted, her expression was playful, I knew that I had a place to sleep. My father might object, but she would handle that. She plucked a thin sheet of fax paper from beneath a fridge-magnet and handed it to me.

'From J. She know you move out?'

'I plan to tell Sunday next. Now need-not.'

Ring me—Jill. I propped the fax by the phone; I would ring later. First things first. I peeled off my wetsuit in the bathroom and stepped into the shower cubicle, turning my face upwards against the gush of steam and water. The shower is another kind of immersion, different, but complementary; the massage of its high-pressure fingers also offers a temporary amnesia. The sound of tapping on the foggy glass roused me after some minutes. I slid open the door, my mother's V-hand appeared through the escaping steam. 'Visitor.'

Her grim expression alerted me: grave concern.

'Who?'

'Police,' she signed, simply: right hand gripping left wrist, a handcuffing mime.

3

I wasn't handcuffed. Nor did the two police officers sitting politely in the living room fit the vernacular sign, common among the younger Deaf: the Fist Hand snout. Introductions were brief: Detective Sergeant Crilly, a big middle-aged man wearing a bored expression on a blunted boxer's face, and Detective Senior Constable Vogel, a young sharp-faced woman in a skirt and business jacket, with a pocket full of pens. Vogel, the junior partner, was carrying a radio handset, a clipboard, and a thick torch that looked more like a baton; Crilly's hands were free, a privilege of rank, perhaps.

He informed me that, acting on 'information received', he needed to ask me certain questions. His tone was world-weary, a been-there-done-that tone. He glanced briefly towards my mother, hovering at the edges of our conversation, and suggested that it might help his inquiries if I would agree to accompany him to Headquarters.

'Am I under arrest?'

'No—but we have a lot of ground to cover, sir. It might be best to do that in privacy.'

My mother signed: 'What wrong?'

'Nothing,' I signed back, an emphatic Okay Hand zero. It failed to reassure her. I repeated the sign, with variations. 'Routine.' 'Police need help'—'help' being a taking-of-the-arm mime, as if to help the police across a busy street, an irony that might have made her laugh in any other context.

Vogel watched our fluttering hands, curiously. Even Crilly raised an eyebrow, willing to be diverted from the day's tedium. I repeated the signs, several times, as my mother followed us outside.

'Back soon,' I signed. 'Worry-not.'

Literally 'think-too-much-not'. Sitting alone in the back seat of the car I couldn't avoid a surfeit of thinking. I stared unfocused from the window. Information received? From whom? And where was Wish, what was *she* thinking? Vogel drove, upright and prim, her jacket neatly suspended from a coat-hanger at my shoulder. Crilly sat with his seat reclined, his elbow jutting illegally from the open window, a big man completely at ease. Twice he turned my way and winked, for no apparent reason. In the confines of the car I noticed for the first time that his broad face was flushed, his breath, on-duty, in the early afternoon, was winey.

We entered Police Headquarters on Angas Street from the back, hidden from public view by the high walls of the carpark. I was ushered up three flights of stairs and into a bare interview room—three chairs, a single table—and questioned, civilly enough, by my male-female tag-team. Neither shone a lamp in my face, neither offered me a cigarette. We talked for a few minutes, in generalities, giving nothing away; finally Crilly said: 'I am about to ask you some further questions relating to this matter. You do not have to answer any of these questions, however, if you do your answers may be taken down in writing and given in evidence in a court. Do you understand?'

The textbook warning, delivered in a textbook tone of voice.

Vogel left the room, returning with an ancient mechanical typewriter which she eased onto the table in front of her. From that point she typed my answers as I spoke.

I answered each question truthfully. There was no point in lying; Crilly claimed to have a signed statement from an unnamed 'eyewitness' and I didn't doubt it for a minute. I'd like to believe my frankness was more than that, however—due more to courage and conviction than coercion. I'd come to terms with my feelings for Wish; to deny the accusations was also surely to deny her, and to deny the depth of those feelings.

Was I deceiving myself? I don't think so; it seemed—still seems—an important distinction. The notion that I was acting with dignity sustained me through the burlesque of that interview. Crilly's expression became slightly less pained and more amused as time passed. He wasn't about to judge me; I had novelty value, if nothing else: a lonely fat man in love with a gorilla. Vogel was also amused, but it was an amused contempt. The questions she occasionally interjected as she typed seemed sharper than Crilly's, and more to the point; verbal tweezers, turning me this way and that.

Peeping out from time to time from behind both his amusement and her contempt was the same curious question: what was it *like*? The question was never put, baldly. Crilly would shift in his seat, his eyebrow would lift at a certain line of questioning. Vogel, crouched behind her huge clacking machine, hid her prurience even more obliquely, in the search for what she liked to call 'the facts of the case', the 'precise details'.

'A gentleman never tells,' Crilly murmured to her at one point, teasingly. Caught out, she buried her face in the typewriter.

Both showed far less interest in my teaching relationship with Wish. The fact that a gorilla had been taught to communicate with her hands was accepted without argument; it aroused no more curiosity than might the begging of a dog, or the speech of a parrot. This was due more to a low opinion of Sign, than to a high opinion of the intelligence of Wish. And due also to the fact that they were only half-listening to what I said; more amused with

330

themselves, finally, than with me. There was a lot of light-hearted flipping through of the statute book—a huge, green door-stop—trying to find the precise wording of an offence which was clearly a first for both.

'Crimes Act, Section 69,' Vogel announced. '"A person must not commit an act of bestiality. Penalty: imprisonment for five years."'

I murmured, unheard: 'She's not a beast, she's a person.'

'"An act of bestiality is any of the following: penetration of the vagina of an animal by the penis of a man; or penetration of the vagina of a woman by the penis of an animal; or buggery committed…"'

'Whoa,' Crilly said, 'run that last one past me again.'

'Buggery?'

'No, the woman bit.'

'Penetration of the vagina of a woman by the penis of an animal?'

He nodded. 'Funny wording. Who gets arrested—the woman, or Rin Tin Tin?'

For the first time he laughed out loud; Vogel managed a short, sharp smile.

I repeated, more loudly: 'She's not a beast. She's a person.'

I was serious; I also saw immediately that I would not be taken seriously. My lines were clown lines, whether I played them straight or bent. My role was cast: less pervert than buffoon.

Crilly said: 'This is not some kind of publicity stunt is it, big feller?'

'What do you mean?'

'This professor—the Animal Rights bloke. He used the same words. You in it together?'

'What *exactly* did he say?'

Vogel flipped through a notebook on the table. 'That we should charge you with unlawful carnal knowledge. Of a minor. That he would refuse to testify to a charge of bestiality.'

She glanced at her colleague, rolled her eyes upwards; he wearily shook his head from side to side, a connoisseur of human types. She flipped another page and read on. 'He says the law of bestiality is demeaning to animals. Animals should have the same protections—and rights—as humans.'

'He has a very logical mind,' I said.

'Tell me about it.'

Crilly added: 'He'll need it.'

'What do you mean?'

They glanced at each other; Vogel finally said: 'The Federal Police are throwing the book at him. And his wife. Vertebrate Pest Control Act. Quarantine Act. They're in more trouble than you are.'

'They've been arrested?'

'They're being questioned. Charges may follow. Illegal Animal Keeping.'

The news filled me with panic. If Clive and Stella had been arrested, *where was Wish?*

'Where's who?'

'The gorilla. That's her name. Wish. Where is she?'

'Can't help you there, big feller. But the Federal Police will want to take a statement from you. You can ask them.'

He stretched his arms, leant back in his chair. 'My guess— the RSPCA have her in safekeeping.'

Vogel said: 'The Act clearly states, Tom—she would have to be kept in an A-class zoo.'

I rose at this, unable to keep still. 'I really need to know where she is.'

'Sit down please, sir,' Vogel said, her tone more serious.

My hands were signing as I spoke, breaking imaginary shackles. 'I have to get *out* of here.'

Her own hand went to the handle of her torch, a heavy blunt instrument. 'I won't ask you again, sir.'

I forced myself to sit, restless and fidgety. 'When can I get out?'

'When': the Spread Hand wriggling its fingers against the cheek, an obscure sign I couldn't help repeating as I spoke, spastically. I must have looked as if I were having some sort of seizure.

Vogel watched me carefully. 'First you sign your statement.'

'That's all?'

'Then we charge you. Then we consider granting police bail.'

'What do you mean?'

'I mean you became visibly agitated during questioning. I don't want the responsibility if we release you tonight. A night in the watchhouse might cool you down.'

I was on my feet again. 'You don't understand! I *can't* stay!'

Vogel's hand went to the torch on the table again. 'For the last time, sir—*sit down*!'

I sat. She said, more reasonably: 'Your lawyer can apply for bail tomorrow. Magistrate's Court.'

'Then you cross your fingers,' Crilly said, and winked, reassuringly. I had provided an hour or two of entertainment, something out of the ordinary. I had helped him get through another morning—he was feeling more mellow.

'So what *am* I being charged with?'

He turned to his companion. 'Good question. What say you, Girl Wonder? Gross indecency?'

She reached again for the heavy statute book, riffled through a few pages, read for a moment, shook her small sharp head, and pushed the book across the table to Crilly, her finger pressed to some key passage.

'Has to be bestiality, Tom.'

'Five years jail?' I said.

Crilly shook his head. 'First offence—a slap over the wrist with a wet noodle.'

Vogel added, more primly: 'With the proviso, of course, that you get some form of counselling.'

'You mean see a psychiatrist?'

'Rabbit on about how your father abused you and you'll be in the clear in no time. Your friends are in much deeper shit. Federal offences.'

My statement, a 'record of interview', was handed to me: I signed with agitated fingers. The detachment of those words—'statement', 'record of interview'—seemed proper; in no sense did I feel I was signing a confession. To confess was to accept some burden of guilt. I hadn't asked for a lawyer to be present at the interview, or during the signing

334

of the statement; I felt I had nothing to hide. Now, desperate to reach Wish, I needed a lawyer urgently.

'You can ring from the watchhouse,' Vogel said. 'Stand up, sir. Hands behind your back.'

She deftly handcuffed me, increasing my agitation.

'Are these necessary?'

'Regulations.'

No one in that small bare room understood Sign, but I felt as if I had been gagged. Those cold cuffs seemed to somehow restrict my thinking. Even speech was difficult.

'Please—I need my hands to think with.'

Crilly shrugged, smiling—regulations were regulations, the gesture seemed to be saying. He opened the door and ushered us through. 'See you in court, big feller.'

Vogel marched me down the same three flights of stairs, then down a further flight into a brightly lit underground tunnel. At the far end another flight led up into what I took to be the watchhouse. A uniformed desk sergeant greeted her, paperwork was exchanged, the cuffs were removed, my belt and shoelaces were confiscated. After the taking of fingerprints, I was allowed access to a phone. I rang the only lawyer I knew: Linda Kelly, the Family Court solicitor who had handled, or mis-handled, my divorce. Her answering machine advised that she wasn't available; I left a message after the beep.

'Can I send a fax?'

The desk-sergeant, a tubby grey-beard, friendly to that point, assumed I was joking.

'It's hardly a laughing matter, sir,' he said, gravely, a phrase straight from the police manual of stern clichés.

He topped it with another. 'I would have thought you were in enough trouble already.'

'My mother is deaf. I have no way of reaching her.'

His expression softened a little, but remained sceptical. 'I'm sorry, sir. That's not my problem.'

He took me by the elbow and 'helped' me to my holding cell, a small clean room with a bed, washbasin, toilet-bowl. A video camera was secured, out of reach, in a high corner. The cell was comfortable apart from the smell: some sickly sweet deodorant-cum-disinfectant. I lay sleepless under a single blanket, with that hygienic chemical stink filling my nostrils. It was the smell of motel rooms and hire-cars, but I was travelling nowhere. At first I could think of nothing but Wish; other, lesser worries then began to seep into my head: my parents' reaction, Jill's reaction, how to contact Rosie who was expecting an access visit in the morning. In the smallest hours I entered a state of delirium where I could no longer even choose what to think, the twilight zone of insomnia where thoughts choose themselves.

I rose with a thick headache and a numbed, exhausted mind, badly in need of my wetsuit and the water cure.

Breakfast arrived on a tin tray at six: a can of Coke and a stale meat pie which obscured, at least temporarily, the motel-stink.

I asked the guard, a thickset tough with a rugby neck, for a morning paper. He laughed. 'You wouldn't want to see it.'

Linda arrived shortly afterwards. She sat on the edge of my bed, a plump woman with a disproportionately small head, clearly ill at ease in those surrounds, but trying to fake confidence.

336

'I have to get out of here.'

'Patience, J.J.'

She glanced around the small cell, nervously. 'Not exactly five-star accommodation.'

'You haven't been here before?'

'I'm not a criminal lawyer, J.J. My clients don't usually end up in places like these.' She smiled uncomfortably. A folded newspaper peeped from her valise. I asked to see it, but she refused to hand it over until after we had talked.

'I haven't read it myself yet. I saw the headlines—but wanted to hear your side first.'

More involuntary hand movements as I spoke. 'The *headlines*?'

'Not *front* page headlines. Not yet. And we can apply for a suppression order to prevent the publication of your name, or any details which might identify you.'

Despite her evident discomfort, her tone of voice slowly soothed me, a cooing dove-like voice. Her small smooth head nodded back and forth as she spoke, a habit, also strangely dove-like, that I found calming as well. Was I clutching at straws? Too self-effacing to succeed in court, her best performances always came afterwards, I suspected, calming her disappointed clients.

'I'll get you out of here, J.J. But first things first. There is a problem with the charge. It may change before the committal hearing. My sources tells me that the Crown's star witness might refuse to testify if bestiality is the charge.'

'No might about it.'

'I understand you've already signed a confession.'

My hands flared again, adjuncts to speech. '*Not* to bestiality. I confessed to making love to Wish—which is not the same thing at all.'

Same-*not*! The adjacent forefingers of 'near' or 'close' disrupting, flying apart.

'You intend to plead not guilty?'

I nodded. 'Of course.'

She screwed up her face, as if my words were unpalatable, bitter-tasting.

'I want to make a point,' I said, standing firm. 'Wish isn't an animal. And even if I'm convicted the police say I'll only get a suspended sentence.'

'*If* you plead guilty. If you make it hard for them they'll raise the stakes.' She fossicked in her valise and withdrew a single sheet of paper. 'Tell me about the statement from the alleged eyewitness.'

'She saw me on the bed. It's as simple as that.'

Puzzlement spread across her face. '*Who* saw you?'

My hands signed an angry twinkling star as I spoke. 'Stella.'

Linda referred again to her notes. 'Stella Todd? The wife of Professor Kinnear?'

'Of course. She made the statement. She was jealous.'

Jealousy: an emphatic J shaped with the baddest of Bad Hands.

'I think you're under a misapprehension, J.J. I'm not talking about whether Stella is *jealous*, I'm talking about the statement itself. *Kinnear* dobbed you in—not his wife.'

I sat, silenced, bewildered.

'I also understand that his wife has left him as a result of his action.'

More news that was difficult to decipher; she took my stunned silence as a cue to continue.

'Professor Kinnear is demanding that the charge be changed to unlawful carnal knowledge. He held a press conference last night.'

She finally tossed over the morning paper, and its comic-book heading: TEACHER CHARGED OVER SEX WITH APE. I wasn't named and the details were scanty. Clive's face stared out from beneath another, smaller headline. GORILLA ENTITLED TO FULL PROTECTION OF HUMAN LAW: PROFESSOR.

'Did he also see you, J.J.? I need to know.'

I lifted my eyes from the paper, and returned her stare, unashamed. 'Yes, he did.'

'*In flagrante?*'

'Not actually in the *act*. But we were naked.'

She seemed to think this important; she cross-hatched a large asterisk on her paper.

'What about Stella?' I asked. 'She, ah, walked in on us too. She saw it all.'

'My sources tell me that she is refusing to testify. She claims that she saw nothing.'

As I tried to digest this, Linda pressed on. 'The police have two alternatives. Either they persist with a charge of bestiality—and they could subpoena Kinnear as a hostile witness—or they change the charge, perhaps to gross indecency. I can't see them accepting a charge of carnal knowledge in a million years.'

The details didn't interest me; all I cared about was the fate of Wish. 'I'm sure this is all very riveting, Linda, but I need to get out.'

'You're stuck here till tomorrow. The hearing is set for ten. After that I don't foresee any problem.' She paused, looked up at me: 'No problem *in* the court, that is.' She tapped the open newspaper. 'I should warn you, this is only the beginning. There is bound to be a lot of interest from the media. Television.'

'Just what I need.'

'I can possibly arrange for you to leave through the back exit.'

'You don't sound too certain.'

'I've never done this before. I've only seen it on TV.'

'No. I'll go out the front. I'm not ashamed. As I said—I want to make a point.'

Although not yet, perhaps, to my parents. Or to Jill and Rosie.

Linda took a deep breath, as if making a reluctant decision, and added: 'I should also advise you—I'm a bit out of my depth. It's not exactly your everyday common or garden Family Court brief. *If* you insist on pleading not guilty—against my advice—then I would urge you to retain a top criminal barrister. Preferably a silk. Can you afford it?'

'Jill got all my money, remember?'

She zipped her valise, avoiding my eyes, chastened. The sign for lawyer: right forefinger striking left palm, firmly laying down the law. When I think of Linda I see the shape of something far more hesitant, a finger never quite reaching

340

its destination, or arriving by roundabout route, without force or conviction.

'I'm sure we can come to some arrangement, J.J. I know a few media junkies who would pay *you* to let them take the case. I'll see you in court at ten.'

'Meanwhile, can you find out about Wish?'

'I'll do my best.'

'Please. It's *crucial*.'

She gave me a look that was half-bemusement, half-pity, and rose and walked out of the room.

The committal hearing, Crown versus John James, was fifth on the morning list. Half a dozen clean-cut boys and well-groomed girls sat in the body of the court, clutching notepads. Their pens remained still during the first four cases: two breakings and enterings, a receiving charge, a common assault. When the clerk called my name, the notepads flipped open as one, the pens clicked on like safety catches. There wasn't much to write home about. No discussion of the case took place. The charge remained bestiality, Linda reserved my plea, I was remanded on bail. The trial date was set; I followed Linda out of the courtroom.

'Where's Wish?'

'Later,' she murmured. 'We've got our own problems.'

She nodded to the glass doors of the building. The cub reporters had reassembled on the steps outside, a single television camera looming behind and above, like a periscope.

'I could still bring the car round the back.'

Her tone was hopeful; I sensed that she was beginning to enjoy the drama.

'I'm *not* ashamed.'

'Your decision. But I have to warn you—if you open your mouth they'll eat you alive.'

'I want to state my case. *Wish's* case.'

She laughed, dismissively. 'No one out there is interested in your opinions about the case. They've already decided what you will say. Look at them, J.J.—sharks in a feeding frenzy.'

I looked: half a dozen fresh-faced innocents, not a tooth or dorsal fin in sight. Linda had watched too much television, surely, a first-time celebrity lawyer, keen to amplify her fifteen minutes of fame into sixteen.

'Even if you *think* you're saying something else, J.J., you'll turn on the TV and find you didn't. My advice is to say nothing—yet. When we talk to the press it must be on our terms. To the sources we choose. Besides, anything more could be construed as contempt of court.'

She sounded almost competent. I mutely followed her through the pens and notebooks. A microphone was offered to my mouth like a single-cone, close enough to lick; I ignored it. The smallish mob parted without offering resistance; perhaps it was merely a journalism class, on a random field trip. A pocketful of Stella's sugar cubes would have come in handy, if only to make a point to Linda. Once we were safely sealed inside the car I asked the question again: 'So where is she?'

Linda opened her mouth to speak, then closed it again. I could almost hear the swallowed answer—'where

343

is who?'—but speaking with a long-tongue, or even a disingenuous tongue, was beyond her.

'She's at the zoo.'

'Take me there.'

'You're joking, surely.'

'Have you been to the zoo recently, Linda? How would you like to be kept in a pit?'

'If I was a gorilla, I might enjoy it.'

'Bullshit!'

'J.J.—you *mustn't* see her. It's that simple. I strongly advise—I *insist* that you keep away.'

I sat, stewing. Escape was impossible. She was driving at speed, I was belted in, the doors were centrally locked.

'There are more urgent matters to discuss. You want the bad news or the good news?'

I shaped a Bad Hand, unthinkingly; she seemed to comprehend, or perhaps merely read my face.

'Jill's lawyer rang. Jill has taken out a temporary injunction to prevent you seeing Rosie—pending a Family Court hearing. She wants to stop all access.'

'How did *she* know? The papers didn't even mention my name.'

'It was bound to get out sooner or later.' She hurried on, as if to forestall brooding. 'The good news is that I think we can mount a not-guilty defence.'

'You've changed your tune since yesterday.'

'I've been asking around. Talking to people.'

Her body language was a little evasive, even shifty. I tried to find her eyes, she refused contact, pretending to be absorbed in driving. 'I believe a defence can be mounted on the issue of the legal definition of an animal. And—by implication—the definition of a person.'

I waited, still curious about her evasiveness, but willing to listen.

'The problem is, to accept that a gorilla is a human, with human entitlements under law, might expose you to a more serious charge. Unlawful sexual intercourse, for one.'

Her tone of voice turned sing-song, as if accessing parts of her memory where knowledge had been stored by rote, and never previously used, or understood.

'A person who has sexual intercourse with a person under the age of twelve years shall be guilty of a felony and liable to be imprisoned for life.'

'She's sixteen or seventeen, in human years, Linda. Fully mature.'

'She's *eight* on her birth certificate. But that's a worst case scenario. It won't happen. The key is the definition of "person".'

'You're very enthusiastic all of a sudden. I'm broke, remember? Are you doing this for love?'

'Not necessarily.'

I turned towards her, surprised, waiting for an explanation. She had braked at a red light, but kept her eyes fixed ahead, avoiding my gaze.

'You have rich friends,' she finally said, and paused, leaving a conversational door ajar.

Surprise became incredulity. 'Someone has offered to pay my costs?'

'He feels in part responsible.'

He? No intuition was required, the opacity of that pronoun was instantly transparent. I felt even more of a pawn, a bit-player in someone else's script. I felt, above all, that I was being used. 'Saint', my hands signed to myself, a terse, angry halo.

The light changed, the car moved on, heading away from the city centre towards Glenelg, and my parents' home on the beach.

'Isn't he under arrest himself?'

'Out on bail. You must be aware that your interests and his coincide.'

This I refused to accept. 'Not at all. Not even *remotely*. I just want to protect Wish. Clive wants a show trial on a world stage. He wants a *spokes*-animal.'

Linda's face glowed, her little pigeon head bobbed excitedly on her body.

'He wants a *what*?'

'A prophet for the Animal Rights movement. An animal Messiah.'

My hands moved, simultaneously, emphatically. The official sign for Jesus, the middle finger of the one hand punching crucifixion-wounds in the palm of the other.

346

Another bifocal sign, surely—revealing an extra dimension, putting shape to thoughts that were still half-formed. Wish, too, my hands were telling me, might become a sacrifice if Clive had his way.

The shapes went unnoticed by Linda. She stared straight ahead, laughing softly, increasingly at home in a case that only a few hours before had seemed completely alien.

'I *love* it, J.J. It gets better and better. He's crazy, yes. But if that craziness includes paying for your defence, why argue?'

'He's not crazy. Crazy is exactly what he *isn't*.'

'Clive is a side-issue, J.J. I'm representing you, not him. If your interests diverge—it's yours I protect. So, what do you think?'

'I think I need to think.'

My hands moved again, more worrying than thinking. She turned to me for the first time. 'Look, if you want to pay the costs yourself, fine. But we need to talk this out. And Professor Kinnear will be crucial to your defence. I've pencilled in a meeting tomorrow.'

'Drop me here,' I said.

'I can drop you at home.'

'Don't worry. I just need to walk.'

She pulled to the side of the road, and turned her head and gave me a long, suspicious look. She clearly wanted to believe me.

'Tomorrow then? Twelve?'

'Tomorrow,' I lied.

5

I needed no directions to the Primate Section, a well-trodden path in my memory. The same colony of bored adult chimps and frisky infants filled the first of the stucco squash courts. Orang-utans still occupied the second and third. A fourth pit, the last in the terrace row, was barricaded from public access: STAFF ONLY. I stepped across the makeshift barrier and up onto the wooden viewing platform. The enclosure seemed empty. Wooden scaffolding filled much of the space: an artificial 'tree' which seemed to have been thrown together in a hurry. Thick hemp ropes were suspended in loops from the topmost strut; rubber tyres were attached to two of these.

I turned away, disappointed. As I stepped back across the barrier, I heard a familiar soft bleat and turned again to see Wish appear from behind a fallen log at the back of the pit. She waved frantically; pain written on her face. She slipped through the tangle of scaffolding and squatted at the slimy edge of the moat, staring beseechingly up at me, brandishing her hands.

'Wish out. Wish free.'

The unshackling of bound hands. My heart sank. Her body was still hairless; even those scant tufts of hair spared by the razor had vanished. The black crepe of her skin was red and raw in places; her hands, between signs, itched at those sores, obsessively. Even her signing was more a kind of nervous, desperate itching at the air.

I signed back: 'Worry—not. I help.'

A small family group, viewing the chimps next door, turned to watch me curiously across the barrier. One or two craned their necks to peer into the pit. Wish was screened by shrubbery, they could see nothing.

'Patience,' I signed.

She knew the sign well: a rhythmic stroking of the chest, the act of calming oneself. I had often used that shape in lessons, to control her excitement. She teetered at the brink of the moat, clearly wanting to jump, or swim—and just as clearly unable to overcome her aversion to water. She would cross an open field for me, but not a river.

I signed: 'I free you.'

She crossed her heart frantically. 'Promise?'

A young, efficient-looking woman in khaki shorts and desert boots appeared from behind the barrier. Her green shirt bore the zoo logo.

'Excuse me, sir. This display is not open to public viewing.'

'Just a few minutes. Please.'

349

'I'm afraid I can't allow it, sir. There are other exhibitions available to the public.'

She gestured towards the apes; I didn't move.

'She's *ill*,' I said. 'Look at her skin.'

'The gorilla is in good hands, sir. Whatever can be done is being done.'

'I refuse to leave her like this. Is she having her cortisone?'

The word startled her. She peered into my face more closely, as if matching my features with some verbal description. Her expression of firm politeness changed, became a mix of anxiety and disapproval. 'Is your name James?'

'J.J.,' I signed.

She took a single step back, alert, careful. 'You shouldn't be here.'

'Have a heart, for Christ's sake—she's out of her *mind*!'

She turned, reluctantly, and looked down into the pit. Wish still sat at the edge of the moat, thickset, pot-bellied, brandishing her arms.

'Mr James, we know her medical history. Dr Todd was very helpful.'

'Then you know about her intelligence?'

A puzzled expression; clearly she didn't. 'I do know that she's lonely. I spend as much time with her as I can.'

'Look at her skin. She's flaying herself alive!'

'Our vets have prescribed a cream—I apply it twice a day.'

'It's not a *skin* condition. It's her mind.'

She stepped forward and took my elbow, but gently, more a suggestion of guidance than a wrestling-hold.

'Please let me stay.'

'It would cost my job.'

'Then maybe you should get a job you can live with.'

Her grip on my elbow tightened. 'You think *you* know best? Using a gorilla for your own...your own... *purposes*!'

She leaned against me; I stood my ground, passive, immoveable. Frustrated, she dropped my arm, and vanished up the path in search of reinforcements. I turned back to Wish. I didn't have much time.

'We go—now!' she signed, the Flat Hand pushed downwards, emphatic: *this* moment, here and now.

'Soon,' I signed back; an opaque shape, a bouncing of the Write Hand, forefinger and thumb pinched as if holding a pen.

351

She watched the gesture with dismay, then abruptly turned her back. A small crowd—several family groups—had now gathered on the far side of the barrier; unfazed I spoke aloud to Wish for the first time.

'Please! Wish—sign to me.'

Incredulous laughter from the barrier; increasing as I repeated the request: 'Please.'

She turned slowly back. All animation had now vanished from her hands; her movements were slow and depressed, monotonous in tone. The Wish Hand, her signature hand, was nowhere in sight; with it had vanished the implicit sense of hope, and possibility, that always coloured her signing. I had failed her; I couldn't help.

'Tomorrow. I here tomorrow. I promise.'

Several khaki uniforms were pushing their way through the onlookers; I added quickly: 'I love you.'

'I love you—not!' she signed back.

A folded net was slung over the shoulder of the largest keeper. For that big silverback me? The thought might have amused me, at other times, in other places. Momentarily I imagined myself at bay, backed into a corner—forcing them to keep their distance, or even to fire tranquillising darts. But the net was for Wish, surely—a precaution in case I had managed to set her free. Against these reinforcements resistance was futile. I allowed myself to be hustled off the viewing platform and through a STAFF ONLY gate, out of public view. I had walked every inch of the zoo with Rosie a dozen times, but I now found myself in a hidden, alternative universe of access paths, maintenance sheds, food supplies, and holding cages; the real zoo perhaps, interlocking with, and screened behind, the public facade. As we hurried through the maze I wondered, absurdly, if I might be destined for a holding cage myself; instead I was escorted up the steps of a large administration building. A door marked JONATHON TIDDY, CURATOR OF PRIMATES opened, an older man, grey-bearded, wearing a T-shirt printed with bright orange orang-utan motifs, waved away his khaki troops and ushered me into his office. The police were on their way, he advised me calmly—while we waited would I care for a coffee? His manner was one of friendly regret, less judgemental than his minions.

'How unfortunate that it's all come to court, Mr James.'

'It wasn't exactly my idea.'

'Quite.'

A small electric kettle on a sideboard boiled, and clicked off; he spooned coffee into two mugs. I sensed that here might be a kindred spirit, a mind vulnerable to reason, or at least to the seeding of a little moral uncertainty.

'You realise you have a human mind locked up there.'

'A mind, perhaps,' he conceded. 'But hardly human.'

What could I tell him? Her brain had been artificially enlarged, grown on hormones like some hydroponic cauliflower? That way lay tragedy, I was certain: the vivisectionists, the brain physiologists, would get their blood-spattered hands on her.

I said: 'Whether it's human or animal is immaterial. It's a *sick* mind—you must see that. She's scratching herself to death. Imagine what she's going through—cooped up in that hole. Imagine taking a human child from her family and dropping her into some snake-pit. She's terrified!'

353

'It's hardly a snake-pit,' he said, mildly. 'And it's only temporary. We simply have no other place to put her.'

'She should be with humans. She *thinks* she is human. Couldn't you find somewhere else—this office, for instance?'

'She'll only be in the holding pit for another day,' he said, and passed me a coffee.

I set it down on his desk, alarmed. 'Then what?'

'There's a large gorilla troop in the Melbourne Zoo—and a lot more space.'

'She's *not* a gorilla!'

My hands beat my chest, involuntarily: gorilla-*not*! For the first time his patience showed signs of wearing thin. 'I hardly think you are the one to lecture me on her care and well-being, Mr James. Exploiting an eight-year-old gorilla for your own sexual pleasure is a serious allegation...'

An odd choice of words. Would he deem the crime less serious with an eighteen-year-old gorilla? It seemed a promising line to explore; a chink in his armour.

'She's not a child. Sixteen or seventeen in human years. And what I am accused of, and what happened, are entirely different things.'

He nodded and waved a hand, calm again, acknowledging the point. 'I'm sorry, I don't wish to prejudge you. Of course I must give you the benefit of the doubt. But until the court case is concluded, surely it's in everyone's best interests if you stay away from her.'

The words might have been Clive's. His civilised calm began to irk me as much as Clive's—as much as Jill's. People without feelings, I was beginning to think

354

them—people whose hands were always frozen, expressionless, at their sides. I tried to hide my own hostile feelings, there was a more important issue at stake.

I said: 'My sole concern is what it has always been—her well-being.'

His eyes held mine for a moment; reassured, he nodded. 'I've spoken to my colleagues in Melbourne. She will be introduced slowly to the members of the troop—there is a strict protocol we follow in such matters. If socialisation doesn't work, then some other avenue will be explored. There have even been cases of gorillas successfully repatriated to West Africa.'

Another promising choice of words: 'repatriated', with its human connotations. I forced myself to remain calm, to say, as reasonably as I was able: 'She's *not* wild and never has been.'

A knock at the door interrupted his reply; the young keeper stuck her head through the gap and announced the arrival of the police. Expecting the nearest highway patrol, I was surprised to see Crilly appear in the doorway. Vogel followed close on his heels, clipboard in one hand, heavy torch, broad daylight notwithstanding, in the other.

They seemed to know Tiddy; I realised that he would probably have been interviewed already.

'The big feller wasn't actually *in* the cage with his girlfriend was he, Dr Tiddy?'

Crilly grinned, amusing himself. Tiddy answered, icily: 'We don't keep primates in cages at the Adelaide Zoo, Detective.'

Water off a duck's back. Crilly turned back to me. What *are* we going to do with you, Tarzan? Maybe they should keep you here. Join the colony.'

He seemed more expansive than previously, less world-weary. I said: 'I don't understand what you're doing here. It's none of your business if I choose to visit the zoo. I haven't broken any law.'

Vogel was terse, and to the point. 'You *are* on bail.'

I was feeling more sure of myself than at my first arrest, a slightly older hand, now, certain of my rights.

'It wasn't a condition of my bail that I keep away from the zoo.'

Crilly said, his amusement a little pained: 'We could charge you with harassing a witness.'

He glanced to Vogel, collusively, then back to me. I put a Fist Hand snout over my nose and stared him in the eye. He hadn't a clue what I was saying.

Vogel took control. 'We're charging you with trespassing.'

I was handcuffed again. Tiddy, with an air of apologetic regret, led us out of the building and through his hidden world. At the high perimeter fence he pressed a lever, an electric gate rolled ponderously to one side. We found ourselves disgorged from the back of the zoo; a familiar car waited among the trees. As the large gate began to roll shut behind us I glanced back. Tiddy was watching from the narrowing gap. He waved, tentatively, and although I couldn't answer in kind, my spirits rose, slightly. I nodded, hoping that I had given him food for thought.

6

'I can get you out again if you promise to behave.'

'What do you mean?'

'You know what I mean. I've prepared an agreement. And spoken with the Police Prosecutor—he agrees.'

Linda slid a sheet of paper from her valise, and passed it over. A close reading wasn't essential, I knew exactly what it would say.

'If I sign this I can get out?'

'It would still need a rubber-stamp from the magistrate. But I foresee no problems.'

'When can I go?'

'Tomorrow morning.'

'Tomorrow? Jesus, Linda—I have to get out of here *tonight*.'

She stared at me, lips pursed, saying nothing, waiting. At length I took the pen, the longest tongue that I had ever wielded, and signed. Linda slipped the sheet carefully back into her valise, and slid out another, rice-paper thin.

'I also have a message for you. A fax. From your mother.'

She passed it across, snapped shut her valise, and rose to leave. 'If I am to continue acting as your legal counsel, I expect, in future, that you will act on my advice.'

An answer was not required; this was a rebuke, not a question.

'I'll see you in court, J.J. In the morning.'

She knocked on the door of the cell, it opened as if by touch to release her. Such magic did not extend to me; I remained imprisoned. I scanned the fax. The message was flavoured more with concern than blame, and somehow managed to avoid all mention of my predicament, although the addendum at the bottom of the page—*Father Sends His Love*—was a fiction, I was certain.

I cast the page aside. My own problems paled in comparison with those of Wish. Dinner arrived: a meat pie and can of Coke, with a coffee and cream bun afterwards to differentiate it from breakfast. I couldn't sleep. I tossed all night amid the stink of disinfectant and stale meat pie. Images of Wish at the edge of a filthy moat, her skin raw and bleeding, her hands frantically signing for help, filled my mind.

My court appearance was brief, a thirty-second lecture from the magistrate. Word of my zoo visit must have spread, the small crowd of reporters in the courtroom had swollen, and aged. Several of the new faces had a distinctly preda-tory look. Linda seemed increasingly at home, but to me the notion of fighting for justice in the courts, or even in the media, was clearly impossible. Wish was suffering, now—a solution was required, immediately. Desperate to make a quick escape, I accepted Linda's offer to bring her car to the back. She directed me to the exit, suggesting that I didn't show my face until she had fetched her car from the carpark. I wasn't about to wait. I stuck my head through the back door, a kind of service entrance. No reporters were in sight. I walked out into the road and hailed the first vacant cab.

7

The Auslan shape for 'worry' is a misnomer: literally too-much-thinking. A value judgement, surely. Worry is often a necessity, worry alone can provide the sheer energy that is needed to search for possibilities, solutions, ways out. This type of worry requires another sign—not-enough-thinking, perhaps. Or tenacious thinking, resolute thinking.

No one was home at my parents' house. I pulled on my wetsuit, crossed the esplanade and waded out into the surf in a state of controlled worry, methodical worry.

Or is 'methodical' another misnomer? Sign uses the shape of 'street', a straight road ahead.

My worrying was less methodical than bent, an exploration of every fork in the road, every single back alley and detour. Exhaustive thinking, perhaps. Thinking that was whole, complete, all-embracing.

A plan of action had been forming in my mind overnight, to succeed would require absolute attention to detail. As the swell lifted and lowered me those details began to accumulate. And yet time was of the essence—I was unsure how long Wish could survive in her prison. After an hour or so I emerged, sluiced away the salt in the warmer cold water of the shower at the bottom of the beach steps, towelled my hair and my wetsuit, and climbed up to the empty house.

I scribbled a brief note on the back of my mother's fax, explaining, bluntly and without apology, the facts as I saw them, adding *Love to Father* as an ironic postscript. Then I pulled the *Yellow Pages* from the phone cupboard, and opened to *Car Rental*.

8

Rosie's school is in the foothills, in the heart of the eastern suburbs Volvo belt: an expensive single-sex school set in leafy grounds. As talented academically as she is socially, her fees are paid by scholarship.

I arrived at lunchtime. The din of children at play filled my ears as I parked in the side lane, a continuous joyous screaming.

I thought of Wish, huddled in her pit, and those carefree voices seemed unbearably poignant.

Rosie spotted me immediately—I'm an unmistakable figure. Normally diffident about acknowledging me in front of friends, she waved and approached with clear pleasure. Was it the sight of the hire-car parked behind me—a gleaming, four-wheel-drive people-mover, more minibus than car? She had always refused to permit me to collect her from school in the old Fiat. There might be fatter dads in the Volvo Belt, but there were no more shameful cars.

'New car, Dad?'

Her tone surprised me as much as her smile, happy, pleased to see me.

'I'm going on a trip.'

'Where are you going?'

'Not sure yet.'

'I can't come,' she said, in case I was about to ask. 'Mum doesn't want me to see you at present. I hope you're not disappointed.'

Her tone—solicitous, even gentle—continued to surprise me. Perhaps I had been wrong about the attraction of the car. She had acted as a precocious teenager for years, but now, twelve years old, on true teen-brink, she seemed to have suddenly passed through adolescence into a more sensitive, adult state.

'Did she say why?'

She hesitated, as if deciding whether to protect me from the truth. 'She said you were unstable at present. Behaving...erratically.'

To prove she understood the adult-jargon, she whirled her index finger about her temple. Her expression was amused, as if this was hardly news. I had always been crazy. Lovably crazy.

'I just wanted to say goodbye,' I said. 'I might not be seeing you for a while.'

'Don't worry, Dad. Mum will change her mind.'

'It's not her. It's me. Whatever happens—whatever you read about me—I wanted you to know I love you.'

She looked behind her, embarrassed. I was starting to get sentimental, testing the limits of her new-found maturity. But she turned back to me again, smiled with radiance, and crossed her arms over her chest, the hug of love.

'Me too, Dad.'

'Thank you.'

She eyed me up and down. 'You put on weight?'

With finger and thumb I prised open a small gap between the buttons of my shirt, revealing my black wetsuit.

'I'm going swimming.'

'Crazy—true!' she signed, giggling.

A teacher on yard-duty—a young woman, thirtyish, stylishly dressed—moved our way.

'Excuse me, Mr James?'

'Yes.'

'I must ask you to leave the vicinity of the school. Your wife rang this morning—about the injunction. The Headmistress has advised us to watch out for you.'

'I'm harmless,' I said. 'I just came to say goodbye.'

She moved in front of my daughter, a human shield. 'Then please leave,' she said. 'Or I will be forced to call the police.'

I looked back as I climbed into the car. Rosie was walking backwards into the school, shepherded by the teacher but still watching me. She lifted her Wish Hand as I drove away—Good Luck.

I left the car at the rear of the zoo, beneath the trees outside the service gate, and followed the high-walled perimeter on foot to the Children's Zoo entrance. I had a feeling that the staff might be watching for me at the main entrance, might even have been issued with my photograph. I donned sunglasses and attached myself informally to a mother and two children in the ticket queue, as if belonging to the same loose family group. Paranoia, or intuition? Paranoia is another modification of the shape for 'think', the Good Hand replaced by the Bad:

Not so much bad thinking as safe thinking, I'd argue; I couldn't afford to take risks. And I was beginning to trust my powers of intuition, they had often proved right.

As my adopted wife passed through the turnstile and out of earshot, I murmured to the cashier: 'Jill didn't pay for me?'

'No, sir—she didn't.'

I slid a handful of coins beneath the glass partition, pushed through the turnstile and immediately headed out of the Children's Zoo, abandoning my new family.

Another fatherless family clump was staring into the squash court that contained the chimp colony; I joined them. No keepers were in sight; as the mother and her children moved away I stepped quickly across the STAFF ONLY barrier, and onto the viewing platform above the holding pit. I couldn't see Wish at first, but she had spotted me; she materialised in the back of the enclosure as if from thin air, poured herself effortlessly through the scaffolding, and in a moment was standing at the lip of the moat, signing frantically.

'Lonely,' she shaped, repeatedly, her own familiar invention.

'I know. I feel too.'

I took a last quick look around, then stripped to my wetsuit, stepped over the low guard-rail and slid, as noise-lessly as I could, into the filthy moat. My head went under, momentarily—but this was my element, after all. I surfaced, spitting, and breast-stroked through a broth of food wrappers, decayed vegetation and cigarette butts. Emerging on the far side was not so easy. The rim was green-slimed and

slippery, the smooth submerged wall of the moat offered no
foothold. I was struggling, chest-deep when two powerful
arms seized me, and hauled me from the mire.

'Hide,' I signed, urgently, one Flat Hand covering,
concealing, the other.

She turned; I followed her through the tangle of scaffolding

to the back of the pit. A small shelter had been constructed
there: a roof of bark placed between two horizontal logs.
I squeezed beneath, she followed me, obscuring me from
outside view. The water that had found its way between
wetsuit and skin had not yet warmed to body temperature, I was shivering with cold. Wish clasped me tightly
to her body, nuzzling me gently, her hands too busy
touching and holding me to sign. I was cramped and painfully uncomfortable, and covered in slime—but I couldn't
risk leaving the shelter till nightfall. I ran my fingers over
her skin, the raw abrasions and deep scratches. Stubble
pricked my fingertips here and there, new-growth, tough
as steel wool.

Remembering this, writing these words, my hands
still fly involuntarily to hide my face. I feel no shame for
my feelings for Wish, but I feel enormous shame for the
stupidity, the sheer comic idiocy, of that attempted zoo-
break. Where did I think I was going to take her? My plans
were still vague, half-formed—the fruits of panic. First,

367

to smuggle her through the service gate after dark. Then to head south to Cape Jervis—an hour's drive—and take the ferry to Kangaroo Island. After that the details were murky—but at least I would have bought time. The ferry crossing—an hour across Backstairs Passage—would prove difficult; she could never pass as human. My plan was to hide her on the floor of the car, cover her with blankets, and cross my fingers.

Squashed into her makeshift shelter, I tried to think it through. Tiddy's idea of releasing Wish into the wilds of Africa, among her own species, had infuriated me—but as a last resort I believed that she could, at least, survive in the wild. A herbivore, she would never starve. Kangaroo Island contained no predator but man: the nearest crocodiles were on the other side of the continent. Snakes abounded, but here Wish had a built-in preservation-sense. I had shown her a flash-card picture of a snake during our first days together; she had instantly ascended the nearest tree, panicking, unable to distinguish between the representation of the thing and the thing itself.

Ferries crossed hourly from Cape Jervis; this I had checked. There had been no time to arrange accommodation—my plan was to camp out till I could find some abandoned farm, or fisherman's shack, on the thickly wooded western end of the island. That the foliage of Kangaroo Island was eucalypt not sclerophyll, and therefore probably poisonous to a gorilla, didn't cross my mind; I reasoned only that the forest would offer sanctuary if and when our safe-house was found. On this point I was not optimistic, but to snatch a few weeks with Wish—even a few precious days—would allow me to prepare her for the ordeals which must inevitably follow.

She still had an important lesson to learn, perhaps the most important: that the stupidity and cruelty of her cousin species, Homo sapiens, was limitless.

The zoo closed at five; the ringing of distant bells carried to us, followed by a vague, distorted announcement on the PA system. I waited another half an hour then crept from the hide, stretching cramped legs. The coast seemed clear; I followed Wish through the scaffolding, dragging a log to the edge of the moat. If she refused to swim perhaps I could tow her across. At the water's edge, I looked up. Tiddy, the Curator of Primates, was standing on the viewing platform, staring down into the pit, astonished, a copy of *Sign for Beginners* in his hand.

Linda refused to represent me; I had ignored her advice once too often. Not even my growing fame could tempt her back. Bail was rescinded; I was remanded in custody until the trial. My protests went unheeded, a testy magistrate advised me merely that a lawyer appointed by the court would 'probably' visit me the following day.

I spent another restless, agitated night in the same deodorised cell.

The morning paper arrived, neatly folded, on the breakfast tray between the Coke and the stale meat pie. The presence of a newspaper, the first I had been given in the watchhouse, should have been a clue. I ignored it for some time, preoccupied. Even when I flipped the paper open, seeking distraction, and scanned the front page, the sense failed to register at first.

LOVE APE DIES IN FREAK ACCIDENT.

A formulaic headline of the kind the mind learns to skip past, without noticing. But the horror of the accompanying photograph would not be denied.

Wish, clearly dead, hung from one of the ropes in her zoo enclosure. Definition was poor, but some sort of noose seemed to have been knotted around her neck. The tyre was still pendant below her. Her limbs were skewed, twisted in a death rictus, the expression on her face—tormented.

These are the bare facts, best left to speak for themselves. Neither words nor signs can offer more.

Crilly visited me later that morning, alone, placing another copy of the morning paper in my hands as if it were a gift.

'Your girlfriend couldn't live without you, big feller.'

He sat on the bed and watched me closely, a student of human nature, jaded, but still willing to learn—or wanting at least to tease his palate with some last thrill. Miffed that I had already seen the headlines, he rose to leave after a few minutes.

'Yes,' I called after him, '*I loved her.*' Not so much to gratify him, as to tell someone. Anyone.

Loved. Love. Past tense in Sign is less economical, but as always, more expressive: the verb, preceded by the sign for past, for finished, already, done.

Past-love, finished-love. Perhaps there is something in that backwards jerk of the hand, in the physical act itself that is therapeutic, a closing off and casting out. Or does it merely prevent the thinking of certain thoughts, the feeling of certain emotions? The tenses of Auslan have an inbuilt optimism, structured into the actual movement and direction of the hands. Tomorrow lies forwards, a road ahead. Yesterday is behind us, backwards, over the shoulder. English is no different. We put the past 'behind' us, we move 'ahead' into the future. But do we? Struggling with grief, it seemed to me that Sign was suddenly, hopelessly inadequate. The structure of my language permitted one way of thinking, my heart demanded another. Sitting in my cell I tried to imagine a sign-language in which the movement of the hands was reversed, in which the direction of the past was straight ahead, the future behind. Because surely we are all walking backwards, blindly, into the future. We know not where we go—we cannot *see* it. It is the past that is always with us; we must face it forever.

I was sent, pending trial, to a low-security prison on the river: less prison, at first glance, than summer camp. The days passed with infinite slowness; to describe their routines and repetitions would be pointless. There is simply nothing important to tell. My mother visited in my first week, but not my father. The visit was not a success. She still avoided all mention of my alleged crime; we signed for half an hour or so, not so much beating about the bush as beating empty air.

'I bring anything next week?

'Wetsuit. Flippers.'

The prison contained a large pool; I was permitted a daily dip. Grieving, I kept largely to myself; my fellow prisoners seemed to respect my grief, and kept their distance. From time to time I was teased—the nickname Tarzan, inevitably, might have been tattooed on my forehead—but perhaps that teasing was more an attempt to communicate with someone who resisted communication, who wished to remain incommunicado. Perhaps it was also a form of probing, teasing sharpened by curiosity. These, after all, were men who had pushed further into forbidden regions than most. Only the paedophiles had passed completely beyond the pale: the lowest of the low, 'rockspiders' in the patois, a term that is even more contemptuous in Sign, making the flesh crawl, literally, the spider of one hand creeping up the opposite arm.

What was I compared to these? A harmless eccentric. I was content to play the role of clown, a role whose lines I had learnt by rote, as a fat boy at school. A strange thing: the ribbing of my fellow inmates was far less ferocious than the teasing of my schoolmates.

At times I felt a perverse jealousy for the rockspiders who were carried off to the sick bay after falling in the communal showers, or scalding themselves with boiling water from the tea urn. Theirs, at least, was perceived as a real crime, worthy of hatred. They were taken seriously. More importantly, their victims were taken seriously, deemed worthy of protection, and respect. One or two old hands seemed to find a certain larrikin ambition in my crime, worthy of at least some respect—like a difficult circus trick. That's the bloke who fucked the monkey. But, finally, I was a joke, and therefore Wish also was a joke, consigned, again, to the inhuman world, and perhaps even to the inanimate. A thing, a sex object. A crime object, like a gun, or a payroll.

A surprise visitor came to see me several weeks after that terrible photograph appeared. At first I refused to accept the visit—she had come to apportion blame, I suspected. Almost immediately I changed my mind; I needed someone to talk with, to vent my own anger on.

And even perhaps someone to share my grief with.

We sat on the lawn outside the Visitors' Centre, away from the various family clumps. I saw immediately that she had not come to blame me—she reserved the largest share of blame for herself, the remainder for Clive.

'I've left him. He's a monomaniac.'

Immense changes in Stella's attitudes were reflected in her body language, more subdued, more contrite, than I had ever seen.

'You know what I think—he hasn't given up vivisection at all. This is one *huge* vivisection. The biggest of them all.'

'You were part of it,' I reminded her.

She knelt beside me on the grass, as if penitent.

'Is it legal to smoke in here?'

'You name it, we smoke it.'

She took a pack from her bag, I held out my hand. 'Let me.'

I found it difficult to remain angry. I put a cigarette between my lips, lit it, passed it across. She managed a feeble smile, remembering. I lit a second cigarette myself, and inhaled deeply, a pleasure I had begun to appreciate in recent weeks.

'I was more than part of it, J.J. It's my fault it went that far. I gave him the idea.'

If she was seeking contradiction, and therefore absolution, I wasn't prepared to offer it—yet.

'Yes, you did.'

'He was always going to *use* Wish. I should have seen it.'

It would have been too easy to sit there and make common cause against Clive, a lynch mob of two.

'Yes, you should have.'

'I've thought about it a lot, J.J. You were right. You gave her more, ah, affection, than any of us. You *loved* her, in your way. It was just so difficult for me to accept.'

A lump clogged my throat, I turned away. Bound up in her apologies, Stella didn't notice.

'I've written some poems about Wish—would you like to hear one?'

I was too surprised to answer. I felt myself harden against her again—the sheer egotism of it. She read my face and smiled apologetically. 'Maybe some other day.'

We sat in silence, smoking. I lit another pair, we smoked those. The sun was shining, a premature spring day, misplaced at the tail-end of winter. Various family clumps were scattered about the lawns and beneath the big river gums. Fathers in their prison Sunday best kicked footballs with their sons, cuddled their daughters and wives. It looked like a church picnic in the park.

'Clive is withdrawing his complaint, J.J. His dream was to have Wish in the witness box—testifying, through a Sign translator.'

An image came to me of Miss-The-Point translating the hand-shapes of a gorilla, in a court of law. I almost smiled.

'He saw it as a huge publicity stunt. Of course it's not over. He wants to try other avenues.'

'The Federal Court?'

She nodded. 'I'll have nothing to do with it. We had a furious argument.' She paused, corrected herself. '*I* was furious. Clive argued that Wish was dead—and that was sad—but the work must go on. We have to make *use* of her death.'

I lit another cigarette, and kept it myself, this time leaving her to light her own.

'I need to know where she is, Stella.'

'I tried to reclaim the body. I had in mind some sort of burial. A ceremony at home.'

'Your graveyard?'

She nodded, then shook her head, almost simultaneously, her signals confused, tears filling her eyes.

'They wouldn't return her body?'

'There wasn't anything to return, J.J. There was an autopsy to confirm the cause of death.'

'Suicide?'

376

She took a long suck on her cigarette, then laughed with some bitterness, a series of smoky explosions. '*That* possibility wouldn't have entered their tiny minds. An animal committing suicide?'

'Tiddy would have known.'

'If he does, he's keeping quiet. Bad publicity for the zoo.'

'So where is she?'

'Some of her is in the Institute of Medical and Veterinary Science—next to the hospital on Frome Road. Her brain. Various organs.'

'Her hands?' I asked, horrified.

She didn't seem capable of answering this.

'The rest was burnt.'

'Cremated?'

'*Burnt*. In the hospital furnace. Behind the Institute.'

1 1

I visited the hospital the day the charges against me were dropped, after my release. A security guard refused me entry to the carpark, another STAFF ONLY precinct. I parked outside in Frome Road, and passed unhindered through the checkpoint on foot. The furnace room behind the main complex was easily found: a tall chimney rising like a beacon above a square red-brick windowless bunker. The metal double-doors were locked; there were no windows. I stood outside, trying to compose my mind. Grief had drawn me to the place, but for what? To seek some sign of her passing? Something tangible, some last memory I could take away? Less this, perhaps, than an obsession to know, and see, everything that I could. A worker in blue overalls arrived pushing a train of linked green garbage bins: BIOLOGICAL HAZARD. He gave me a quizzical look, then unlocked the door and entered the blockhouse. Smoke shortly began to issue from the high chimney. Perhaps it was human smoke: burning gallbladders, tonsils, amputated limbs, the superfluous flesh of surgery, by-products from the manufacture of health. Perhaps it was animal. Perhaps it was merely the unbiological waste of hospital administration offices.

I sat on a nearby postage-stamp of lawn and watched the slender filament of smoke rising in the cold morning air. I remembered the first and last conversation I had shared with Wish on the subject of death, the heaven-euphemisms I had brandished about, her blunt insistence on pinching her nose, the shape of 'stink'.

'Maybe heaven,' I had signed, 'maybe stink.'

She had watched my hands, sceptical.

'But to find out—what an adventure.'

Adventure was my own invention, a mix of the meandering path of journey, the winged hands of flight. Another euphemism? At the time I had toyed with the idea of taking her to Deaf Church on Sunday mornings. I soon rejected the plan. The congregation would have tarred and feathered me, not so much for the blasphemy of taking an animal to Church—the notion that animals might have souls reaches back at least as far as the original St Francis—but for the crime of debauching their beautiful language by teaching it to an ape, a far greater sacrilege.

What could Wish have learnt in a church—even in a Sign church? Sign, the most natural of languages, seems as lost as English in the world of the unnatural, and supernatural. The inbuilt tenses, the structural optimism that sees the future as an endless road—such notions can only lead to grief. I lay back on the soft winter grass and tried again to imagine a different language, a truly religious language which might allow more resonant concepts of past and future, life and death. Could I put the future behind me? Could someone who had lived and died in the past always be with me, ahead of me, facing me? It seemed a shallow consolation, another euphemism, but better than none. Perhaps religious belief is beyond the grasp of language, by definition. Perhaps that's what faith *is*.

At least I could hope—fingers tightly crossed—that her last thoughts might have been softened by her own consolations, by some sense, however implausible, of making a fresh start.

A breeze stirred somewhere; I heard the shiver of the treetops, the sweepings of approaching debris across the carpark, then saw the wind catch and embroider and then divide the rising column of smoke, two fingers which briefly tangled, as if crossing index and middle, before joining again in a single smooth column rising upwards into the blue.

HAND SIGNS

MOTHER

SPOON

OKAY

CUP

WRITE

GOOD

FIST

BAD

RUDE

GUN

AMBIVALENT

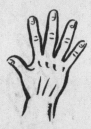

SPREAD

FLAT

ANIMAL

WISH

POINT

QUEER

HOOK

TWO

ACKNOWLEDGEMENTS

I would like to thank Trevor Johnston of the Department of Linguistics, University of Sydney, for his invaluable advice and assistance. His *Auslan Dictionary: A Dictionary of the Sign Language of the Australian Deaf Community* (published by Deafness Resources Australia Ltd) is a classic of its kind.

I would also like to thank my Basic Auslan teacher at the Royal South Australian Deaf Society, Barry Priori, for his wonderful lessons. He bears no responsibility for the monster those lessons have created.

Christopher Pearson gave editorial shape to this book. Clare Forster, Lisa Mills and Angelo Loukakis of HarperCollins, together with Bernadette Foley, supplied further invaluable advice and fine tuning. Thanks to Steven Bray for the illustrations which add poetry to the text.

Andrew Male, Michael Jacobs and Lindy Powell, QC, acted as interactive reference 'works'. Sandy McFarlane alerted me to the work of Rachel Yehuda on enhanced rat intelligence.

Invaluable criticism as always came also from my family— Helen, Anna, Daniel and Alexandra.

Those readers interested in pursuing some of the issues at the core of this novel might choose to consult more standard reference works. An initial list would include the following: Douglas Keith Candland, *Feral Children and Clever Animals*, OUP, 1993; Paola Cavalieri and Peter Singer (eds), *The Great Ape Project*, Fourth Estate, 1993; Jared Diamond, *The Rise of the Third Chimpanzee*, Vintage, 1991; Francine Patterson, *The Education of Koko*, Holt, Rinehart & Winston, 1981; Dale Peterson, *The Deluge and the Ark*, Vintage, 1989; Oliver Sacks, *Seeing Voices*, Picador, 1990.

A concise criticism, from a post-Chomskian perspective, of the various Sign language projects involving great apes is to be found in Steven Pinker's *The Language Instinct*, Penguin, 1984.

P.G., 1994

Text Classics

Dancing on Coral
Glenda Adams
Introduced by Susan Wyndham

The Commandant
Jessica Anderson
Introduced by Carmen Callil

Homesickness
Murray Bail
Introduced by Peter Conrad

Sydney Bridge Upside Down
David Ballantyne
Introduced by Kate De Goldi

Bush Studies
Barbara Baynton
Introduced by Helen Garner

The Cardboard Crown
Martin Boyd
Introduced by Brenda Niall

A Difficult Young Man
Martin Boyd
Introduced by Sonya Hartnett

Outbreak of Love
Martin Boyd
Introduced by Chris Womersley

The Australian Ugliness
Robin Boyd
Introduced by Christos Tsiolkas

All the Green Year
Don Charlwood
Introduced by Michael McGirr

They Found a Cave
Nan Chauncy
Introduced by John Marsden

The Even More Complete
Book of Australian Verse
John Clarke

Diary of a Bad Year
J. M. Coetzee
Introduced by Peter Goldsworthy

Wake in Fright
Kenneth Cook
Introduced by Peter Temple

The Dying Trade
Peter Corris
Introduced by Charles Waterstreet

They're a Weird Mob
Nino Culotta
Introduced by Jacinta Tynan

The Songs of a Sentimental Bloke
C. J. Dennis
Introduced by Jack Thompson

Careful, He Might Hear You
Sumner Locke Elliott
Introduced by Robyn Nevin

Fairyland
Sumner Locke Elliott
Introduced by Dennis Altman

Terra Australis
Matthew Flinders
Introduced by Tim Flannery

textclassics.com.au